MY HUSBAND'S WIFE

Also by Alice Feeney

Beautiful Ugly

Good Bad Girl

Daisy Darker

Rock Paper Scissors

His & Hers

I Know Who You Are

Sometimes I Lie

MY HUSBAND'S WIFE

ALICE FEENEY

MACMILLAN

First published 2026 by Flatiron Books

First published in the UK 2026 by Macmillan
an imprint of Pan Macmillan
The Smithson, 6 Briset Street, London EC1M 5NR
EU representative: Macmillan Publishers Ireland Ltd, 1st Floor,
The Liffey Trust Centre, 117–126 Sheriff Street Upper,
Dublin 1 D01 YC43
Associated companies throughout the world

ISBN 978-1-0350-8300-8 HB
ISBN 978-1-0350-8301-5 TPB

1 3 5 7 9 8 6 4 2

A CIP catalogue record for this book is available from the British Library.

Chapter numbers from HandMadeFont.com / Shutterstock
Key from Nigel Stripe / Shutterstock
Designed by Donna Sinisgalli Noetzel

Printed and bound in the UK using 100% Renewable Electricity by CPI Group (UK) Ltd

FSC
www.fsc.org
MIX
Paper | Supporting
responsible forestry
FSC® C116313

For Daniel, my favourite husband

1

EDEN

30th October

Everybody lies and everybody dies. Those are two of the only things you can be certain of in an uncertain world. The half dark is my happy place. That thin sliver of time that separates night from day, and day from night. Twilight. Sunset. Nightfall. If we give things a different name, it's easier to pretend they aren't the same. Like love and heartbreak. No joy lasts forever. No sorrow lasts forever either, and time is too precious to be wasted. So, even though it is getting late, and the sky is already dressing itself for dusk, I head out into the night and I run.

The cool evening air slaps my face and stings my skin and I see clouds of my own breath in front of me, but I like the cold almost as much as I like the dark. The smell of the sea floods my senses, and I can hear relentless waves crashing in the distance, getting louder as I run closer. The next sixty minutes are mine. For the next hour I am not just the wife, or a mother, or a woman trying to find her way in an increasingly lost world. For the next hour I am just me. I leave my worries behind, along with my phone, knowing that my problems will all still be waiting for me when I get home.

I jog down the hill towards the village, my long blonde ponytail swinging from side to side as my trainers pound the pavement. I live for these moments of feeling young and free again. Thirtysomething isn't old, but the milestone of a big birthday motivated me to make a few changes. Running was just one of them. I'm so grateful for everything that I have – my husband, our home, my health, our freedom – but sometimes I can't help wondering how things might have turned out if I had made different choices when I was younger. Life is filled with sliding doors and dead ends, and I'm sure everyone wonders *what if* from time to time. I run a little faster, as though I can escape the thoughts if I put enough distance between me and them. I'm good at running away from the world when real life gets too loud.

The picturesque fishing village that recently became our home is small and quaint and quiet. Hope Falls is bordered by the Cornish coast on one side and wild moors on the other. Stepping into the village feels like stepping back in time, and I like living somewhere with so much history. Modern places rarely have a good story to tell, a bit like modern people. A network of narrow lanes and cobbled streets tightly packed with tiny, terraced houses and quirky independent shops lead downhill to the seafront. Almost all the shops are closed, as are the cafés and restaurants at this time of year when the tourists retreat to the cities they came from. Former fishermen's cottages painted in pretty pastel shades line the harbour, but most of them are now holiday homes so sit empty in winter. The ghost-town vibe might bother some people, but I like the peace and quiet. I find it calming.

I keep running, only slowing down when I reach the art gallery, but I still don't stop.

Not even when I see my name on a poster in the window.

EDEN FOX

Local artist exhibition

8 PM tonight

My first exhibition still feels like a dream come true.

A dream that I've had for so long. Too long.

That's what happens when you live someone else's dreams instead of your own.

I got married young. For years, being a wife and a mother seemed to take up all my time, but I finally have some spare to do something for me again now that our daughter no longer lives with us. Once I got over the initial guilt of putting myself first for a change, it felt good to rehabilitate my ambition, and painting is my one true passion. Dreams deflate as we get older. Sometimes they disappear completely, real life sucks all the air out of them, but I'm trying to resuscitate mine. Tonight will be the first time I've shown my work, and it's the first time my husband and I will meet our new neighbours. People who I hope might become friends, because I don't have too many of those. Remembering why hurts, so I concentrate on my breathing, find my rhythm and run away from my worries.

They soon catch up with me again.

My husband hasn't been himself since our daughter moved out and we moved here. I can't decide whether it's just empty-nest syndrome or something more. Moving out of the city was my idea, but moving to Cornwall was his, despite his job in London. Harrison kept our old flat in the city and sometimes stays there instead of coming home to me. I don't mind; his work is important. I do mind that he secretly sees our daughter without me and thinks I don't know, but the two of them always had a closer bond. Even though I'm the one who gave up their life to care for her and raise her because he was too busy.

It's almost completely dark when I reach the scenic harbour where I am greeted by panoramic views of the ocean. The tall, black granite harbour walls have protected this village for over two hundred years, and will no doubt still be standing long after I am gone. Sturdy. Strong. Safe. These walls are all the things I am not but wish to be, and I touch the stone for good luck even though I know there's no such thing. Lines of bobbing fishing boats decorate the waterfront, their different colours now shaded by shadows, and the night air is still and cool and quiet. By the time I turn onto the coast path, the last of the light has been swallowed by the horizon and the only thing lighting the sea now is the reflection of a full moon: a shimmering silver path dancing on blackened waves. There is an infinite black blanket of sky covered in star-shaped sequins, a whole universe of endless possibility and wonder, and it reminds me how small and insignificant we and our sometimes seemingly insurmountable problems are.

I am painfully shy. The thought of meeting so many strangers at the gallery tonight, knowing that they'll all be silently judging *me*, not just my work, fills me with fear. Some people love a good party; personally, I prefer a good book. I spent years alone at home taking care of our daughter. Things might have been different if she was *normal*, but she needed me twenty-four seven, and as a result I am out of practice when it comes to social situations. I rarely leave the house at all these days, except to run. Harrison is the opposite. He has always known how to charm strangers and make them fall in love with him. Just like he did with me. I have never been a people person. I have spent a lifetime feeling as though I don't fit and don't belong, but I hope things might be different now that we have moved here.

A brand-new start for a brand-new me.

I run with the sea-salt wind in my face and the soothing sound of the ocean in my ears and propel myself along the steepest part of the coast path to the top of the hill, where there is a waterfall crashing and cascading down the cliff. Harrison and I shared a romantic picnic here recently to watch the sunset. He called it *our special place*, but the scenic spot that gave Hope Falls its name is also the place where many people give up hope. The carefully positioned suicide hotline poster always dampens my mood. I guess sometimes hope fails. I continue on my circular route for a mile or so, then turn off the coast path, heading further inland and onto the moor. I run to get away from it all but always end up back where I started. The irony is not lost on me.

Our house is just outside the village, all on its own at the top of a steep hill, literally built into the cliffs overlooking Hope Falls. It was called Spyglass when we bought it and the name suits the quirky building with its huge windows that look like eyes. The house has white, wonky, wavelike walls, and knowing it is our forever home makes me so happy. It's an emotion I haven't worn for a while and I'm relieved it still fits. Hopefully the vintage black velvet dress I have chosen to wear later will still fit too.

Spyglass was built in the sixteenth century; it was previously owned by a woman who had lived there for almost one hundred years. It looked more like a museum than a home when we first stepped inside, couldn't have been more different from our modern flat in London, and I could tell Harrison wasn't sure. The potential cost almost blinded him from the potential, but when I fall in love with something I have to have it. Renovating is more my bag than his – my husband doesn't have the patience – but sometimes even the simplest of makeovers can transform a place – or a person – making them almost unrecognizable.

When I reach the front gate I see that Harrison's midlife-crisis car is in the driveway. I'm so happy that he is home from London on time for the exhibition that I run down the garden path, excited to see him. We've had more than our fair share of hard times and heartbreak over the years, but all of that is behind us now. Hope Falls is a fresh start for our marriage, not just for me, and I'm hoping he'll be proud of me tonight. Maybe look at me the way he used to, when we were still just us. Who I used to be is always doing battle with who I want to be.

The only thing I take with me when I run is my key to the front door.

When I go to slot it in the lock it doesn't seem to fit, so I try again.

It still won't go in and I don't understand.

It's as though it's the wrong key, or the wrong house, which isn't possible. This is the only property on this quiet country lane overlooking the village.

I stare at the key, then at the door. The key is on a key chain Harrison gave me the day we got the house. We shared a bottle of champagne in our special place by the waterfall, watching the sun set and the moon rise, and he handed me a beautiful gift box. Inside was the key to the house attached to a silver key chain with my name – Eden – surrounded by stars on the front, and the words *Love you to the moon and back* on the other side.

I try to open the door again and when the key still doesn't work, I tap the fox-shaped knocker three times. There must be some simple explanation. Harri will probably take the key from my hand and slot it straight in the lock and make me feel like a fool. The thought makes me smile again, but the smile is soon replaced with a frown.

My husband doesn't open the door.

A woman does.

I've never seen her before but there is something familiar about her.

She looks a lot like me.

"Can I help you?" she asks, and I'm shocked by how much she sounds like me too.

At first, I don't speak. It feels like I can't. Instead, I just stand and stare.

She's wearing my black velvet dress, the one I was going to put on tonight.

"Who are you?" I ask, but my voice comes out as a whisper.

"I'm Eden Fox. I live here."

2

EDEN

I'*m* Eden Fox. What are you talking about?"

The woman stares at the key I am still holding as though I am brandishing a weapon. She looks down on me in every way, making me feel oddly self-conscious about my running clothes, when she is wearing *my* dress and standing in *my* home. Then she looks at me as if she thinks I am crazy or dangerous or both.

For a moment I wonder if I am.

But I *am* Eden Fox and this *is* my house.

We might have only moved in a few weeks ago, but I've barely left Spyglass since then. The previous owner lived here for almost one hundred years. To say that the house was in a state of disrepair would be putting it politely, but things that get broken can often be fixed with a little love and hard work. Despite my husband's impressive salary as the CEO of a company in London, there still wasn't much spare cash after the move, so I did a lot of the work myself. I haven't forgotten ripping up carpets, sanding floors or painting the walls all on my own while Harrison was still in the city. I put my blood, sweat and soul into the place.

This house is mine.

"I think you've made a mistake," says the woman claiming it's hers and that *she* is *me*.

She does look a bit like me.

She's wearing my clothes.

She even smells of my perfume.

The woman starts to close the door, and I feel off-kilter and strange, like when you know you're having a bad dream and try to wake yourself up. But this isn't a dream and I don't understand what is happening.

I put my foot in the entrance, preventing her from closing the door, and she stares down at my running shoes. Her mouth forms a perfect O. She looks so shocked I almost apologize.

"I don't know who you are, but this is *my* house," I insist.

"You're clearly confused. I moved here a few weeks ago," she says, sounding afraid.

But she's lying.

She didn't move here a few weeks ago, *I* did.

A million thoughts race through my mind, but none of them make sense.

I worry that this is some kind of elaborate identity theft, but there is very little of any value inside. Harrison has a well-paid job, but with the mortgage and our daughter's fees to pay, we are not cash rich. There is no logical reason for anyone to want to steal my name or my life or my things. We're just normal people, living in a normal house, leading normal lives. I wish I hadn't left my phone behind on the kitchen counter. At least then I'd be able to call someone, though I'm not sure who. I study the woman's face, unnerved by how similar we look. Her long blonde hair is even styled the same way as mine, her skin is painted with the same minimal makeup and I know that's my dress. It was from a tiny little boutique in London and I've had it for years, fixed it myself when it got torn at a party. I tend to make do and mend everything about my life.

She really does look like me. A slightly older, more polished version of me. Like the me I could have been if I cared more about what I looked like. If I'd been able to spend the last ten years only looking after myself instead of my family.

The woman is clutching the front door and I see something else I recognize on her hand.

She's wearing my engagement and wedding rings.

I always take them off when I run. Never wanting to attract attention to myself when out running alone at night. Stripping myself of anything valuable when I am vulnerable, because of a deep-rooted fear of having the things I love, things I worked so hard to get and to keep, taken from me.

I stare at my ring. My dress. My home. Her face.

Confusion transforms into rage, and my fear twists into fury.

"What the fuck is going on?" I blurt out.

She tries to close the door again. "I've asked you to leave my property."

"It isn't *your* property, you crazy bitch," I say, raising my voice. She suddenly looks terrified and stares over my shoulder as though there might be someone standing behind me in the darkness. I look too, there isn't, but when I turn to check I see Harrison's car in the driveway again. "Where is my husband?"

"I don't know who you are, or who your husband is," she says, regaining her composure. "But if you don't leave right now, I will call the police."

"Good. Go ahead and call them," I tell her. "If I had my phone I'd call them myself."

And then I hear his voice and it is such a relief.

"Is everything okay?" Harrison says, hurrying down the hallway behind her and staring in my direction. He's still dressed in his suit from the office – the black Armani accompanied by a black shirt and tie. Despite being ten years older than me, his well-groomed appearance and immaculate dress sense often make him seem younger than his years. Some men get more handsome with age and my husband is one of them. He's my rock. My lover. My best friend. Whatever this is will be okay now that he is here.

She answers before I can.

"This *woman* thinks she lives here," she tells him. "She's making all kinds of threats and won't take her foot out of the door."

I expect him to demand to know who the hell *she* is and let me inside.

But Harrison stands in our doorway, places a protective arm around a woman I've never seen before, then glares at me before speaking.

"This is our home. I don't know you. Please leave," he says.

Then my husband slams the door in my face.

3

EDEN

I never cared about what goes on behind closed doors until the door was mine.

I stand and stare at it in disbelief, then I pound my fist on the door.

Nobody answers and it doesn't open.

In desperation, I try my key again but of course it doesn't fit.

Did someone change the locks while I was out for a run?

If this is a joke, it's not funny. I have my first exhibition tonight, I don't have time for this, whatever *this* is. I need to get showered and changed and ready. I need to get into *my* house. I need someone to explain what the fuck is going on.

I ring the doorbell repeatedly, then I push the letterbox open and peer inside, but all I can see is an empty hallway.

It's cold tonight and now that I've stopped running, I'm freezing.

And I'm trembling, but I don't think that's because of the temperature.

"Open this bloody door!" I yell.

Nobody replies.

Nothing about this makes sense. I need my mobile but it is inside the house, along with my purse and my car keys. I could walk to the village but where would I go? I don't know anyone here yet. I only ever spoke to the art gallery owner over email and once on the phone. I was hoping to meet them in person and make a good impression tonight.

I bang on the door again. This time, when nobody answers, I walk around to the rear of the house. I try the back door but it's locked, as are the windows. The closed curtains and blinds prevent me from seeing inside, but the lights are on. I know they're in there. I'm so cold and confused and I can feel myself starting to crumble. This feels like a bad dream, but I can't seem to wake up. Tonight was important for me, for us. I don't know why Harrison would go along with something like this.

And then the realization hits me. He wouldn't. At least not willingly.

I make my way to the front of the house again and stop when I hear a car in the distance. We live on a lane with no name at the top of the village, there is rarely any traffic, and I wonder if I flag down the driver whether they might be able to help me. But what would I tell them? What could I possibly say that wouldn't make me sound crazy? What I really need to do is contact the police. There is a small police station in Hope Falls – housed inside a former fisherman's cottage – but I doubt it is staffed twenty-four hours. This place isn't exactly a hotbed of crime. Harrison is clearly doing this against his will, which must mean that the woman is dangerous. If I had my phone I'd dial 999, but without it, running to the police station seems like my next best option.

I don't need to.

The sound I heard was a police car, and something like instinct makes me stay in the shadows as it pulls into the drive. I crouch down in the darkness and watch as a uniformed police officer makes his way to the front door. He looks too young, too handsome and surely too inexperienced to handle the situation. Like a child playing dress-up. I wait and watch as Harrison opens the door, then I listen to him lie.

"I'm sorry to have called you but we didn't know what else to do. There was a woman banging on the door, insisting that she lives here," my husband explains to the police officer. "She seemed confused and unstable. She threatened my wife."

I'm his wife.

I never knew my husband could lie like this.

Hearing him do so makes me feel unsteady on my feet.

The young officer nods his pretty head, runs his hand through his floppy hair, then scribbles something in his notebook before asking for their names.

"I'm Harrison Woolf and my wife is Eden Fox."

That's my name, not hers.

An angry voice inside my head tells me to march over there and say something. Demand that he tell the truth. But a calmer voice tells me to stay hidden, keep quiet for now, try to understand what is going on here.

"And you've never seen this woman before?" the officer asks.

"No. Never," Harrison says, and the lie is so convincing I almost believe it myself. "My wife and I only moved in a few weeks ago and this area felt so safe until now."

"I assure you Hope Falls is one of the safest places to live in the county. Lowest crime rates in all of Cornwall," the child police officer tells him proudly, as though he is personally responsible for this statistic. He seems to believe everything Harrison is telling him, but why wouldn't he? My husband has outsmarted him, but then my husband outsmarts everyone, that's just who he is.

"Would it be possible to speak to your wife?" the officer asks Harrison then, and I experience a tiny glimmer of hope. "It would be helpful to get a description of the woman from both of you."

"I'm afraid my wife suffers from migraines and has had to take some pills and lie down. Tonight was supposed to be a happy occasion – her first art exhibition – but being threatened on her own doorstep by a woman who is clearly unhinged has left her feeling a bit out of sorts."

The officer nods. "I understand—"

"But in terms of a description, the woman was petite, thirty-something, with long blonde hair tied back in a ponytail. She was dressed all in black. I only saw her briefly and that's all I can remember."

My head is spinning.

My chest hurts as though my heart might actually be breaking.

Why is my own husband pretending not to know me?

"We'll get to the bottom of this. Try not to worry. Like I said, this is a very safe area, and just to make sure things stay that way, we actually have a new senior detective starting tomorrow," the officer says.

"Well, perhaps I could talk to him?" Harrison asks. He's a man who always wants to deal with the most senior person in the room, as though he believes that's the only one he'll have anything in common with.

"Of course. Until then, I'm Sergeant Carter and my mobile number is on the back of this card. If the woman comes back, or if you remember anything else in the meantime—"

"There was something," Harrison says. "This might sound strange, but she did *look* a little bit like my wife. Like a younger version of her. And her voice . . . it was almost as though she was trying to imitate her."

The officer frowns. "Well, I'll check around the property, but I want to reassure you, and your wife, that Hope Falls is a safe place. I've lived here all my life . . ."

Says the child police officer.

". . . That said, maybe lock all your windows and doors. This sounds personal to me."

It sounds personal to me too.

I feel like I have fallen down the rabbit hole to a world where I don't belong.

A world where I don't exist.

I stare at my husband standing in the doorway of our home, and a police officer writing a description of me in his notebook, and I feel the panic take hold of my body and mind. I try to calm down, slow my breathing, but I can't seem to get enough air into my lungs.

I stumble, a twig snaps beneath my feet, and they both look in my direction.

I duck down, but the policeman reaches for his flashlight and I know that the shadows won't hide me for long.

So I do what I always do when real life gets too loud. I run.

4

BIRDY

Six months earlier

Nobody wants to be themselves anymore, everybody wants to be somebody else.

Including me.

I wish I could be her.

I lie on the cool metal bed wearing nothing except a flimsy hospital gown. I am in a white room and I am alone. Again. Like always. The fake-friendly nurse made me remove my jewellery when I arrived. All of it. Taking off my rings made me feel even more naked and my fingers feel too light without them. All of me feels weightless in this moment, untethered to a reality that is too loud, and in my imagination I float up to the ceiling and stare down at myself. I do not look like me. Or her. My long black hair – it wasn't always this colour – looks untamed and wild, having been released from the braids I normally wear. My skin looks too pale, having been starved of sunlight for too long. The only familiar things about me are the tattoos stretching from the top of my right arm to my wrist. I trace the outline of the swallow on my right hand with my fingertips as though stroking a pet. Without my rings, my skinny fingers and short, neat nails remind me of my mother's hands instead, and for a moment I wish she was here with me. I'm forty years old. My mother has been dead for most of my life, and yet I still miss her every day.

Selfish fucking bitch.

I tell myself that it isn't really *her* that I miss. It's the idea of her. The concept of unconditional love. Fuck her for abandoning me the way she did. Some relationships are harder than others but sometimes we use the word *complicated* to describe something that is surprisingly simple. The parent is always the parent, the child is always the child. Time and age shouldn't bend those rules, because things can get broken when they do. The sense of loss I still feel seems illogical – you can't lose something you never had – and there wasn't enough love to go around when I was a little girl. Besides, what happened was a lifetime ago – another life, another time, another version of me – and our memories can make liars of us all.

She'd hate my tattoos. She'd hate what I've done with my life.

I often wonder, if she were still alive, whether my mother might hate me.

I loved her so much it still hurts.

There is a clock on the wall and it ticks loudly, reminding me that my appointment was meant to start an hour ago. I fucking hate hospitals. The only reason I'd ever set foot in one is if I was presented with symptoms and facts suggesting I might die if I didn't. The thought fuels my fear, which soon translates into anger, an emotion I am fluent in. First, they kept me waiting in the aptly named waiting room, now again here in this white-walled room. I hate it when people behave as though their time is more important than mine. As though I have all the bloody time in the world.

When maybe I don't.

I want to cry but I won't.

I want to leave but I can't.

I need to know what's wrong with me because I know that something is.

So I stay. And the clock ticks my time away. And I wait a while longer.

The fake-friendly nurse comes back into the room and smiles. She's pretty and young and inexplicably cheerful and I do not like her. Her voice is too high pitched and she sounds like a fucking mouse. I tell my face to smile back anyway, but I am too terrified to function normally so it doesn't listen. I can't do hospitals. I can't do *this*. I have an overwhelming urge to get up and get the fuck out of here—

"So sorry for the delay," she squeaks.

"Oh, no problem at all. I know how busy you must be."

You insincere bitch.

The sound of my own voice out loud – instead of the one I am more familiar with inside my head – surprises me. I sound like the polite and friendly person everyone thinks I am. The person they expect me to be. I suppose we're all actors on the stage of our own lives, some of us are just better at it than others. I can smell the cigarettes on the nurse's breath. She's probably just been on an elongated smoking break, and I hate her for that too. I'd kill for a smoke right now even though I gave up years ago. She starts wrapping a contraption around my arm to take my blood pressure and I can feel it rising already. Her fingers touch my skin and I recoil.

"Sorry. Cold hands, warm heart," she chirps.

That wasn't why I flinched. I don't like to be touched. By anyone.

I can't remember the last time someone did, and the thought makes me shrink inside myself a little bit further.

"Trust me, this won't hurt a bit," the nurse lies, smiling with all her teeth.

What a warmhearted bitch.

I wasn't always the person I am now. A life of crime has turned me into someone else. I suspect *my* heart is cold, and hard, and smaller than it used to be, and I don't trust anyone. When you have seen firsthand what people are really capable of doing to each other, the way I have, it is only logical to never let anyone ever get too close. Not a lot of people could do what I do for a living. Or see what I have seen. Or feel what I have felt. My job is easier when I feel nothing at all. Self-preservation meant flicking off my feelings the way you might flick off a light, and I learned to see in the dark. There are things I have done because of my job that still keep me awake at night, but I'm good at what I do. Sometimes I think it might be the only thing I am good at.

"Try not to look so worried," the nurse says, and I imagine taking the pencil from her pocket and stabbing it in her eyeball. I wish she'd stop talking and get on with it. "The MRI machine looks and sounds scarier than it is," she adds, pushing buttons on the enormous contraption I will shortly be inside.

I am not used to people speaking to me as though I were a child. Nobody ever has. Even when I *was* a child. Before she died my mother often said that I was born old.

I wonder if that means I might die young?

Stop it.

Is forty considered young?

Isn't it?

I try to shake the negative thoughts from my mind, but they linger and join all the others. Fear can kill a person far faster than anything real so I try to ignore it.

If only I'd ignored the damn letter from my GP inviting me for a routine health check when I turned forty, I'd still be none the wiser and none of this would be happening. That's a lie. I knew I was ill, but I thought it was just my body reacting to grief. Grief is the Grim Reaper of hope and without hope we are nothing. Blood tests resulted in more blood tests. A CT scan followed. Then there was the call from the doctor, which I have replayed in my mind so many times since.

"Is this a convenient time to talk?" she asked a few weeks ago. The answer was no, but it was never going to be yes, so I told her to tell me. "I'm afraid the CT scan revealed some sinister-looking shadows," she said, and then there was a pause. I didn't know what to say so I said nothing. Life has taught me that the whole world is full of sinister-looking shadows and people are almost always responsible for causing them. I had sinister-looking shadows beneath my eyes as a result of lack of sleep. I thought it might not be as bad as it sounded—

"We're putting you on the cancer pathway," she added, interrupting my thoughts.

That didn't sound good.

"We'll need to do some more tests. An MRI and some biopsies."

That didn't sound good either.

Then she put me on a waiting list, and the waiting began to find out how bad the bad thing might be.

Thinking about the last few months of appointments and anxiety and endless *waiting* makes my heart beat faster. It feels like someone is pushing down on my chest and I can't remember how to breathe. I try to get a grip, but my fingers have balled themselves into fists and are clinging to the bottom of my hospital gown. I have an overwhelming urge to get off the bed and run right out of here.

But then I still won't know what is wrong with me.

Or if I can be fixed.

How much longer is this going to take?

"We just need to go through a few more questions before we start," the nurse says as though reading my mind. She stares down at me and then at the clipboard in her hand. "Can you tell me your full name again?" she asks.

"Olivia Bird."

"That's a pretty name."

"Thank you, but I didn't choose it."

She pulls a face that suggests I said something wrong, and I want to say something right to cancel it out. To try to make her like me. I could tell her that my friends call me Birdy but that would be a lie. I don't have any friends.

"Any chance you could be pregnant?" she asks.

Not unless it's an immaculate conception.

"No."

"And you've chosen *not* to have a sedative, is that right?" I nod. "Just to remind you that if you change your mind once you're inside the machine – people often do – we can still sedate you. But you won't be able to drive yourself home, and you'll need someone to stay with you and monitor you for twenty-four hours."

"I'm fine without. Thank you."

I would very much like a sedative, but I don't have anyone who could take me home and stay with me. Nobody even knows that I am here. My scooter is parked outside.

"Okey doke, we're all set. Ready?" the nurse asks. She touches my shoulder and I know she is just trying to be kind, but I flinch again.

"Lie back and try to relax. Think of it as a day off work. What do you do?"

None of your fucking business.

"Admin mostly," I tell her. It's not a complete lie.

She looks sufficiently bored by my answer and I'm glad. I never tell people what I do for a living. Aside from the obvious reasons, I'm not sure why. I guess, if people know what I do it makes them look at me differently, and I'd rather they didn't look at me at all.

"I just need to double-check that you have removed all your jewellery?" the nurse asks before pressing the button that will slide me inside a giant magnet. I nod again, but she looks down at my hands as though I might be lying, checking for a wedding ring I might have forgotten to take off. There's no need. That's the only finger I never wear a ring on.

"I'm going to leave the room now, but there is an intercom and a camera inside the scanner, so I'll be able to see you and talk to you at all times."

Just when I thought things couldn't get any bloody worse.

I wonder how many times she says this. I wonder how many patients have already been through this today, and whether she remembers any of them once her shift is over. People who pretend to care are even worse than those who don't. It's like she's just reeling off a script she's had to repeat a thousand times before.

"Once you're inside it's going to feel a little cosy," she says, even though nothing about this situation feels cosy to me. "And it's going to get a bit loud, so I'm just going to pop these earplugs in for you."

"Thank you."

Fuck you and all who sail in you.

The nurse presses a button and the motorized metal bed I am lying on starts to move backwards. The MRI machine swallows me headfirst until I am deep inside it, and she was right, it is loud. My ringless fingers ball into fists again, and I hold my breath while the machine scans my body.

"You're doing really well, Olivia," says the voice on the intercom. "You okay in there?"

No.

"Yes," I lie.

"Good. Only twenty minutes to go."

The roar of magnets flying around me at tremendous speed is too loud in my ears. The space is too small, like a coffin, so I keep my eyes shut. I imagine being by the sea, in the place where I was happiest as a child – Hope Falls – and I tell myself that it is the roar of waves crashing on the rocks around the pretty little harbour that I can hear. Not a man-made machine that will predict my fate and future.

Afterwards, I wait in a different waiting room. The hospital seems to have a lot of them. I stare at the other patients and wonder why they are here and what is wrong with them, as though you can tell just by looking at someone whether they are seriously ill. Trust me, you can't. I try to see myself through their eyes: my long dark hair now restrained in an elaborate plaited bun, my tortoiseshell glasses, the tweed jacket, white shirt, skinny jeans, polished laced shoes. My rings are back on my fingers, and my polite smile is fixed on my face. We all choose a costume to wear every time we open the wardrobe, and this is my armour. I feel vulnerable without it. My tattoos are hidden, except for the swallow, and I look like me again. Even if I don't feel like myself.

The doctor appears, calls my name, and I follow her to a private consulting room. She invites me to take a seat and I do. She sits behind a desk and her face gives me the diagnosis before her words do, but it is still a shock when they confirm it. Turns out those shadows on the previous scan didn't just *look* sinister, they are.

"I'm afraid there are multiple tumours growing inside your body . . ." she says, and the room seems to get smaller, colder, darker. I hear the sound of waves inside my head again, so loud that they drown out a lot of what the doctor is saying. I see her lips moving but I don't hear another word. Can't. Won't. It's as though the sea is calling me home and that is all that matters.

"How long do I have?" I ask, interrupting her. Everything is suddenly silent, as though the room itself is holding its breath.

"It's hard to say."

"Then give me your best guess."

Her eyes fill with sympathy. "Not long."

It feels as though someone just shook the Etch A Sketch of my life; one minute it was there, now it's gone. She talks about options and opportunities but none of them are really that. She talks about choices as though I still have any. Then she tells me she is sorry, and I wonder why and what for. I don't cry.

Fuck that.

And fuck her.

And fuck this life because it's been out to get me from the start.

I don't want to waste whatever time I have left feeling sorry for myself.

Sometimes you just have to accept the shitty hand life dealt you and play to win anyway.

There are things I need to do before it is too late.

5

EDEN

30th October

I hide in the shadows until the police officer leaves, trying to understand the situation I am in, my eyes fixed on the door of the house that was supposed to be our forever home. Trying to run only drew more attention to myself, so I hid, stayed perfectly still and held my breath. Running from something dangerous can make it even more determined to chase you. Moving to Hope Falls was meant to be a dream come true but now it feels like a nightmare.

How can my husband pretend not to know who I am?

Who is the woman in my house claiming to be me?

Why are they doing this?

It's pitch-black and bitterly cold now. I've been crouching in the same spot for a long time and all of me hurts. The freezing air nips at my skin, my teeth chatter and my body shivers, but I stay where I am. Watching. Waiting. Not knowing what else to do. If I had my phone I could call someone, but I left it on the kitchen counter like I always do before my run. I have no phone, no money, no ID; everything I own is inside the house. I need to think, but I'm so cold it physically hurts. Who would I call if I could? And what would I tell them? I have never been good at making friends or holding on to them, and finders doesn't always mean keepers when it comes to friendships. My husband has friends in London – people he works with mostly, people I have little or nothing in common with – and although I force my face to smile on the rare occasions I get dragged along to see them, his friends are not my friends. I'm just the wife.

The front door of Spyglass opens and I see them.

First Harrison, then *her*. I watch with fascination and bewilderment as they walk towards his Porsche. He opens the car door for her – something he never does for me – before climbing into the driver's seat and turning on the engine. I don't know what to do. I consider throwing myself in front of the car but it seems a bit dramatic, and before I know it they have driven away.

Where are they going?

I run again, chasing after the car from a distance, but I can't keep up.

I retrace my steps back down the hill towards the village, retracing my thoughts at the same time. Trying to make sense of something that simply doesn't make any. I stop to catch my breath when I reach the harbour. I'm doubled over with exhaustion and fear, hugging myself for comfort and warmth, feeling like I might be sick. The black water mirrors the sky and is perfectly still, reflecting the moon, and Hope Falls is eerily quiet tonight. I look around me but everywhere is closed. The bars and restaurants don't open until the tourists come back. Even the local pub, The Smuggler's Inn, always looks empty. I haven't met anyone here yet, I only spoke to the owner of the art gallery on the phone, but maybe she can help me. I start to walk in that direction, not knowing where else to go.

Even from a distance, I can see that the gallery is full of people. Their chatter and laughter spill out onto the cobbled street through the open doors and windows, and I'm so angry that tonight has not gone according to plan. This exhibition meant so much to me. I wonder if there might be a way to salvage the situation, but I don't know how to explain what has happened, or my appearance, without sounding completely mad. Turning up in my running gear wasn't the first impression I was hoping for, but maybe there is still a way for the exhibition to go ahead. I could find the gallery owner and explain that I got locked out of my house while out on a run. That's not a lie.

The loud babble of conversation from inside the gallery stops abruptly just before I reach the entrance. The place is filled to the rafters with people I have never met, and the turnout is much bigger than I expected. I stay outside on the cobbled street, take a breath and try to calm my breathing. I was right to be nervous about tonight but wrong about why. I hear the sound of glass clinking to signal the start of a speech, and when I stare inside through the gallery window I see that someone is about to give one.

It's her.

The woman who was at my house earlier is standing in the middle of the gallery, wearing my black velvet dress. I can see her more clearly now, under the bright lights. I'd say she is around forty, a good ten years older than me, and clearly far more confident. Her long blonde hair has been perfectly styled into loose waves framing her face, and her lips are painted a shade of red I would never dare wear. She's holding a glass of champagne in one hand and my husband's hand in the other, and everyone – including me – is staring at her.

"Without further ado, it's my great pleasure to introduce you all to the very lovely and very talented Eden Fox," says another woman I do not recognize. She's talking about *me*, but she's looking at *her* – they all are – and I feel as though I have been sucker-punched when the woman pretending to be me starts to speak.

"When Harrison and I moved to Hope Falls I knew it was going to be a very special place for our family. Thank you for making us feel so welcome these past few weeks, and for this, my first ever art exhibition. As you can probably tell from my work, I am obsessed with the sea. I'm so grateful to the Saltwater Gallery, to all of you for coming tonight, and last, but never least, to my Harri for encouraging me to paint again and for being the best husband in the world.

Cheers to you all. I hope you have a wonderful evening, and please buy my work!"

What the actual—

The packed gallery erupts into spontaneous applause and laughter and it feels like they are all laughing at me. Because this has to be a joke.

Harrison is smiling at her. He looks so proud. I don't understand.

This was my night. My paintings. My exhibition.

I am not going to let this woman steal my work, my husband, my life.

I won't let her take what is mine.

I push my way through the clapping crowd, trying to reach Harrison, and her, ready to confront them both about whatever this is, when a hand grabs my arm. I am not used to being manhandled and look up in shock to see the police officer who was at my home earlier. He smiles but it is not kind.

"I think it's time to go."

6

BIRDY

Six months earlier

I leave the hospital in a trance, still trying to process what the doctor said. Death is just a fact of life, but it still manages to take so many people by surprise. Including me. The diagnosis doesn't feel real, perhaps because I don't want it to be. London, which is always loud, is too loud all of a sudden. There is too much noise, too many people, and they are all behaving as though the world didn't just end. I retreat inside myself, switch to autopilot, pull on my helmet and start the red Vespa. I shouldn't really drive the scooter – not when I'm feeling like this – but where I need to go isn't far. I concentrate hard on the road ahead, the traffic, the tourists, the people. Time stretches and contracts into something I can no longer tell, and it feels disorientating when, what feels like only a few seconds later, I arrive at Cecil Court, the little lane in Soho where I live. This place has been home for over a decade and home is where I know I need to be.

Cecil Court is Diagon Alley for bookshops. The tiny, pedestrian street, hidden away but only a stone's throw from Leicester Square, with its quirky Victorian buildings and old-fashioned gas lamps, is home to a collection of beautiful independent bookshops. One of them is dedicated to all things *Alice's Adventures in Wonderland* and I live in the flat above it. The bookshop is closed now. They all are.

And this is normally my favourite part of the day, coming home to a street filled with books, perhaps because I like reading stories that have happier endings than my own.

I take out my key for the flat I call home, slot it in the lock and give an audible sigh of relief when I step over the threshold and close the door behind me. The relief doesn't last. Having longed for silence and sanctuary from the noise of real life, the place is too quiet. Something is wrong. Someone is missing.

"Where are you?" I say, removing my shoes.

He does this when I go out for too long.

He does not like to be left alone.

Today should have been a day off together, but instead I was at the hospital. Not that he knows that. Nobody does. I take off my jacket, hang it by the door, then I walk further into the flat, appreciating the soft rugs and parquet floor and bookcases filled with all the stories I have collected and hidden inside over the years. My own story is less inspiring. If I were to read the manuscript of my life there are so many scenes I would want to delete. But maybe I'm too hard on myself. We all forget our lines from time to time, and sometimes the best and only option is to improvise.

I catch a glimpse of my reflection in the mirror above the fireplace before I collapse into my favourite armchair with a book. I look too thin. Too pale. Too weak. Like someone who might be—

I don't know how or why I keep forgetting.

It's as though my mind is determined to delete the diagnosis.

I need to eat something, that will make me feel better. Unlike the fact he still isn't speaking to me, which makes me feel overwhelmingly sad.

"Please don't sulk. I've had a horrible day and I need someone to be nice to me," I say, getting up and walking into the kitchen, but he isn't there either. "I know you're here somewhere," I call out, not in the mood to play games.

It's true. I can smell him. And then I hear him.

The creaking floorboards in this place give everyone away.

The sound of quiet steps starts in the bedroom then continues down the hallway until he is standing right in front of me. Looking very sad and sorry for himself, as though he is the one who just got told he has less time than he thought.

"I'm sorry I was gone so long," I tell him. "Do you want some dinner?"

And then Sunday's eyes light up and he wags his tail and I am forgiven.

Sunday was just a puppy when we met. I found him crying and shivering in a shoebox outside the bookshop one morning. Abandoned, as though he had been put out with the rubbish. I carried him up to the flat just to get him warm, with the intention of taking him to a vet or an animal shelter. As much as I have always loved dogs, having a Siberian husky when you live in a little London flat and have a busy job is not ideal, and I knew that the tiny puppy would one day be the size of a wolf. So I did take him to a vet, but I didn't leave him there. Couldn't. I got him checked out and then I adopted him. Love is the only thing that is real in this world and you know when you've met your soulmate.

I don't know what I'd do without him.

I don't know what he'll do without me, and the thought of there not being anyone to take care of him and love him the way he deserves after I am gone dismantles me. My legs seem to give way and I fold down onto the kitchen floor and I let myself cry. I'm too young to die. I'm not ready. But life is an unreliable waitress. Sometimes you order ice cream and instead life serves you a triple-decker shit sandwich with a side order of completely fucked.

Sunday knows me better than anyone and he knows when something is wrong. He comes to rest his head on my lap and I stroke his soft fur until I start to feel like myself again. Pull together what is left of me. I need to be strong for everything that I need to do next, but it can all wait until tomorrow. Today is the last day I can afford to let myself carry on as normal, then I'll need to see her. Even if it's the hardest thing I'll ever do and despite all the years I have avoided it. Sunday barks, snapping me out of my melancholy state.

"Yes, I know you want dinner," I tell him. "Come on then, let's see what we've got." We both peer around the fridge door when I open it. There isn't a lot to see. The cupboards are equally bare. So I open a cutlery drawer containing just one knife, one fork and one spoon. I take them out and set a tray, adding the only plate I own. I've never felt it necessary to buy more – there is only one of me and I never have guests.

"Takeaway it is. Cheeseburger and fries for me and chicken nuggets for you?"

Sunday barks and wags his tail.

An hour later, we are sitting side by side on the sofa after a satisfying feast. We're about to watch *The Shining* – my favourite film – when there is a knock on the door. I pause the film just as Jack Nicholson's car is driving along a winding road through the forest. I am especially fond of the music at the start – an adaptation of a medieval hymn for the dead called "Day of Wrath" – so interrupting it rather spoils the mood and puts me in a worse one.

"Who the fuck is that?" I say beneath my breath, hitting pause on the remote.

Nobody should be knocking on my door at this time of night.

I haven't invited anyone. Not tonight. Not ever.

This happens sometimes. People think the downstairs door that leads to my flat has something to do with the bookshop below. It doesn't. More often than not it will be a tourist who has arrived after the shop has closed but is desperate to buy a rare book before they head to the airport. I'm dressed in short Winnie-the-Pooh pyjamas and fluffy socks, my tattooed arm and long bare legs on show, not suitable attire for talking to strangers. I'm comfortable on the sofa. The dog is comfortable. I can't really be bothered to go all the way downstairs to deal with someone who has nothing to do with me. So I wait, hoping whoever it is will take a hint and fuck off.

They knock again.

I get up and stomp along the hallway and down the stairs, flinging open the door, ready to take my bad day out on whoever has dared to interrupt it.

"The bookshop is closed," I say, my words filled with irritation.

A man in a cheap suit smiles at me. "I can see that. I'm looking for Olivia Bird."

I take a small step back, suddenly aware that I have clearly misjudged this situation, and feeling vulnerable without my normal clothes. He's middle-aged – on first glance middle-everything – and is carrying a leather briefcase in one hand and a large black umbrella in the other, as though he might have just blown in over the rooftops à la Mary Poppins. He does not *look* dangerous, but that does not mean that he isn't. The world is full of monsters masquerading as normal people who look like you and me.

Nobody knows that I live here. So I don't understand who this man is or how he knew where to find me. He doesn't seem threatening, but I don't plan on taking any chances. I whistle a high note followed by a low note and within seconds Sunday is by my side.

"I'm sorry to interrupt your evening," the man says, looking a little wary of the large white wolflike creature now staring at him. "But *are* you Olivia Bird?"

"Who wants to know?"

"If you are the Olivia Bird I've been looking for then I'm sorry to inform you that a family member has died."

I don't have any family.

"Your grandmother passed away a few weeks ago and I am the solicitor she appointed to look after her affairs."

"I don't have a grandmother."

"Everyone has a grandmother," he says politely. "It's biologically impossible not to. Just like everyone has a mother. Sorry," he adds then, as though he knows what happened to mine, which seems unlikely. Unless what he is saying is true. "I understand parts of the family were estranged, but according to our – very thorough – research, you are your grandmother's only surviving relative and, well, she left you a little something in a place called Hope Falls. To be honest, she's left you rather a lot. May I come inside?" he asks, looking more hopeful than he did before.

"No," I say and close the door in his face.

Because I know he's lying.

7

EDEN

30th October

I'm telling you the truth," I say to the young police officer who marched me out of the art gallery and down to the old fisherman's cottage that serves as the station in Hope Falls. Sergeant Carter, as he introduced himself, looks like he could have been a mediocre film star had he chosen a different path in life. His floppy hair has a habit of falling over his big brown eyes, and his good looks are just as distracting.

He sighs, suddenly looking older than his years and sounding weary for his age.

"You're telling me that *you* are Eden Fox?"

"Yes."

"That you live in the house on the hill?"

"Spyglass. Yes."

"That the exhibition at the gallery tonight is displaying *your* work, and that the artist inside is pretending to be you?"

"Exactly."

"And that your husband is going along with this elaborate identity theft for reasons you can't explain?"

"That's right."

He looks a little befuddled and I'm guessing this sort of thing doesn't happen very often in a rural fishing village like Hope Falls.

After an excruciating silence he asks, "Would you like a cup of tea?"

I nod and take a seat in what was probably once a fisherman's front room, which is now dominated by a large desk, two chairs and a filing cabinet. Sergeant Carter disappears into an adjacent room, where I hear the sound of mugs clinking together and a kettle. He clearly doesn't believe me, which makes me think he won't be able to help me, but I am at least grateful for the hot drink. A ribbon of steam rises from the cup he puts on the table, and I greedily gulp down the tea, burning my mouth but not caring.

"Thank you."

"You're welcome," he says. "Perhaps we could start at the beginning?" he suggests, then offers a head tilt of sympathy as though I might be confused or lost or unwell.

But I am none of those things.

"I told you already," I tell him, unable to hide my frustration. "There is a woman pretending to be me. I went for a run, the same way I do every Thursday evening, and when I got home, to *my* house, she was in it. My key didn't work in the door – she must have changed the locks – and somehow she has tricked my husband into going along with it. And all those people at the art gallery who also seem to think she is me! I don't understand what is happening, but she's the one you need to arrest."

"Nobody is being arrested. We're just here to have a chat. Hopefully we can get this straightened out in no time. I'm afraid there is an abundance of admin with all police work these days, so let's start with the paperwork." He takes a black pen with a chewed lid from the pot on his desk, then his hand hovers over a blank form.

"Name?" he asks, staring at the page.

"Eden Fox."

He frowns. Looks up. "Well, there's our first problem. The lady who lives in Spyglass and is having an exhibition tonight is called Eden Fox. It's *your* name I'm after."

"That *is* my name."

"Okay then. Let's suppose for a moment that it is. You must have some ID on you? A driver's licence perhaps?"

"I left my purse at home, along with everything else when I went for my run."

"How about online?" he says, opening up a laptop. "You must have a social media account? Something with your name and a picture of you?"

"I don't do social media," I tell him.

"Well, let's just see, shall we?" He starts to type my name into a search engine. "A digital footprint is often more useful than fingerprints these days."

I really hope he isn't going to scan my fingerprints.

"This is a waste of time. I already told you. I value my privacy and I don't do Facebook or Twitter—"

"But you *do* have an Instagram account," he interrupts, turning the laptop around so that I can see the screen. "Or at least the Eden Fox who is at the art gallery this evening does." My chest feels tight as I stare at the Instagram account I have never seen before. It belongs to someone called "Eden Fox Artist" and there is a picture of the woman pretending to be me at the top. I don't understand what I am seeing. "And this isn't a new account by the looks of things," he adds, looking at a patchwork screen of square images. He scrolls down the page and I see endless pictures of my paintings and photos of our new home. Before and after shots of all the renovations. There is even one of me in my overalls on a ladder, painting the walls in the kitchen, but you can't see my face. And from the back, I suppose I do look a bit like her. Harrison must have taken the photo without me knowing, but the rest are all mine, and there must be a hundred of them. All from the last few weeks. All from my phone.

But I didn't post them.

I don't even have an Instagram account.

"I don't understand—"

"Looks pretty definitive to me. These are pictures of her work, her home, her life. I have no reason to think that Eden Fox isn't who she claims to be," he says. "You, on the other hand—"

"Those are pictures of my work, my home, taken on *my* phone."

"But you can't show me your phone?"

"Because I—"

"And you're saying that you *didn't* share these pictures online?"

"No. She must have."

He sighs. "Why would she do that? How would she? These pictures have been posted over several weeks. There is even a picture of her husband—"

"*My* husband."

The head tilt of sympathy is replaced with a look of irritation.

"Well, there is a picture of them together at the village pub a couple of weeks ago. And he isn't the only one who says she is Eden Fox. The gallery owner confirmed it. So did the girls at the bakery where Eden pops in to get fresh bread once a week."

"What?"

"She's the only Eden Fox anyone in the village has seen since the new owners bought Spyglass a few weeks ago. I met Eden myself, only last week. She came in here to the police station to introduce herself and gave me a poster for the exhibition to put in the window," he says. "So I think we can be fairly certain that *she* is the real Eden Fox. What we need to figure out is who *you* are."

"I . . . don't understand—"

"If you don't want to tell me your real name, is there someone we can call? A friend or a relative?"

"My husband," I whisper.

"Great. What's his name?"

"Harrison Woolf."

The sergeant shakes his head. "Anyone else?" I don't answer because there isn't. "You mentioned that you went for a run. Do you think there is a possibility that you slipped and hit your head?" He rolls up his sleeves and I can see the muscles on his toned arms. I can't tell whether he knows how good-looking he is. Men like him used to look at women like me when I was younger. Really look. Not anymore.

"No, I didn't hit my head," I tell him. "I know this sounds crazy, but I'm telling you the truth."

"I believe that you believe that. But you need to understand that you can't go around pretending to be someone that you're not, threatening people, trying to break into houses." I frown and feel my cheeks burn. "Hope Falls has almost zero crime and I plan to keep it that way. Which means I can't let you leave until we get this sorted. So is there anyone else you can think of to call? Someone who can help verify who you are?"

"No."

"Then I have no option but to drive you to Falmouth, where they have a bigger station with better facilities and more staff. They'll keep you overnight."

"What? No. Wait. You can't lock me up, I haven't done anything wrong."

"Sorry, this is way above my pay grade."

"Please. I don't know why any of this is happening. I'm not a bad person."

"Then tell me someone I can call. Someone who can back up your story."

Any contact details for people I know are in my phone. The only numbers I know off by heart are my husband's and—

"Gabriella. My daughter."

"Okay, good. Now we might be getting somewhere. How old is she?"

"Eighteen."

"Great. Want to call her now?"

"I don't have my phone."

"Use mine," he says, offering me his mobile.

"I can't."

He looks as though he is completely out of patience. "Why not?"

"She won't talk to me."

8

BIRDY

Six months earlier

I try to avoid talking to strangers, and never let outsiders into my home, so I ask the man on my doorstep to wait there while I put on some clothes, then suggest we talk in the pub on the corner of my street. Some private conversations are best had in public; it's safer that way. He claims to be a solicitor, but the man looks like a saggy boob dressed in a suit, and I don't trust him. That said, I don't trust anyone. I quietly explain what I do for a living, and promise that if this is some sort of trick, I will fucking end him. He looks scared when I say that – people often are when they find out what I do – and he is quick to show me his ID and some paperwork. A big part of my job is knowing when someone is lying, but despite everything I thought I knew, this strange little man is telling the truth. Turns out I had a grandmother I didn't know about, and she has left me a house in her will.

Sometimes what we don't know can teach us more than what we do. I get a nonalcoholic cocktail from the bar and make myself listen while the solicitor sips a ginger beer and tells a story about me that includes a few missing chapters. Hope Falls used to be home a long time ago, I knew that already. It's where we lived when I was a little girl, it's where my mother died when I was ten years old, and I have never been back since. What I didn't know is that I had a grandmother living in the same village. And what I want to know now is why I was sent into care at the age of ten and forced to endure a series of foster "homes" when it turns out I still had family. Finding this out now, when I have spent my whole life feeling so alone, is nothing less than devastating.

"Your grandmother and mother were estranged," the solicitor says in a matter-of-fact tone. He does not say why. I didn't know my grandmother, but I knew Mum, and I can't help thinking that she must have had a good reason for cutting her own mother out of her life. Home isn't always where the heart is; sometimes home is where the hurt lives.

When I think about my childhood before Mum died – and I make a conscious effort to rarely do so – I remember the sound of the sea outside my bedroom window in Hope Falls. The watery lullaby was the soundtrack of my dreams, and my nightmares. She used to say that we were both mermaids and that one day we would return to a secret world beneath the waves where nobody could hurt us. Then she went there without me. The memory of the sea frequently wraps around me like a blanket of comfort all these years later, and strange as it sounds – even to me – it has often felt as though something about Hope Falls has always been calling me back. Like an unfinished story you just have to know the ending to. The last page torn out of the book of me. Lost. Missing. Incomplete.

I named my dog Sunday because that's my favourite day and he is my favourite everything. The following morning, back in my flat, he sits on the bed and watches me while I get dressed and I feel bad about leaving him again so soon. He's smart enough to know that the clothes I am wearing mean I am going out, and I can see him wondering if he is coming too. My wardrobe contains ten white shirts, five identical pairs of jeans, three pairs of polished brogues, and a selection of very similar tweed jackets. I am a creature of habit, as is my dog. I have always preferred dogs to people. Dogs are loyal and can be trusted. Humans are the ouroboros of the world. Going in circles, eating themselves, making the same mistakes over and over in history as well as in our own puny, pointless lives. Humans may have evolved but humanity has not. We do not learn. Instead, we self-destruct on repeat until oblivion, and we're too stupid to see it.

My dog normally goes everywhere with me, but this is a journey I need to make on my own, so I leave Sunday downstairs in the bookshop. I have never been good at trusting people – but the booksellers always take excellent care of my dog when I can't. Booksellers are almost always the best variety of humans. I worry about the last-minute nature of it all – I am not a spontaneous person, I am someone who likes a plan – but I guess sometimes life takes us on unexpected detours that we simply cannot plan for.

I don't do cars, and Hope Falls is too far away for the scooter, so I head to Paddington Station and take a train. It isn't until I am far away from London and my job and the life I have made for myself that I start to feel afraid. Away from my little flat above the bookshop. Away from my dog. Away from what the doctor told me yesterday. Away from everything familiar. Heading towards the unknown and a house called Spyglass, which apparently now belongs to me. The time passes surprisingly quickly; I'm lost in my own thoughts and regrets, and as the train hurtles through Blackmoor National Park things start to feel strangely familiar.

The park is huge. Over fifty square miles of open moorlands dotted with sheep, craggy granite hills, hidden valleys and waterfalls. Its beauty stretches far and wide in every direction, and I stare out of the train window, trying to take it all in. Blackmoor is also home to a handful of small, fairly isolated villages, and none of them are more remote than Hope Falls. The nearest train station is in another town, miles away. There is only one road in and one road out of Hope Falls, so when I get off the train I take a taxi, and by the time I finally arrive it is getting late. The harbour wall protects the village from the Atlantic Ocean on one side, and ancient moorland borders it on the other. Blackmoor cannot be built on, so the village is protected in lots of ways. People are harder to protect than places, I think, and then I wonder if that is true. The view of the sun setting over Hope Falls is breathtaking, and I am hit by an unexpected wave of memories and a tsunami of emotions.

This was where my mother abandoned me.

I've been alone ever since.

Even when I wasn't.

My mother's voice used to narrate my life. She lived on inside my head long after she stopped living. It was only when I got older I found the off-switch, and learned to dictate a life of my own. My views of parenting have changed over the years. These days I think part of a parent's job is to figure out how to hurt you so that you can learn how to heal yourself.

The village still looks exactly as it did when I was a child and I can remember the house on the hill called Spyglass even though I have never set foot in it before. It's an iconic part of the skyline above Hope Falls, with its oversized eye-shaped windows and curved white walls, built into the cliffs it sits on. I climb out of the taxi and stare up at the house I have just inherited from a grandmother I never knew. She must have known I existed. She probably saw me. From up here on the top of the hill, you can see everything and everyone down below. The sun sets fast in this little corner of the country, and by the time I reach the front door it is almost dark. I look up and glimpse the first stars shining down on me from light years away. A variety of time travel I find astonishing and comforting at the same time. I have never visited any other place where you can see so much sky; it's beautiful.

Spyglass is at the end of a lane with no name, high above and far from the other houses in the village. The way it has been built into the cliff gives it a slightly unreal quality, and although it is still very striking, up close it looks a little tired and broken. But then I have always felt there is much beauty to be found in imperfection. Lavender bushes line the path that leads to a wooden front door with a shiny, brass bird-shaped knocker. The sight of it stops me in my tracks, though I'm not sure why. It's beautiful. This place is so peaceful and still and quiet, the contrast to London is profound. There are no neighbours. No traffic. No one and nothing at all. Other than the calming sound of the sea in the distance, it's completely silent.

I can't quite get my head around the idea of owning this place. I go to put the key the solicitor gave me in the lock but then stop. For some reason it feels wrong, so I tentatively knock on the door, my fingers flinching at the touch of the cool brass bird, but nobody answers. The solicitor did say it was empty and that it was mine, but life has taught me that when something seems too good to be true it almost always is. I have a word with myself and use the key he gave me.

It fits and turns and the door opens.

I hover in the dark doorway, unsure what to expect. Surprised because I feel scared and I don't know why. It is not a familiar feeling for me. My feet seem to be stuck to the spot, not ready to go in, as though my body knows something I don't about this place. But it's too late to turn back. I'm here now. So, for lack of a better idea, I reach for a light switch in the gloom, and am relieved when I find one. The lights flicker to life and although I can now see, the first thing that really hits me when I step inside is the smell.

It's not unpleasant, it's just so overwhelmingly *familiar*. Even though I thought I'd never been here. I recognize the hallway and the staircase too, and I feel as though I have been pulled back in time or tumbled down the rabbit hole. I *have* been here before. Even if I don't remember it. I don't know if all homes have a distinctive smell, but this one definitely does. It smells of old books, wet dogs, Shake n' Vac, chocolate brownies and tea.

It smells like my mother.

It smells of my childhood.

But we didn't live here and I didn't think I had ever set foot in the place until now, so I don't understand what I am remembering.

I hesitate in the hallway, lingering in the shadows of forgotten memories, still uncertain about going any further inside. Stepping into the hall feels like stepping back in time. The decor is faded and old, the furniture looks as though it belongs in a museum and the elderly, elaborate carpet is threadbare in places. The wood-panelled walls are covered in framed photographs of what I suspect might be family. But when I venture closer, I see that every one of the expensive-looking frames contains a photograph of a dog. Some big, some small, all different. Every frame has two dates engraved into the bottom of it, and I'm guessing they were all beloved pets that lived here. I had presumed we would have little in common but my grandmother was clearly a dog person too. One picture is of a huge husky that looks the spitting image of Sunday, but according to the date on the frame the dog died over thirty years ago. I don't recall the dog, or the house, or the woman who owned them, but now I'm here, I'm almost certain I spent time in this house as a child. Maybe I was just too young to remember it. Memories and feelings coexist in a close relationship. They'll lie to you if it means they can stay together.

I close the front door, sealing myself inside the house in a way that makes me uncomfortable. When I do, I notice that there is a large, untidy pile of unopened post on the floor behind the door. I experience a lightning bolt of pain through my body when I stoop to pick it up. The pain is getting harder to ignore. I wish I knew exactly how much time I had left – the doctor was predictably vague – it would make it so much easier to plan and make decisions if I knew how long I've got.

I try to forget about the future and focus on the present, but everything about this situation feels peculiar, as though I have been dragged inside an unfamiliar version of my past. I feel off-kilter and uncertain, and am uncomfortable looking through a dead woman's mail. She might have been family, but to me she was a stranger and I can't help thinking I am intruding. I also can't shake the feeling of being watched, but when I look outside there is nobody there.

The post I have picked up consists mostly of unopened envelopes and far too many flyers. Several of them are for retirement villages, funeral homes, stair lifts and hearing aids, and the way advertisers target the elderly sparks a small flame of fury inside me. I'm about to leave it all on an antique bureau by the front door that is already covered in papers when something catches my eye. The envelope looks fancy. It's like a wedding invitation, except that it's black, with pretty rose-gold foil letters printed on expensive-looking card stock. There are just two sentences on the front:

Everyone knows their birthday.

If you could know your deathday, would you want to?

"For fuck's sake," I say beneath my breath. What a terrible thing to be sending to elderly people. Some scam, no doubt, to relieve them of their savings. The cruel things people do to other people never fail to shock me, even after all the years I have spent doing what I do and seeing what I have seen. I know it's nonsense but the envelope has still managed to pique my interest, and it's already been opened, so I pull out the letter inside.

At Thanatos we believe that

everyone deserves to live their best life.

The only way to do that is to know how long you've got.

Millions of people spend their lives

saving for a future they'll never know.

Millions of people pay into pensions

they'll never receive a penny of.

Millions of people never get

to say goodbye to their loved ones.

The world is full of people who put off living their dreams,

because they've been fooled into thinking

there will always be a tomorrow.

Nobody needs to live, or die, that way anymore.

We can offer you the certainty to make the most of your time.

Here at Thanatos, after years of tireless research,

our friendly team of scientists and doctors

have discovered how to predict the date of your death.

There are **no** scary medical tests involved.*

Unlike most private health clinics, there are **no** fees.*

We care about our clients and we keep anxiety to a minimum,

so there is **no** waiting list.*

We believe knowing your future is your right

and that your time is precious.

Let us help you make the most of whatever time you have left.

For a free consultation, please call this number.

*Terms and conditions apply and only clients named on this letter can participate.

The name at the top of the letter is mine.

9

EDEN

30th October

"I already told you my name."

The young police officer stares at me and shakes his head in despair. I do the same, as though it might be contagious, then I try to convince him again.

"I bought Spyglass and moved in a few weeks ago with my husband. All I know about the woman who lived there before is that she died. I am the real Eden Fox. I don't know who this other woman is or why she is in my house pretending to be me—"

"Okay, I think I've heard enough," he interrupts. "It's getting late and I'm going to have to drive you to Falmouth where they have the facilities to hold you overnight—"

"No, wait," I tell him. "I've thought of someone who I can call to confirm who I am."

I'm not lying. There are only three telephone numbers that I know by heart. The first is my mother's landline in my childhood home. Back then, before mobile phones existed, it was the only number I knew. Despite not calling it for decades the digits are still burned into my brain, but that isn't who I plan to call now. My mother stockpiled pleasantries for other people, but when it came to kindness for her own family the cupboard was always bare. She wouldn't help me then and she can't help me now.

Sergeant Carter drops his car keys back on the desk and reaches inside his pocket.

"Be my guest," he says, holding out his phone. *More like your prisoner*, I feel like saying, but keep the thought to myself. It's the latest iPhone – just like everyone his age seems to have – but it looks intimidating to me. Something I am scared of breaking. He is probably only a few years younger than I am and yet I feel like part of a much older generation. Perhaps the last generation to have not spent their whole lives staring at the world and themselves through a screen. I take the phone from his hand and our fingertips touch. It's such a small thing and yet I feel my cheeks burn.

I type the number into the keypad, my fingers shaking a little, then lift the phone to my ear. The weight of his stare is too heavy so I look down at my running shoes to avoid eye contact. If only I hadn't gone out for a run tonight maybe none of this would have happened.

The phone rings once.

Twice.

Three times and I'm starting to lose hope.

I feel like I am running out of options. My imagination wanders and I fantasize about seducing the young police officer and persuading him to let me go. The thoughts that unfold inside my mind excite and then humiliate me. I can't remember the last time I slept with my husband – Harrison hasn't touched me for weeks – he's been cold and distant since we moved into the new house. It's not like me to have X-rated daydreams – perhaps I am lonelier than I thought – but I imagine Carter fucking me on this desk, the sound of his body pounding mine, flesh slapping flesh, and wonder how it might feel to have a stranger inside me after so many years of marriage. The fantasy turns me on so much I almost don't notice the phone has stopped ringing. The person I called has answered. They clearly already have the sergeant's number in their contacts because they think it is him calling, not me.

"Have you found her?" Harrison asks. I can hear what sounds like a party in the background and I realize he must still be at the art exhibition. *My* exhibition. With *her*. The other woman.

"Harri, it's me."

"Who is this?" he asks.

How can he not recognize my voice?

"It's Eden. Your wife. Why are you pretending not to know who I—"

The officer snatches the phone from my hand. "I'm very sorry, sir. I have the woman in custody and this won't happen again," he says before hanging up.

"In custody? I thought you weren't arresting me," I say.

"You've left me with no choice. You do not have to say anything but it may harm your defence if you do not mention when questioned—"

I start to cry. "I don't understand why my husband is doing this to me—"

"Nobody is doing anything to you. We just need to get this straightened out."

"How would I know his number off by heart if he wasn't my husband?"

Sergeant Carter, who doesn't have an answer for that one, just stares at me. Tears are streaming down my face. I don't understand what is happening, or why, but Harrison being a part of it is devastating. And the thought of being locked in a cell for the night is terrifying. I sob more loudly.

"Stay there. I'll get you a tissue, then we really must get going," the police officer says, sounding uncomfortable. Tears seem to have that effect on most men.

I stop crying as soon as he leaves the room.

I have no intention of spending a night locked up. I take Sergeant

Carter's car keys from the desk and leave through the door we came in. I throw his keys into the harbour – I don't need his, I need mine – then I start running up the hill towards Spyglass.

If nobody will believe me then I'll have to find a way to make them.

10

BIRDY

Six months earlier

I've made some bad choices in my life, but hasn't everyone? Nobody gets it right all the time. Hopefully coming back to Hope Falls won't turn out to be yet another mistake. I explore the rest of Spyglass, and as I turn the lights on in each room I have to keep reminding myself that I own this place now. The solicitor warned me that the property was historically significant and as such came with various ancient covenants attached. One was that the original bookcases in the library at the back of the house were not to be renovated or removed. He explained that they were installed over a hundred years ago by a famous local carpenter who went on to work for the royal family. "Well, whoop-de-fucking-do," I told him, and my reaction was clearly not what he was hoping for.

I hate disappointing people, despite being so good at it.

The paperwork the solicitor gave me – which made excellent bedtime reading as it sent me straight to sleep – said the house came with another covenant which, to me, seemed far more interesting than the first. There was a photocopy of what I think was an original handwritten document from the 1800s declaring in elaborate ink-stained writing that "No merriment making is to be had within these walls." Looking around the place now, I don't think there is much danger of that. The solicitor explained it was something to do with liquor licences, as the owner of Spyglass also once owned the pub in the village. I guess they didn't want any competition in the merriment-making business if the property ever changed hands.

I find the little library at the back of the house, and although the bookcases are rather beautiful, and crammed with books, having a preservation order attached to them seems a little overkill. But what do I know? All I do know is that I have inherited this old house from a grandmother I thought I never knew, and yet, each room fills me with an unfamiliar sense of nostalgia. I often feel as though I have lived lots of different lives in one lifetime. I had to grow up fast and I've had to move, and move on, more often than I should. But I wish I could remember more about this place and the time I spent here as a child.

The blue room is the one that conjures the loudest feeling of déjà vu. The formal sitting room has navy walls and a matching ceiling decorated with painted gold stars. I remember *this*. There is a chandelier that looks far too big and grand for the house, and a huge stone fireplace. There is a single stocking hanging over it, as though it were Christmas, even though it is not. I reach inside and find a small square jewellery box. When I open it I see an enormous ruby ring, so big it must surely be fake or it would be worth a fortune. I slip it on my wedding finger – the only one without a ring – and to my surprise it is a perfect fit.

I stare at the blue velvet sofas on the other side of the room, knowing that I once sat on them, even if I don't know when or with who. There is an ancient TV built into a wooden cabinet on legs in the corner. Now that I see it, I think I remember watching cartoons on this old TV set as a child. A hazy memory of doing so, sitting next to a dog on this blue rug, seeps into my mind, but I'm not sure if it's real. I continue to look around, and I guess the library was too small for all my grandmother's books, because there are piles of them everywhere in this room too. Stacked on shelves, leaning against walls, arranged in teetering piles in the middle of the floor. There must be hundreds of novels just in this one room. My mother always said books were the best company. It seems *her* mother felt the same way.

I'm about to leave the room when something catches my eye: a framed photo on the mantelpiece above the fireplace. But unlike the photos I found in the hallway, this one isn't of a dog. It's me, maybe age five or six, sitting on the lap of a grey-haired woman in *this* room. I guess that's her, my grandmother, but even when I pick up the picture for a closer look I do not recognize her face. I wish I could remember something about this woman who clearly played more of a role in my life than I knew. But I can't.

Next to the photo is a stack of envelopes tied with string wedged between some dusty old novels. There must be over thirty envelopes here, and each one has my name written on the front in the most beautiful calligraphy. I trace the black ink with my fingertips, my rings reflecting the light of the ostentatious chandelier. I open one of the envelopes and find a Christmas card for me.

To dearest Olivia, my favourite little birdy. Why won't you fly home?

The others are all the same, just with a different year scrawled at the top. Tucked inside each card is a swallow's feather, and I instinctively touch the tattoo on my hand.

Maybe my grandmother did love me after all.

Perhaps she just didn't know where to find me.

Why else would there be decades of cards here all with my name on them?

There is a large antique freestanding globe in the corner of the room. It sits inside an elaborate wooden stand. I spin it and my mind is filled with the memory of a grey-haired woman doing the same. She walked her fingers from England on the vintage sphere-shaped map, around the slowly spinning globe, then said, *Life is too short to stay in one place. But however far we travel, we all find ourselves back where we started eventually.* Her fingers came to rest on England again, exactly the spot I am touching now. I pull my fingers away, as though the globe might be haunted, or cursed, wondering if the memory is real or just my tired mind playing tricks on me.

There is a wingback armchair covered in a patchwork design by the fireplace, like a hideous comfy throne. I recognize it from the photo. This is the chair my grandmother was sitting in when the picture of me on her lap was taken. It's clearly very old, and she must have used it a lot over the years because I can see the indentation of where she sat. As though she is still sitting in it. There is one other framed photo in the room, so small I almost miss it. It's of a little girl holding a flashlight in what looks like a dark tunnel. She is me, but I do not remember this photo being taken either.

A loud knock on the front door startles me.

I drop the frame and the glass smashes on the parquet floor.

Shit.

I ignore whoever knocked and look for something to sweep up the mess with. It's probably just a nosy neighbour outside and I can do without that right now – I can do without that, period – but they knock again just as I step into the hall. Almost as though they know I am there. I mutter a few profanities beneath my breath then unbolt the door and open it just enough to politely tell them to fuck off. Except I don't. I'm surprised to see a rudely handsome young man standing on the doorstep. He's wearing a black shirt and blue jeans and an expression that suggests he is equally surprised to see me.

"Can I help you?" I ask.

He frowns, as though he was expecting someone else. "I was down in the village and noticed that the lights were on up here."

"How very observant of you," I say.

"I wanted to check that everything was all right."

"Fine, thank you," I tell him, already starting to close the door.

He puts his hand on the door to stop me. "Can I ask what you're doing here?"

"You could ask but I'm not sure it's any of your business."

He hesitates before speaking again, as though he can't quite make up his mind about me. He isn't the first and he won't be the last.

"I'm sorry. I don't mean to intrude and I don't want to scare you."

What a patronizing fucker. As if I'd be scared of a little shit like him.

"Do I need to call the police?" I ask.

He smiles. "I am the police around here," he says with a baffling dose of pride. "That's why I came to check on the place. It's my night off, but I couldn't understand why the lights were on at Spyglass when I knew nobody was home."

I look him up and down and I believe him. He looks like a police officer, albeit a young one. Too inexperienced to know what he is doing, too arrogant to know it. I am not remotely intimidated by a boy playing detective; I've outsmarted people like him my whole life. I can already tell he falls into the category of oh-so-fucking-predictable. "Can I ask your name and what you are doing here?" he says, and I almost feel sorry for him.

Almost.

"I'm Olivia Bird," I tell him.

But then his face folds into a frown and he shakes his head. "Olivia Bird is dead."

11

EDEN

30th October

I feel like something inside me has died. This morning I was looking forward to spending quality time with my husband and meeting some of the people who live in Hope Falls at my first exhibition. Now my whole life has turned upside down and, just to add to the chaos, I think I might have broken the law by throwing a policeman's car keys into the sea. I don't want him to drive me to the next town and have me locked up; I needed to slow him down. I have never been in trouble with the police, never been accused of any crime. But I am so far out of my comfort zone I can't see my way back, so I do what I always do and run. Up the hill and towards the house I know is mine.

It's raining now and I'm soaked to the skin by the time I reach Spyglass. I'm pleased to see that Harrison's car is still gone, and that my Range Rover is still parked in the driveway. Once I have found what I'm looking for inside the house I plan to get out of here. I presume Harrison and the woman pretending to be me are still at the art gallery; it certainly doesn't look like there is anyone home, but I have no intention of trying the front door again. I just need to get inside, find something to prove that I am the real Eden Fox – I'm guessing my passport should do it – then get out.

I walk to the back of the property, pick up a rock and smash the glass door. Then I reach inside, twist the handle and let myself in. I search the kitchen for my phone but it isn't on the counter where I left it. I can't find my purse either, which means I can't find my driver's licence. I stop and stare at the room, remembering our first night in this house. It was the last time Harrison and I made love.

We christened our new home right here on the kitchen counter. Harri seemed reluctant at first, which was not like him. I didn't take it personally – I thought he was just tired from the move and the long drive from London – and after I got a little champagne inside him he relaxed. I've always known how to turn him on, and once we got going it felt like the good old days when we first met. Back then we couldn't keep our hands off each other. I remember how he picked me up and lay me down on this wooden worktop the night we moved in. Then he unbuttoned the front of my dress from top to bottom until all of me was exposed. I remember his head between my legs and closing my eyes. I only opened them again to see the look on his face when he thrust himself inside me. The sex wasn't like normal. It felt almost animal-like, and he looked angry with me, but maybe I just imagined it.

I push the memories of us from my mind and race through every downstairs room – rooms I decorated – hunting inside the drawers of furniture I lovingly restored. There is no doubt about it in my mind. This *is* my home. How else would I know where to look?

But then why can't I find anything?

Downstairs looks as though it has been completely ransacked by the time I am finished searching for something I can't find. Anything to prove who I am. It's as though all traces of me have been removed. Hidden. Taken. There are pictures in the lounge of our daughter, Gabriella. Various shots of her since she was a baby. But there are none of us as a family; any photos of me are gone. There is one of Harri and Gabby when she was a little girl – an old favourite of mine – but the ones of the three of us together are all missing. As is the wedding photo of me and Harrison that is normally here.

I hurry upstairs to the bedroom I share with my husband. Everything looks exactly as it did before I went for my run. I open the wardrobe, pull out some jeans and a clean white T-shirt and quickly get changed out of my dripping wet running gear. The jeans feel a bit loose around the waist, but I suppose I have lost weight recently. Then I grab a pretty cashmere sweater covered in stars I don't remember buying and put it in a bag with some other things I might need later. I catch a glimpse of my reflection in the mirror on the bedroom wall and I barely recognize the woman who stares back. No wonder the police officer was looking at me as though I might be crazy. I guess the house move, combined with countless sleepless nights worrying about why Harrison was being so distant, anxiety about the exhibition, guilt about my daughter and weeks spent renovating this place have taken their toll. I still look good – long blonde hair suits me – but I look tired, a shadow of my former self. The version of me my husband fell in love with is long gone.

I search inside the drawer in the bedroom where I keep my passport but it isn't there. My laptop is missing too. All traces of me seem to have been removed. I discover an old birthday card from Harrison to me with the words *I love you to death* scrawled inside. I don't remember the card, but reading it now makes me shiver. I find some money hidden in the back of my underwear drawer – if ever I needed a secret rainy day stash of cash this is it – and shove the banknotes into my pockets.

Our bedroom is at the front of the house, and when I hear what sounds like footsteps coming up the gravel drive I freeze. Could Sergeant Carter really have got here that quickly? I creep onto the landing and peer out of one of the eye-shaped windows that must have gifted this house its name. Spyglass is at the top of the hill overlooking the entire village, and from here you really can spy on everything and everyone below. I look out now but there is nobody there. Maybe I imagined it. Either way, I'm sure someone will be here soon, and I need to hurry.

So far I have failed to find my phone, my ID, my purse, my laptop, my passport or my handbag – which also contained my car keys. I know I had a spare set of keys for the Range Rover somewhere, but it's hard to think straight with everything that has happened tonight. I rush back into the main bedroom to search for them. If I can't find anything to prove who I am then I need to get as far away from here as possible until I can come up with a plan.

I think I hear a noise downstairs, and I panic that I'm going to be arrested for breaking and entering on top of everything else. Then I remind myself that I own this house. I stop and stand still, hear nothing, and carry on opening drawers. That's when I notice the silver frame on the dresser in the bedroom. This frame is normally downstairs. I remember carefully choosing it years ago for my favourite picture of us on our wedding day. But when I take a closer look at the photo now, it is not of Harri and me. It's of him and her. It's the *same* photo, but it must have been photoshopped or something, I don't understand. I am not a violent person but something inside me snaps and I throw the frame across the room. It hits the wall, falls to the floor and the glass shatters.

I keep opening drawers, pulling everything out of them, tossing it all on the carpet, and I'm so happy when I find the spare set of car keys I almost cry again. I know what to do now. I know where to go. I'm going to visit my daughter. Gabriella won't talk to me, but going there will help me prove who I am.

I hurry out of the bedroom and along the landing. I hear the creak of a floorboard just as I'm about to head downstairs. It all happens too fast – so fast I don't know whether I tripped or if someone pushed me – but I lose my balance, my arms reaching out for something that isn't there, and then I am falling down the staircase.

Tumbling. Twisting. Breaking.

I hear a loud crack as I land on the stone floor.

There is an explosion of pain in the back of my head, and a shadowy figure slowly walks towards me. My world fades to black before I can see who it is, and I think I might be dying.

12

BIRDY

Six months earlier

"Olivia Bird is dead," says the handsome young police officer standing on the doorstep. Overconfident, underprepared, but good-looking enough to get away with both. He's the kind of guy I would have gone after when I was younger. These days I much prefer the company of dogs. "Can I see some ID, please?" he asks, and I think I'm going to enjoy this.

"The Olivia Bird that died was my grandmother. I was named after her, so we share the same name. She died, I inherited this house, case solved, good night."

The solicitor informed me that my grandmother liked to be known as Mrs Bird even though she never married. My mother – who also never married – preferred to be known as Ms Bird, as though she thought the slight difference was sufficient to tell them apart. They both had a daughter outside of marriage, and neither of them ever said who the father of their child was. That section on my birth certificate was blank. I imagine it was quite the scandal back then. I am not a fan of titles. I go by Bird or Birdy, and have never felt the need to label myself for the benefit of others. What other people choose to call me is up to them.

The boy cop looks a little less sure of himself. "I'd still like to see some ID," he says.

My insufficient stockpile of patience expires.

"So would I."

Not because I don't believe this pretty pipsqueak is a police officer, I just want to know his name. He shows me his badge and it still looks shiny and new. I make a mental note of the name – Carter – and rank – sergeant. He's very junior, nothing I need to worry about. I show Carter my driver's licence and he seems satisfied.

"Sorry to have disturbed you," he says then, looking a little sheepish and stepping back from the door. "I just wanted to make sure everything was okay. We have zero tolerance of crime here in Hope Falls and Blackmoor National Park, which borders the village. So much so they are advertising for a new detective to cover the area. It's statistically one of the safest places to live in England and we want to keep it that way. Now that I know who you are I'll leave you to it."

He starts to walk away and at first I'm glad. But there is something he could help me with, given he has lived in Hope Falls for so long.

"Did you know her? My grandmother?" I ask.

He stops and turns back to face me. "I'm not sure anyone *knew* her. Your grandmother was a woman who liked to keep herself to herself. She lived in the village longer than anyone else; I think she was born here, and was almost one hundred years old when she died. I know she had a live-in carer – I'd see their red Mini parked outside – but nobody ever saw much of either of them. I didn't know your grandmother but I knew of her."

"Was she a good person?" I find myself asking without meaning to.

He shrugs. "I don't think she was a bad one. Like I said, I never met her. She didn't like to leave the house and I don't think she ever had any visitors. Strange how you can live in the same place as a person and know almost nothing about them. I guess some people are very private. Or maybe she just felt the need to shut the rest of the world out."

I can relate to that.

"Do you know the name of the live-in carer?" I ask him.

"Sorry, no."

"At least there was someone with her when she died."

"Actually, she was alone. I was the one who found her. But if it's any comfort, I think she died in her sleep."

Something about that doesn't quite add up no matter which way I do the sums.

"How come *you* found her if she had a live-in carer?"

"The carer was on holiday for a couple of days and your grandmother wouldn't accept any replacement. Insisted she could cope for forty-eight hours on her own."

"Then how did *you* know she was dead?"

"She wrote me a letter."

I can't tell if he's yanking my chain.

"What do you mean, she wrote you a letter?"

"Three days before she died, your grandmother sent a note addressed to me to the police station. Her carer said she couldn't walk very far on her own, but she could clearly walk far enough," he says, nodding towards the red post box built into the dry stone wall in front of the house. "She wrote that she knew she was going to die, and when, and that she had sent her carer away because she wanted to die with dignity and in privacy. The letter said that she had left the back door open so I could let myself in, and that she would be dead when I did. Obviously I didn't believe any of it when I read the letter. I thought perhaps she'd had too much Cornish gin, but sure enough, when I did come to check on her, the door was open and she was dead in her armchair. She'd sent the letter second class or I'd have come up here sooner."

"Evidence of foul play?" I ask.

"None. The coroner concluded natural causes."

Well, that's clearly bullshit.

"Obviously she can't have known the exact day she was going

to die from natural causes," I say, suddenly feeling protective of an elderly woman I didn't even know had existed until recently. "Are you sure it wasn't suicide?" I ask, aware of that dark river running in the family.

He shakes his head. "That's what I thought, but the coroner insisted no. She died peacefully, in her sleep, in her library, wearing her reading glasses and with a book in her lap."

"Which book?"

He stares at me as though that is a strange question.

"*Frankenstein.* I remember because her story choice surprised me. I'm sorry, I don't know how your grandmother knew it was her time, but she did and she was right."

I remember the letter I found claiming to predict the day a person will die.

"I'm sorry for your loss," he says, and turns to leave again.

I retreat inside myself a little bit when he says that. It's what people said when my mother died and it used to make me so angry. I didn't *lose* her. The word *loss* suggests I mislaid her, forgot where I left her, as though perhaps if I went to a lost-and-found desk she'd be there waiting for me. What my mother did dismantled me. I didn't *lose* her, but I have felt lost since she died. Untethered. Alone. This is not the same as that.

"Thank you, but I didn't really know my grandmother. Sounds like the people in Hope Falls didn't either."

"We might not have known *her*, but everyone in the village knew the stories about her. The mysterious old woman living at Spyglass has always been a bit of a local legend."

"What stories?"

"I don't want to upset you—"

And I don't want to rearrange your face.

"Tell me."

"Your grandmother was the woman who died twice."

13

EDEN

30th October

I dream I am dead.

When I open my eyes, I don't know where I am at first. But then I see that I am lying on the cold stone floor at the bottom of my staircase. I don't remember how I got here, it's all a blur, but everything hurts.

I do remember going for my run, but the rest of my thoughts feel fractured, like tiny fragments of themselves that don't fit together or make any sense. Then I have the strangest memory of another woman in my home. Harri pretending to not know who I am catches up with me next, then it all comes flooding back: seeing my husband with that woman at my art exhibition, the social media pages I didn't know existed with *my* name but *her* face, the police officer – what was his name – saying that he was going to arrest me. I experience an overwhelming rush of thoughts and fears and it feels like waking from a bad dream to find myself still trapped inside a nightmare. Perhaps that's all it was, just a bad dream. But then why does everything hurt?

"Are you okay?" asks an unfamiliar voice.

Then I remember falling down the stairs. Or was I pushed? I panic that whoever asked the question is here to hurt me. I try to move, but a bolt of pain flashes through my head and my back.

"Can you hear me?" he asks, a face now appearing in my field of vision.

It's him. The young police officer. Standing there in his too tight uniform, so tight I can see his muscles beneath his shirt.

Did *he* push me down the stairs?

"Try to stay calm," he says. But staying calm has become an obsolete objective. "You took quite a tumble. Are you hurt?" he asks. "Do you know who I am?"

"Sergeant Carter," I say through gritted teeth.

"That's right. Now can you please tell me your name?"

"Eden. Fox." I tell him my name for the hundredth time.

He sighs. "Your *real* name. No more games."

"I think someone pushed me down the stairs," I say, but he just shakes his head.

"I don't think so. I thought you might come here, but it took me a while to lock up the station. I saw that someone had smashed the back door as soon as I arrived and guessed it was you. I had just stepped inside when I saw you at the top of the staircase. You tripped and fell. We'll have to add breaking and entering to the list now—"

"This is *my* house. Why don't you believe me?"

"Do you really need me to answer that?"

I reach inside my pocket for my house key. "Look. This is *my* key chain, with *my* name on it – Eden – why would I have this unless I was telling the truth?"

"Perhaps you stole it? Breaking into a house is a strange thing to do if you have a key."

"I told you they changed the locks. I didn't steal a key chain—"

"I'm guessing you *didn't* steal my car keys and throw them in the harbour too? Lucky I have a spare set. Perhaps you *didn't* break into this house, ransack the place and attempt to leave with the owner's belongings either?" he says, staring at the bag next to me.

"I *am* the owner."

"What you are is under arrest. Come on, up you get."

I try to stand but my legs give way. Instead of helping me, Carter just shakes his head as if he thinks I'm faking it. I rarely swear, even in my own head, but *fuck* him. This man-child is no match for me. He clearly isn't an experienced police officer – his face is as uncreased as his shirt – if his brain were a fraction the size of his ego he would realize that I am telling the truth.

I reach up and touch the back of my head; when I look at my hand it's red. Carter sees the blood too and his expression immediately changes. As does his tone.

"We need to get some pressure on that wound," he says, looking for something to use.

"There are clean towels in the cupboard at the top of the stairs," I tell him.

He climbs the steps two at a time, opens the cupboard, then says, "You're right. There are."

How would I know that if this wasn't my house? is what I want to say. But I'm too busy running out the back door, down the driveway and clambering into my car. All I have is the bag of extra clothes and the map of Blackmoor National Park I managed to grab. The spare key to the Range Rover and some cash were all I found in the house, but that's okay, because that's all I need to get where I have to go.

14

BIRDY

Six months earlier

I go through the gate and step into the graveyard in Hope Falls with a man I just met. The evening sky is an agitated palette of black and blue, as though it can't decide what to do with itself. A bit like me. A flight of swallows soar and swoop and dance high above us, making the most of the dying light, and it brings another wave of forgotten memories to mind. My mother taught me that swallows always find their way home, and I touch the swallow tattoo on my hand, as though doing so might turn back time.

I used to play in this cemetery when I was a child, I remember that too. It was a short walk from where Mum and I lived – much closer than the playground – and memories of reading books while sitting among the headstones fill my mind. I'd make up stories about the people buried here, whisper their names out loud and play hide-and-seek among their graves. The pointlessness of playing the game alone didn't bother me until I was older. It didn't occur to me back then that if nobody knows to look for you, you can't be found.

I remember the last time I was here. It was for my mother's funeral when I was ten, so it's hard to forget. I never came back to Hope Falls after that. A plump lady from the council – whose name and face I don't recall – collected me straight after the funeral. She drove me to meet a foster family in London, and left me with a woman who used me as a human ashtray when I didn't do what I was told. I've never forgotten *her* face, or the scars she left on my skin and my soul. Being back here after all this time feels strange. Dreamlike. Almost as though my sad and lonely childhood wasn't really mine, but something that happened to someone else. I don't tell Carter any of that – it's none of his fucking business – and I only followed him here out of morbid curiosity about "the woman who died twice".

Our hands accidently touch as we walk side by side through the cemetery and I hide mine in my pockets. Rows of ancient headstones line up, or in some cases fall over, all the way to the cliff edge with panoramic views of an unforgiving ocean. My mother is buried here somewhere and I have a sudden urge to find her, which is frankly ridiculous after all this time. I think maybe we love some people more when they are gone.

"This graveyard has been full for years," Carter says, oblivious to the thoughts whirring around my head. "There are no more plots available, but your grandmother already had one."

"You mean she had reserved a space?" I ask.

"Not exactly."

He stops in front of an ancient headstone and – even though I knew to expect it – I am still shocked by the sight of my own name. I frown at the two sets of dates carved beneath it. The headstone looks very old, and I don't understand how if my grandmother died recently. The name and first set of dates were clearly engraved years ago, so weathered by sea and sky that they are barely legible. The second date and the epitaph are much easier to read.

Olivia Bird

1926–1944

1944–2025

THE WOMAN WHO DIED TWICE

"According to my grandparents, Olivia Bird – your grandmother – died at age eighteen when she received news that her fiancé had been killed in the war in 1944. She read the telegram then dropped dead on the spot, as though her heart had literally broken, and was buried here the following day. The Bird family – your ancestors – were relatively well off, certainly compared with the rest of the villagers. Most people struggled to make ends meet during the war, but Olivia's parents paid for the most expensive silk-lined coffin money could buy. Her body was dressed in the finest clothes and apparently she wore rings on all of her fingers," he says. Something else I seem to have in common with Granny. "Her family wanted a big send-off, so they splashed out on a huge banquet so that lots of hungry villagers would attend the funeral. The vulgar display of wealth – especially the huge ruby engagement ring on your grandmother's hand in the casket – was the talk of the town. And unfortunately, or fortunately as things turned out, robbing graves was big business back then.

"That night, as soon as it was dark and only a few hours after Olivia was buried, two men came here with shovels to dig her up. They ripped the earrings from her ears, snapped the necklace from around her neck and started to slide the rings off her fingers one by one. It was the ruby engagement ring they wanted most; they knew it was worth a small fortune, but no matter how hard they tried, they could not get the ring off her hand. They decided to cut off her finger with a fishing knife, but as they sliced into Olivia's flesh and bone her eyes opened and she screamed. The grave robbers screamed too – it's not every day a corpse comes back to life – then they ran through the graveyard to the edge of the cliff where they jumped into the sea to get away from her.

"Your eighteen-year-old grandmother was discovered sleeping back in her bed the following morning at Spyglass. She had all of her rings but was missing a finger – her marriage finger – and she wore those rings for the rest of her life. Like she was making a point. She gave her family a fright when they found her alive at home less than twenty-four hours after they buried her, her bedsheets covered in mud and blood. They were scared and confused for lots of reasons, including that all of the doors were locked overnight, so nobody could understand how she got back to her bedroom or which parts of her story were true."

I stare at Carter and wonder what my face is doing.

"You surely don't expect me to believe all that?"

He shrugs. "I'm just telling you the story I was told. All of this happened long before I was born. After dying the first time, your grandmother rarely left Spyglass. She became a bit of a hermit. Old Mrs Bird outlived the family who accidently buried her alive, and by all accounts preferred living with dogs instead of people. She never married but she did have a daughter – your mother – who was another woman nobody really knew, until she . . ." He skips over the part where my mother killed herself. "Old Mrs Bird left clear instructions in her will that when she did die again, she wanted to be remembered as the woman who died twice. She's a Hope Falls legend."

"I guess not a lot happens around here."

He laughs. "Your new home isn't as uneventful as you might think."

"I'm not staying," I say, perhaps too quickly. "I'm going to put the house on the market. I just wanted to see it for myself first."

"That's a shame. If there is a more beautiful corner of the world than Hope Falls I've yet to find it," Carter says.

"Have you looked?"

He smiles again. "My family and friends are all here. I've never wanted to leave."

I stare at him. "You've *never* left Hope Falls?"

"Why would I? I watch the news and I've seen what a shit show the rest of the world has become. Some people spend their whole lives searching for something they had all along, but I know how lucky I am to live in Hope Falls. It's beautiful, safe, familiar. It's home."

How can anyone be so happy leading a PG-13-rated life?

I think I'd die of boredom if I lived somewhere like this now.

"And I love my job, which is another reason why I'll never leave," Carter says. "This isn't the kind of place where bad things happen. There has never been a case too difficult to solve – nobody has ever been *murdered* here – and with a village this size there could never be many suspects! I don't know why my bosses think the area needs a senior detective. There'll be nothing for them to do, which is probably why nobody has bothered to apply."

"Murders aren't really difficult to solve," I say, teasing him. "I've seen enough true crime documentaries to know it's always the husband."

He smiles and I find myself smiling too.

Then I feel the need to retreat.

"Thanks for showing me this place and telling me about my grandmother. But it's getting late and I think I'll probably start heading back to London."

"So soon? You only just arrived."

"Afraid so. Things to do, places to be, you know how it is." He looks as though he doesn't and it makes me think that living here must be lonely for someone his age. What he says next confirms it.

"Do you want to get a drink before you go?" he asks.

It's been a while since I had anything to do with the opposite sex. My relationships are all nonstick, which makes them easier to wipe from my memory. So I'm a little out of practice, but I don't think I'm imagining it. The hot young police officer is asking me out.

15

EDEN

30th October

Someone is out to get me; I'm not imagining it.

The roads are quiet at this time of night but it still takes longer than it should to drive to the place where our daughter lives now. Time seems to stretch and contract as though I can no longer tell it, and nothing about tonight feels real to me, but I know that it is. The woman in my house pretending to be me is lying. My husband is lying. I'm starting to think the police officer is lying too. But I know that I am Eden Fox, and that woman, whoever she is, is an impostor. I hope visiting my daughter will help me prove it.

I don't stop, even when the car displays a warning light. It's electric and isn't fully charged, but I'm sure it has enough juice to get me where I need to go. The roads are pitch-black and all look the same to me, but I think I'm heading in the right direction. Calling them roads seems overly generous when I am rarely on anything more than a single-track lane. Blackmoor is full of them, narrow winding lanes paved with potholes and lined with a labyrinth of high hedges, so you can barely see where you have been or where you are going.

I haven't visited Gabriella since we dropped her off six months ago. She didn't want to live here and the whole thing was very upsetting for all concerned. But it was best for her, and for us. It was definitely best for me, even if Harrison didn't completely agree. He wasn't the one looking after her. Ten years is a long time to take care of someone who needs that level of attention. Even someone you love.

Gabriella was only eight years old when the accident happened.

She wanted to play hide-and-seek in the house – her favourite game – but I'd said no.

I told her to go outside and get some fresh air instead, and she wasn't happy about it. I dressed her in her coat and the matching pink bobble hat and mittens I had knitted for her that winter. She was a little madam back then; tears and tantrums were guaranteed if she didn't get her own way, but that afternoon she did what she was told without the normal fuss. I should have known she was up to something. Gabby was always a daddy's girl. She liked me, but she *adored* Harrison, and wanted him all to herself whenever he was at home. But I wanted to spend time with him too, alone, in a way that an eight-year-old doesn't understand.

We weren't always the us we are now. I think maybe this happens to all couples eventually, but some try to hold on to what they had rather than admit it's gone. Our variety of love is like a sand timer; it was always going to run out and I think I knew that from the beginning. All varieties of love are an equation. Time *plus* life *multiplied by* hard times *plus* heartbreak *equals* love *minus* lust? Maybe relationships are just a matter of maths? My husband doesn't love me the way he used to, but he does still love me, I know he does, and perhaps that is all anyone can hope for when they have been together as long as we have. Love is more important than passion anyway.

Isn't it?

Ten years ago Harrison and I couldn't keep our hands off each other. On the day the accident happened I thought Gabriella was playing outside like I'd told her to – it was a very safe neighbourhood – so when Harri started getting a bit hands-on after lunch, I suggested heading up to the bedroom for a quickie. Back then he could never say no, but with his job and a little girl to look after, we didn't have a lot of time to spend with each other. So when opportunities presented themselves, we took them. I removed my clothing one piece at a time that afternoon, dropping my blouse, my skirt, then my bra on the floor as I walked up the stairs, silently seducing him, wanting him to want me. He followed, just like I knew he would, and when I dropped my knickers on the landing he bent down and picked them up, staring at me the whole time with a smile on his face. I miss that smile. By the time we reached the bedroom I was already naked. He stood in the doorway and drank down the sight of my body. Even with his suit trousers still on I could see it had the desired effect. I always wore my hair down back then; it was so long it almost covered my nipples, and hid some of the tan lines that decorated my bronzed body. Harri liked to slowly trace those whiter-than-white bits of my skin with his finger, then his tongue. But there was no time for foreplay that afternoon. I climbed onto the bed facing away from him, got on all fours and waited. He accepted the unspoken invitation, unzipped his fly and entered me from behind. Then I let him do whatever he wanted to me, just like always.

Afterwards, he had a shower before driving back to work. I lay exhausted on the bed, not wanting to get up, and it was only when I eventually did that I knew Gabriella wasn't where I thought she was. She'd been outside earlier, riding her bike up and down the street, just like children do. She knew not to go too far and she should have been safe. She'd begged Harrison to take the training wheels off the bike the day before, but he refused, said she wasn't ready. When I looked out of the bedroom window after he left there was no sign of Gabby outside. The guilt I felt in that moment was huge, but the fear was overwhelming. Fear of him never forgiving me if something ever happened to her.

I did all the things people do when children disappear.

I looked for her in all her usual hiding places.

I didn't want to worry Harrison until I had to, until I was sure, so he was already back in his office by the time I called to say Gabriella was missing. His assistant heard the panic in my voice and put me straight through.

It was Harri who called the police. He told me to stay calm and that help was on the way. My husband has always been able to keep his head in a crisis.

The sky was dark and it was raining. I stared out of the window. Watching. Wishing. Waiting. Big fat raindrops streamed down the glass like tears, but I didn't weep. I sat and I worried and I waited for the police to arrive. Afterwards, everyone said that I wasn't to blame. That it could have happened to anyone. That it was an accident. But I have always blamed myself for what happened to Gabriella that day. It was my job to keep her safe and I didn't.

I heard the screaming siren of a police car in the distance.

It got louder and closer so fast.

Then I heard the sound of screeching brakes.

I ran out to the front of the house but it was almost impossible to see anything. The rain was so hard it seemed to be falling up as well as down, bouncing off the ground. The police car had stopped on the street almost right outside but at a strange angle. The siren was still wailing and its blue light continued to flash, causing a series of blue reflections on the black, rain-covered road. I saw the bike first. It had become a twisted, flattened metal shape beneath the car's front tyres. I stopped and stared, unable to process what I was seeing, my eyes searching for her. Then the tears started streaming down my face with the rain when I recognized the little pink mittens I had knitted.

I saw Gabriella lying on the road.

She looked so small and still and broken.

Then I heard someone scream and realized it was me.

16

BIRDY

Six months earlier

It was me who said no. I politely turned down Carter's offer of a drink – the only pub in the village looked closed anyway – but I did let him walk me back up the hill to my grandmother's house. Even doing this is out of character for me. I don't need a man to walk me home, especially one ten years younger than I am. I tend to keep myself to myself these days, but maybe I have missed human company more than I thought. When we reach the old front door at Spyglass with its curious bird-shaped brass knocker, I take out the key but hesitate before using it. Carter looks hopeful. Cocky but still unsure of himself. I find myself wondering how young is too young.

"Thank you for telling me about my grandmother."

"You're welcome," he says, standing a little too close. "If you ever come back to Hope Falls and fancy that drink—"

"I won't be coming back."

"Got it." He nods, smiles politely, and starts to turn away.

"And I don't drink . . . but if you want to come in I'm sure we could find something else to do."

His strong hands paw at me as soon as we are inside the house, quickly unbuttoning my shirt and jeans as though worried I might change my mind. I won't. I've been imagining us doing this since we met. We stumble into the quirky-looking lounge where everything is a shade of blue, and collapse onto an old velvet sofa. Carter might be young to be a cop, but he clearly knows what he is doing in this department. His tongue is inside my mouth and his hand is inside my knickers before I have time to think too much about what a bad idea this is. I stare up at the dark blue ceiling covered in stars as he kisses my lips, my neck, my breasts, before moving lower. I've never been intimate with a man ten years younger than me before.

I think I like it.

"You have tattoos all over your arm," he says, stating the obvious when I pull off my shirt. I liked him more when he didn't ruin things by speaking. I flinch when he reaches for them. I don't know why some people think it's okay to touch a person's tattoos.

They're not fucking kittens.

I got my first piece of body art – the swallow – when I was thirteen. It was designed to disguise a cigarette burn my foster mother gave me for Christmas when I was ten. She dug her long nails into my skin to hold my hand in place, burned me, then smiled when I cried. The tattoo hid the hurt. Something ugly can sometimes be turned into something beautiful.

I'm impatient to feel Carter inside me, but he looks serious all of a sudden, as though he can somehow sense that people have hurt me. Or tried to. "If there's anything you don't want me to do just say so and we can—"

"I don't want you to *talk*. Is that okay?" I say, pulling him towards me.

Carter is a fast learner and doesn't need to be told twice.

He has a lot of energy but takes his time taking me. On the blue velvet sofa, up against the mantelpiece, on the floor. He picks me up as though I weigh nothing, and I wrap my legs around him, holding him in place. He seems enthusiastic to try me on for size in as many positions as possible and I'm here for it. We make use of the wingback armchair in ways I'm guessing Granny never did. The only thing that spoils it is remembering my diagnosis and wondering if this might be the last time I sleep with someone. It's hard not to feel down when you start collecting lasts instead of firsts.

"Can I ask you a question . . ." I say afterwards as we lie naked on a sheepskin rug.

"I think after what we just did, you can ask me anything," Carter replies, lying on his side with his head propped up by one strong arm, staring into my eyes as though he might be in love. His face is stretched into a broad smile as though he just won the egg-and-spoon race. "I mean, that was the best sex I've ever had. *Ever.* It was incredible, right?" he says.

It wasn't bad.

"Sure. How do you think my grandmother knew when she was going to die?"

From the expression on his face, that was clearly *not* a question he was expecting.

"I don't know," Carter says. "The letter she sent to the police station said she was going to die on Friday the fourteenth and the coroner concluded after I found her that she did. But *how* she knew . . . maybe when you're that close to the end you just do? She was almost a hundred—"

"So you believe she predicted her own death?" I ask.

"The only thing I believe is that there is a lot we don't know we don't know. Death is never right on time in my experience. I don't know the answer, not sure we ever will, but maybe your grandmother knew something we don't." Or maybe a company called Thanatos predicted her date of death, she believed them and somehow that caused her death.

It can't all just be a coincidence, there's no such thing.

Before we can continue our deep and meaningful post-shag discussion, my phone rings. I reach inside my bag to see who is calling, then I choose not to answer.

"What was that?" Carter asks.

"That was none of your business."

"I said what, not who. Your phone is from the Dark Ages," he says, laughing.

"It's actually only a couple of years old and it works perfectly well. I've never understood the need to replace things that are not broken."

"You don't have a smartphone?"

"No."

"Why?"

"Because I'm smart. Those things listen to every word you say and I value my privacy. So-called social media will stain your brain, and I don't have time for all that shit and shenanigans. I only need a phone to make phone calls. If I want to waste hours of my life staring at a screen I'll buy a TV."

He stares at me as though I might be crazy. "You don't have a TV?"

"Thank you for the questions, and for the sex, but I have a few things to do, so . . ."

It takes a second for the penny to drop and when it does he looks mortified.

"You want me to *leave*?"

What was he expecting? Did he think we were going to go upstairs and spend the night spooning in my dead grandmother's bed?

"Unless you want to do that again? But to be completely honest I'm exhausted," I say. His cheeks turn red and he looks a curious mix of hurt and confused, which makes me feel bad. "That was *lovely* though," I tell him in the voice I normally reserve for young children.

I wait until Carter is gone, then get dressed and go back to the bureau in the hallway by the front door. It's covered in post – some opened, some not – all stacked in precarious piles. I quickly sort through them, not expecting to find what I'm looking for. Not even sure if I want to find it. But sure enough, among all the clutter and chaos, there is another black envelope with gold foil and the same logo as the first. I open it and read the letter inside.

Thank you for joining the Thanatos Family.

You'll find your date of death confirmed below.*

Olivia Bird – Friday, 14th February 2025

We all have a right to know when our last day will be,

and now you can live your best life every day until the day you die,

and make any arrangements with peace of mind.

Do be sure to contact us if you need any further information

at the number below.

We wish you a Happy Deathday.

*Terms and conditions apply.

I stare at the letter that was sent two weeks before my grandmother died, correctly predicting the day that she would. I guess she took Thanatos up on their offer, and my head starts to spin with the effort of trying to make sense of it all. I have a logical mind and I know this can't be real. I don't understand how this company was able to predict the exact date my grandmother was going to die. But I intend to find out.

17

EDEN

30th October

Someone is setting me up and I plan to find out who. Visiting Gabriella will help prove who I am. She survived the accident but was never the same again, which is why I dedicated my whole life to looking after Gabby from then on. But I couldn't do it forever. Ten years is a long time, so I found somewhere else for her to live, a place with people who have more time than I do to take care of her. I thought it was best for all of us, but as I make my way up the winding driveway that leads to The Manor I start to have second thoughts about that.

The Manor looks like a spooky old mansion in the dark, but that is not what it is. Not since a company with a lot of money bought it, renovated it and turned it into something else. I'm just relieved I finally found the place; it feels like I've been driving in circles for hours. The lights are off in almost all the windows and when I check the time I see it's very late. Gabriella is bound to be asleep by now but this can't wait. I park the car outside the imposing entrance, walk up to the door and push the buzzer.

"Can I help you?" asks a weary-sounding voice.

"I need to see my daughter. Gabriella Woolf."

"It's almost *midnight*," the voice says.

"I know. I'm sorry. It's a family emergency."

The only problem with a secure mental health unit is that it is very secure.

There is no response, so I try again.

"I'm so sorry, I know how completely unacceptable it is to turn up like this in the middle of the night, and I would never do such a thing if it wasn't so important. I can't tell you how grateful I am to you and your colleagues for taking such great care of our little girl now that we are no longer able to. I've driven through the night to get here. It's a deeply upsetting family matter, and it is time-sensitive, so won't take long. I would just like Gabby to have the opportunity to say goodbye to someone who loves her before it is too late."

It's strange how true the lie sounds when I say it out loud.

Something I said works because I hear a click, the door is released from its locks, and I am able to push it open. The large wooden door of The Manor gives a theatrical creak as I step inside, and the air feels immediately cooler. A little stale. This place was once a manor house, but it is now home for young people who need the kind of care only somewhere like this can give. The Manor is expensive, secure and discreet. It's where rich broken people go when nobody wants you to know they are broken. Gabriella did not *want* to come here. Harrison didn't like the idea either. But as much as I love her, I cannot care for her every day and night forever.

Is that so wrong of me?

Guilt is a tight-fitting emotion and I wear it a little too well.

A woman dressed in white hurries towards me across the polished parquet floor. *Everything* she wears is white; not just her uniform, but her hair band, glasses and shoes too. She insists on accompanying me to Gabby's room, which is good, because this place is a bit of a rabbit warren and I honestly can't remember the way.

I follow the woman in white. The heels of her white leather shoes squeak on the stone floor as we walk through a grand entrance hall, past a huge grandfather clock and up the steps of an elaborate twisting staircase. I can still hear the ticking clock echoing as we walk along the corridor and it reminds me of the night Gabriella had her accident. I remember feeling more alone than I have ever felt, and counting down the minutes until Harrison would come home and fix everything.

But some things that get broken can't be fixed.

I can still picture eight-year-old Gabby on her shiny new bike.

One minute she was there, then she was gone.

The investigation that followed the accident concluded she was on her bike in a blind spot on the quiet suburban road outside our house. They said the driver of the police car wasn't to blame, despite driving too fast in a residential area in heavy rain, but I have always believed that if they had driven more carefully perhaps they might have seen her and stopped before it was too late. I hate the driver of that car; what happened that day was really their fault, not mine.

I remember Harrison finding us in the hospital and it was like watching his heart break when he saw his broken little girl. *What happened?* he'd whispered over and over again, holding her tiny hands in his. She was unconscious so couldn't answer. I struggled to find the words myself. I think I knew even then that we – Harri and I – would never be the same again. His daughter was his world and his love for her eclipsed his love for me.

Harrison is a man used to getting his own way. He insisted on only the best doctors caring for Gabriella, and when they couldn't fix her he demanded better ones. Until there was nobody left to tell him what he didn't want to hear. None of them thought she would make a full recovery and all of them were right. Over time, and with a series of lengthy and painful operations, her body healed itself. But her mind never did.

"I don't think we've met," I say to the woman in white, wondering how much she knows about me, our daughter, and us.

"No, we haven't," she confirms. Her crisp white uniform looks new and I think she might be too. "I only work nights, so I rarely meet visitors." Which means she can't confirm that I am Eden Fox. I'm pleased she didn't ask to see any ID – given I don't have any – but the fact that she let me in without checking who I am leaves me with more questions than answers. Like wondering how secure this place really is for the residents if they let random people inside late at night.

"Here we are," she says, stopping outside a door that looks exactly like all the other doors we have passed except for the name and number on the front.

Room Thirteen
GABRIELLA WOOLF

"I'm sure you know this already," the woman in white says. "Gabriella has been making good progress." I did not know that, but perhaps the woman is just being polite. I also didn't know that the staff locked the residents in their rooms at night, and feel a little shocked when she takes out a set of keys. It makes the place feel even more like a prison and me feel even more guilty about leaving Gabriella here. What if there was a fire? The woman in white takes an extraordinary length of time to unlock the door, and a small part of me is relieved, scared of what I might find behind it.

Gabriella was a happy child before the accident, but she was never kind. It's a terrible thing to think, but I always thought there was something wrong with her. Even before there was. Gabriella won't be able to say who I am – she hasn't spoken a word since it happened ten years ago. Harrison took her to see every specialist in the country after she recovered from her physical injuries, but none of them could help. All the doctors he took her to said the same thing – that there was nothing wrong with her brain function and that her mutism was a symptom of extreme post-traumatic stress. They all said she'd speak again one day. But she never has. The only thing she does do since the accident is paint.

Painting was always my favourite form of escape. It was something I did to try to find myself again when I was too naive to see that I had lost me in the first place. It was something I did for myself – the *only* thing I did for myself – but the way Gabriella watched me made me think it could be good for her too. So after the accident I taught her to paint, and it seems to be the only way she can express herself. Despite being eighteen now, all the paintings she did with me in our old home were still very childlike. They tended to include animals and birds, clouds and rain. Gabriella's face rarely expresses emotion since the accident; there is no real way to know what she is thinking or how she is feeling, but I like to believe that painting makes her happy. Even if she isn't terribly good at it.

The real reason I came here wasn't to see my daughter, it was to make sure I haven't gone mad and that I am who I think I am. I left a framed photo of the three of us – Harrison, me and Gabby – in her room the day we dropped her off. It must still be here. So even if all traces of me have been removed from the house in Hope Falls, there is something at The Manor to help prove who I am. To prove that I am Eden Fox.

The woman in white opens the door and flicks on the light inside Gabriella's living quarters, which consist of the lounge we are now in, a bathroom, and a bedroom. But I don't see the framed photo I came here to find. I forget to even look for it, I am too distracted by the paintings.

There are so many of them.

And they *don't* look like paintings by a child.

They are perfect. Beautiful. Terrifying.

Because all of them are of Spyglass, with its distinct curved roof and windows like eyes. I stare at the endless, exquisite paintings of my beautiful but strange new house in Cornwall. A place Gabriella has never been. A home she's never seen.

The woman in white leads me into the bedroom and switches on the lamp. Gabriella sits up in bed. She has clearly been asleep, and looks startled when she sees us. As I suppose most people would if woken in the middle of the night. Her eyes flick from me to the woman, blinking as though adjusting to the light.

"Your mother is here to see you," the woman in white tells her.

Gabriella stares at me again, then shakes her head.

She looks confused and afraid.

Then my daughter, who hasn't spoken a single word for ten years, opens her mouth.

The whispered words that come out of it are quiet and fragile and broken, as though it requires a huge amount of effort to speak them, but I still hear what Gabriella says.

"She. Is. Not. My. Mother."

18

BIRDY

Six months earlier

I am not a people person, and it is a relief to be back in London. Back in my flat. Back inside the life that I have built for myself since the life I knew was taken away from me. Everything that has happened over the last few days feels like a dream – the hospital, the inheritance, the grandmother I didn't know I had, the trip to Hope Falls, the one-night stand. It's all a bit overwhelming – even for me – but I will not let this diagnosis define me. Nobody else needs to know that I am terminally ill, that's between me and death. It's time to get back to reality. Back to work. Back to who I am now, not who I was then, before I knew. But first, there are some things I need to know.

I leave Sunday downstairs in the bookshop, walk along the little lane that is Cecil Court and step into real London. I hail a black cab to Harley Street, anxious not to be late for my appointment. The fancy letter I found from Thanatos claimed to predict the exact day of my grandmother's death. I want to know if it's a con. And if it isn't – which of course it is – I want to know if they can predict mine.

The receptionist knows my name before I say it, which is a tad disconcerting. I sit in a waiting room – something I am getting used to – but this is not like any of the NHS hospital waiting rooms I have spent hours in recently. This is a private clinic on Harley Street and it looks like something from the future. Instead of dated, tired furniture and a permanent smell of bleach and despair, everything in this place is brand-new and white. The air has the calming scent of a luxury spa, and the staff all look like models, with perfect hair, flawless makeup, as though their faces have been airbrushed, and permanent white smiles.

I only booked the appointment yesterday and now I am here. The Thanatos website consisted of a landing page with the company's name and a phone number. That was it. No details about who they are or what they do. Nothing. When I called the number, a posh female voice immediately purred that membership was *by invitation only*. I didn't ask membership of what, instead I gave her my grandmother's name that was printed on the invitation I had found at her house in Hope Falls. Because Olivia Bird is my name too. I was put on hold for a long time. So long I almost hung up, but then a voice replaced the soothing music I'd been forced to listed to, and I swear I could hear the woman on the phone smiling as she said *Welcome to Thanatos.*

I was given a different web address – something you would never find unless you knew to look – and asked to complete an online questionnaire. An hour later they called me back, offered me an appointment today, and here I am. No waiting list. No waiting. When I first found the Thanatos letter at my grandmother's home I felt nothing but rage. I was sure that it was a con, just another – albeit elaborate – way to take advantage of the elderly. And take their money. But the anonymous voice on the phone said that there are no fees at Thanatos.

You give us your time and we tell you how much you have left.

That's what the voice said. More than once.

As though it were a line from a script.

I might be here in the waiting room, but I still don't believe that a company can really predict a person's date of death. I know we live in a world ruled by technology capable of things I couldn't have even imagined when I was a child, but this just sounds too far-fetched. A quick Google search soon proves me wrong.

There are literally hundreds of news articles about the subject. Ranging from stories about scientists using blood samples and laser beams to predict how long a person will live, to more recent AI developments involving algorithms that can guess when someone might die with a "high degree of accuracy" based on their DNA. While there seem to be a lot of companies all competing in the race to create an accurate death clock, none of the ones I have found online claim to be able to predict the exact day a person will die. A death date.

There are very few details about Thanatos online, almost none, but I found one tiny mention of it in a recent newspaper article describing it as "one of the world's leading pharma tech companies" – whatever that means. They wouldn't even give me an address until I completed the online questionnaire and was offered an appointment. All I had that proved this place even existed was a paper invitation and the website. Both looked stylish, expensive and minimalistic. A lot like this waiting room.

"If you could just fill out this questionnaire, the doctor will see you shortly," purrs the smiling receptionist, handing me an iPad. She's young, early twenties, and dressed in designer clothes that look like they cost a week's wages. I still can't figure out the scam. I've met more than my fair share of criminals and she doesn't look or sound like one. But she *does* look familiar, even though I can't put my finger on why. I think I might have seen her in a film, but that seems unlikely. I stare at the iPad in her pale, manicured hand.

"I already filled out something online—"

"That's the *first* questionnaire. This is the *second* one. It's all part of the process." She says the words slowly and kindly with a smile so strangely sincere it is unnerving. Her teeth are a dazzling shade of white and too perfect, just like the rest of her. I wonder how many questionnaires there are going to be in total as I take the iPad and start answering the next set of questions. Some of which are the same as last time, almost as though this is a test.

The questionnaire starts with the basics: name, address, age, sex, weight, height. Then there are some questions I didn't expect and feel uncomfortable answering:

Please state your annual income.*

List names and dates of birth for all known family members.*

Any and all social media accounts must be declared below.*

Any and all email addresses (past and present) must be declared below.*

ALL questions are PART OF THE PROCESS.

*Failure to disclose any requested information terminates the process.

I swipe to the next page of the digital questionnaire and see a long list of statements with yes/no options. It seems obvious that I have to say yes to them all if I want to proceed.

I hereby agree to install the Thanatos App on all my electronic devices within my home and those carried on my person. **Yes**/No.

I hereby agree that Thanatos will have access to all previous medical records for me and any immediate family. **Yes**/No.

I understand that I will not have to pay for this service, but I will sign an NDA if selected as a suitable candidate. **Yes**/No.

The list goes on and on, page after page. I fill it all in with true enough answers, then hand the iPad back to the too-perfect receptionist.

"Thank you, this looks wonderful," she says, beaming as though I just baked her a bloody cake. "Now I just need to scan your fingerprints."

I take a tiny step back from the desk. "Why?"

"It's all part of the process," she says again, like a fucking robot. "All of our clients have to complete these steps before meeting with the doctor."

In my line of work the scanning of fingerprints is something best avoided. My mind is racing ahead, wondering why that is *part of the process*.

"Can a person's fingerprints predict when they are going to die?" I ask.

She smiles. Again. "Everything will be explained to you when you see the doctor, and they'll be more than happy to answer any questions you have then. If you would rather leave, you are of course under no obligation to stay."

The unspoken threat is not lost on me. I let her scan my fingers and thumbs on both hands because what choice do I have. "Please leave all your belongings – including any electrical devices and all phones – in the locker provided," she says afterwards. "Then you may proceed to room nine, where the doctor will be waiting for you." Her smile vanishes as soon as she looks back at the screen.

The doctor does not look like a doctor. He doesn't sound like one either. His face is strangely familiar – just like the receptionist – but I'm not sure where I have seen him before. He also smiles a bit too fucking much, and I'm starting to think that smiling is compulsory in this company.

"Hello, I'm the doctor," he says.

I'm guessing if he wanted me to know his actual name he would have told me. He's young, younger than me at least, and everything he is wearing looks expensive and brand-new, the shirt, the fitted waistcoat, the shiny, pointy leather shoes. The room we are in is a white box devoid of decoration. There are two white swivel armchairs, a white table and a discreet camera. It seems they plan to film me.

"Don't worry about that," he says when he notices me staring at it. "Just saves me having to make notes while we chat. Tell me, in your own words, why do you want to know when you will die?" he asks with another dazzling smile. He starts nodding before I have started answering, as though trying to encourage the words out of me.

"I've had a diagnosis of—"

"Yes, I read that," he says, as though hurrying me along. "But why do you want to know your end date?"

"My *end date*?"

"Sorry, that's just what we call it. Your date of death?"

Fuck me. Straight to the point then. I guess that's part of the process too.

"So I can make preparations, I suppose. Say goodbye to loved ones."

He nods and I think I have given the right answer. But then he frowns. "You don't really have any loved ones though, do you."

What variety of tomfuckery is this?

His words were a statement, not a question.

I stare at him, speechless, thinking I must have imagined him saying that to me.

He smiles. "Except for your dog, of course; we understand that you love Sunday. From what we know about you, and we know a lot, you know when a person is telling lies, so it seems strange to us that you would lie yourself. It's just that, you are an intelligent person with an above-average IQ. Your score when you were a child suggests superior intelligence . . ."

How does he know my bloody childhood IQ score?

". . . As does your track record at work."

I deliberately never told them what I do.

I start to stand. "I think I'd like to leave now—"

"Please sit, Birdy. May I call you that?"

"I'd rather you—"

"We know your mother called you Birdy when you were a little girl – before she committed suicide – and that you prefer to be called Birdy than Olivia. And we know you know that with a diagnosis like yours, you'll probably be dead before too long." His insensitivity stuns me into silence. "Your pupils have dilated a little, so I can see that I have upset you, and I apologize for that. Your emotional response level is a little higher than we estimated based on the information you supplied. Causing you further anxiety is not our intention, but I hope you can understand our strict guidelines and the need for checks and balances. What I'm trying to establish is if we tell you the exact date you will die, what will you do with that information?"

"I don't understand how you can claim to predict when—"

"You don't need to know *how*, Birdy. That's our job. We only want what is best for our clients, and we are a highly ethical company, one which takes its role and responsibility seriously. If telling you the date you will die might in any way cause you additional suffering or anxiety, we simply won't do it."

If this is an act it's a bloody good one.

Is he an actor? Is that why I recognize him?

He's waiting for me to say something, and the truth feels like the best option.

"I want to know because there is someone I need to see before it's too late."

He stares back at me for a long time, then nods.

It's only then that I notice the earpiece he is wearing.

"Good," he says, as though I have just passed a test. "I'll be back in just a moment."

He leaves the room and "just a moment" feels like it takes almost an hour. I can't be sure because they made me leave my watch and my phone in the locker and there is no clock in the room. I have never been a patient person, so after what feels like too long to leave me waiting, I stand and walk towards the door to let myself out. As soon as I reach for the handle the door opens, almost as though someone was watching me the whole time.

"Sorry to have kept you," says the doctor. "This is the nurse. She's going to do a few tests, starting with a blood test if that's okay?" I guess we're still on a no-name basis. The nurse, like her colleague in reception, looks like she just stepped off a catwalk. "Please take a seat, this won't take long."

I remove my tweed jacket, roll up my shirt sleeve and reluctantly sit back down. The nurse smiles, wraps a tourniquet around the top of my arm, smiles again, then inserts a needle. I've never been great with needles, so I turn away. The doctor resumes his position sitting on the white chair opposite me, then answers my next question before I have time to ask it. "Our tests involve a blood sample, some nail clippings – think of it as a mini manicure – followed by a scan, which will feel very similar to the MRI you had at the hospital, but works in a different way. Then I just need some skin and hair samples. It's all just part of the process." I turn back to the nurse and see that she is filling a third small tube with my blood. It seems they need quite a lot.

"Okay. After you've carried out these tests, what happens then?" I ask.

The doctor smiles. "Then we'll be in touch."

The letter arrives the next day.

There is no stamp. It has been hand-delivered.

It looks just like the fancy black envelope my grandmother received, with rose-gold foil letters printed on expensive-looking card stock. But this time the name on the front really is mine. My hands tremble a bit as I start to open it. People with my condition, diagnosed at this stage, can sometimes live for another year, possibly two. Or they're dead within six months. The diagnosis was a death sentence without a deadline. This might give me a more accurate time frame, or it might all be nonsense. I understand enough about pharmaceutical companies and the lengths they are willing to go to in order to secure contracts and make money. A lot of money. And it's often when people are at their most desperate and most vulnerable that they fall victim to huge corporations who feed off despair to fulfil their greed. But Thanatos, a so-called pharma tech company, still haven't asked me for a penny. They invited me to see a doctor straight away and haven't even made me wait for the results. Despite my cynical nature, I'm starting to believe they might actually be able to do what they claim to be able to do: accurately predict a person's date of death. If not, it's a very elaborate hoax, and given they don't charge for their services I can't quite fathom what they are getting out of it.

Sunday jumps up on the sofa beside me and rests his head on my lap. We stare at the envelope in my hands as though we're both afraid of what might be inside. I open it and carefully take out the letter. My eyes rush to read the date of death first – of course – but then I read the words printed beneath it several times, as though I can't quite process them.

Thank you for joining the Thanatos Family . . .

We all have a right to know when our last day will be,

and now you can live your best life every day until the day you die,

and make any arrangements with peace of mind.

Do be sure to contact us if you need

any further information on the number below.

We wish you a Happy Deathday.

Seeing my *end date*, as the doctor called it, winds me.

Maybe nobody should know their date of death.

Maybe we should all be allowed to dream that we might live forever.

But then who in their right mind would want to live for fucking ever?

I know what I need to do.

19

EDEN

30th October

I have no idea what to do.

"She. Is. Not. My. Mother."

Gabriella whispers the words again, her eyes wide and wild, sitting up in the bed looking like a ghost. Then she opens her mouth to scream and a strangled sound comes out. She hasn't spoken a word for *ten years*, now *this* after just six months of living at The Manor. The woman in white stares at her in horror, then turns to stare at me, before trying to comfort the girl.

I don't understand what is happening.

Have I gone mad?

Maybe I'm not who I think I am.

But if I'm not me, who am I?

My daughter hasn't spoken, or laughed, or cried, or frowned for a decade. But when the other woman in the room isn't looking, Gabriella turns her face towards me and slowly smiles. It's the creepiest thing I've ever seen.

I can't breathe, my heart is beating too fast and it feels as though someone is pressing on my chest. The room seems to tilt and I lose my balance, stumbling back towards the door. Looking for a way out. This is all too much, *she* is too much – she always was – and I can't take any more. I used to love her but now I *hate* her. I wish she had never been born. They are thoughts no mother should have, and as always, the thoughts soon translate into guilt. Being a good parent and being a good person are not the same thing and I'm so tired of trying to be both.

I run out of Gabriella's room. I run past all her perfect paintings of Spyglass, along the corridor and towards the spiral staircase. The woman in white calls after me but I don't stop, won't turn back, can't answer. I just need to get out of here. It feels like I can't trust anyone, including myself. The grandfather clock in the hallway of The Manor starts to chime midnight as I hurry down the stairs, and I feel a curious sense of relief that this awful day is finally over. But my problems are not behind me, I'm surrounded by them now. I lock myself inside my car. My hands tremble as I switch on the engine and grip the steering wheel. I drive as fast and as far away as I am able, along narrow country lanes, weaving through Blackmoor in the dark. My tears blur my vision, making it almost impossible to see, but I don't pull over. I don't even know where I am going. I have nowhere left to go and nobody to turn to.

The network of lanes that twist through the vast, untamed moorland are silent and empty at this time of night. I'm scared and exhausted and when the car makes an unfamiliar noise I panic. I stare at the dashboard and see the red warning light I ignored earlier. The Range Rover seems to take control of itself and starts to slow down. Damn Harrison for persuading me to get an electric vehicle. It is out of charge and I am out of time. The speedometer slowly decreases until I come to a halt. The car turns itself off and I sit in the dark. There are no streetlights out here. I can't see anything at all.

I am somewhere in Blackmoor National Park but I have no idea where. It is the middle of the night. It is cold. Pitch-black. And I don't have a phone so I can't call for help. I don't dare to get out of the car – there is nothing and no one for miles, I wouldn't even know what direction to walk in, and I don't even have a coat to keep me warm. I find the bag I took from the house earlier, but there is nothing useful inside except for the cashmere sweater covered in stars. I pull it on to combat the cold but it offers little comfort. I'm stuck and I'm trapped and I'm scared. I cry. *Really* cry. And when I close my eyes and rest my head on the steering wheel, I somehow fall asleep.

The sound of a phone ringing wakes me.

At first, I don't know where I am. I'm so cold it hurts, and when I open my eyes I see clouds of my own breath inside the car. It's freezing. I sit perfectly still for a second, trying to isolate the ringing sound. It's coming from the glove compartment. I couldn't find my phone anywhere when I searched the house last night; if I had it I'm sure there must be *someone* in my list of contacts I could call. Someone who could confirm who I am, because even I'm starting to doubt myself. But when I open the glove compartment it is not my mobile that I find. The phone I see is inside a clear plastic bag. It looks cheap and basic, and I do not recognize it. The phone rings again and the display says NO CALLER ID. When I answer it, whoever is calling hangs up. I stare at the screen and almost drop the phone when it vibrates with a text message.

> Eden, everything is going to be okay. Go to our special place at sunrise. I'll be there. Love you to the moon and back. x

I take out the key chain Harri gave me when we bought the house. It has my name on the front and the same words, *love you to the moon and back*, engraved on the other side. He gave it to me during a champagne picnic at the top of the cliffs overlooking Hope Falls. Next to the waterfall that gave the village its name. I don't know where I am now – other than somewhere in the national park – but I know where Harri wants me to meet him. I try to switch on the car but of course it doesn't start, so I begin to panic.

I stare out of the windscreen and see that it *is* dawn. There is just a sliver of light on the dark horizon, but it's enough for me to finally see where I am. Hope Falls is visible in the distance, a mile away at most. I was so close, but I was so lost I didn't know it. I grab the phone, clamber out of the car and start to run. Down the hill and along the deserted country lanes, into Hope Falls and towards the sea. I run past the Saltwater Gallery where I should have had my first exhibition last night. I run past The Smuggler's Inn and the Driftwood Café. Everything is perfectly still and calm and quiet. Too quiet. The silence swells like the incoming tide and I know it might drown me. I'm so tired I can't think straight, but I'll be okay once I see Harrison again. I just need to know that he still loves me. He said to meet at sunrise and I just hope I'm not too late.

I reach the church and run up the coast path towards the cliffs. I pass an old man walking his dog, but there is nobody else out and about at this early hour. The sea gets louder the further I run away from the village. The thoughts swirling inside my head are loud too, and running is normally the only thing that can silence them, but not today.

Can I really trust Harrison after the past twenty-four hours?

I don't have a choice.

I don't have anyone else to turn to or anywhere else to go.

And despite everything, I still love him.

When I reach the top of the cliffs Harrison isn't there.

I'm too hot after running up the hill, so I pull off the pretty cashmere sweater covered in stars and drop it on the ground. Then I try to catch my breath, but it does not want to be caught.

I take out the phone I found in the car, but there is no signal up here so I slip it back inside the bag I found it in and into my pocket. Then I stand at the edge of the cliff while I wait for my husband, peering down at an angry sea and the giant waves crashing on the rocks below, wondering how and why my life has unravelled the way it has.

As though I don't already know.

I try to reassure myself that there is a way to fix this. Remind myself that hearts that get broken can mend. But maybe there are some truths we can never really outrun. The past is a stalker, following us throughout our lives, never completely out of sight, never far away enough to forget to fear. And guilt is a thief that will steal everything if you let it catch up with you.

I notice the suicide hotline poster and step back from the cliff edge. I'm an idiot for standing so close, I could have slipped and tumbled to my death. Maybe I'm a fool for coming here at all; how can I possibly trust Harri now? I must be crazy. We shouldn't meet here. We should meet somewhere public. Somewhere *safe*.

I'm about to leave when I hear someone on the path behind me.

Soon after that I am falling through a waterfall. My body twists and turns and spins until it smashes onto the rocks at the bottom of the cliff. The pain is intense but lasts less than a second. If anyone says *She didn't feel a thing* they're wrong.

I felt everything I have ever felt when I was dying.

The last thought I have before I die surprises me:

True love kills.

20

HARRISON

31st October

Someone knocking on the door downstairs wakes me. It takes a few seconds to remember where I am – the London flat or the Cornish village we moved to a few weeks ago – I have never been a fan of change. It's early, still dark, but my tired eyes adjust to the light and I recognize the bedroom my wife recently decorated. Spyglass was never *my* idea of a dream home – I always thought it looked old and creepy built into the cliff – but Eden *loves* it. Sometimes I wonder if she loves this house more than she loves me.

Whoever is outside knocks again.

My head hurts the way it always does when I drink these days. Memories of the art gallery in Hope Falls and Eden's exhibition flood my mind, and I think I might have had one too many glasses of malbec. I reach for the empty space on the bed next to me on autopilot, before clocking the pillow that has not been slept on.

The sound of knocking starts again, louder this time, more insistent.

Whoever it is clearly isn't going to go away. I sit up, stand up, and the bedroom seems to tilt, then blur. It's as though everything is out of focus. It feels like the mother of all hangovers and yet I didn't drink *that* much.

I put on my glasses. They don't help with the disorientation, but I can see that I've slept in my clothes. That's strange. Now I think about it, I don't actually remember going to bed last night. I must have been really out of it. When whoever is downstairs knocks again something inside me snaps and I stomp out of the room and down the stairs, ready to take my hangover out on whoever has woken me. I unlock the door and yank it open. All the angry words I rehearsed retreat when I see the young police officer from yesterday standing on my doorstep.

Sergeant Carter was here last night before my wife's exhibition, and then again afterwards when we discovered we had been burgled, but he looks different today. Almost as though he has aged overnight. He's still just a boy and it's hard to take someone so young and inexperienced seriously – he can only be a few years older than my daughter.

"May I come in?"

I step aside without answering, a silent invitation to enter our home.

"Is everything all right?" I ask, already knowing that it isn't. If it were, he would not be here. I lead him through to the kitchen. The glass has been swept away but the back door is boarded up. A reminder that someone broke in and ransacked the place while we were at the gallery last night. Maybe that's what this is about.

"Would you like some coffee? I'm making one for myself anyway—"

"No. Thank you," he says. "When did you last see your wife?"

I stop and turn to face him. It is not a difficult question, but I hesitate before answering it. Mainly because my mind is working overtime to understand *why* he is asking.

"Last night when you were here. I keep thinking that if we hadn't stayed for a drink with the gallery owner after everyone else left we might have caught whoever did this in the act. We had a little nightcap after you left, then we went to bed. Or at least, I did. I think

Eden was still buzzing from the exhibition so she stayed up a while longer . . ."

Where is my wife?

I do not ask the question out loud, but I am increasingly desperate to know the answer. I keep expecting her to walk in the room.

"I confess I don't know where Eden is now. You knocking on the door woke me up. She does disappear sometimes to go for a run—"

"There is no easy way to say this," the boy cop interrupts, and my blood seems to turn cold in my veins. "I'm sorry to inform you that a woman matching your wife's description was seen running up to the cliffs this morning by a man walking his dog. He said she looked distracted and upset, that it was clear she had been crying. When he walked back the way he came, he found some clothing abandoned near the waterfall." He's talking about the local suicide spot, but I'm still not sure why he is telling me this.

Or maybe I just don't want to know.

"Do you recognize this?" he asks, showing me a picture on his phone of a pale grey sweater covered in stars.

"It's Eden's." My reply is so quiet I'm surprised he hears it.

"You're sure?"

"Yes. I bought it for her."

"It was found by the cliffs on the coast path," he says, then pauses as though waiting for me to fill in the gaps. I don't want to. An uncomfortable silence parks itself between us like a no-man's-land of unspoken words. Then he stares at me, and I stare at him, both trying to process the things we think but don't say. I blink first.

"Are you saying that my wife has committed suicide?"

"No. We can't be sure of anything yet," he tells me, but his face says something different. "We know that your property was broken into and that her car was stolen last night—"

"By that woman pretending to be Eden. Have you found *her*? Have you found the car?"

"No."

"This must be a mistake. My wife was here last night—" I start to say, then I begin to frantically search for Eden. I leave the kitchen without a word of explanation and look in every room downstairs. When I don't find her there, I run upstairs and do the same. I end my search in our bedroom, where her side of the bed has clearly not been slept in. I snatch my mobile phone from the bedside table, impatiently stab the screen with my finger, find my recent calls and dial Eden. I experience a full range of emotions in the next few seconds when I hear a phone ringing in the distance. I follow the sound, running so fast down the old stairs I almost fall – the top step is bigger than the rest and a terrible trip hazard. I hurry back into the kitchen where the police officer is waiting. The ringing has stopped so I dial my wife's number again. The sound is definitely coming from this room. I trace it to a kitchen drawer next to where the boy cop is standing. I yank the drawer open, and there, right at the back, is Eden's phone. What a strange place for it to be.

The unspoken question is too loud now.

"Is my wife dead?" I ask.

"It's too early to—"

"I am bullshit intolerant, so please don't. Is my wife dead?"

"I'm very sorry. I think she might be."

21

BIRDY

31st October

I think I might be winning at life for a change. It was surprisingly easy and dirt cheap to rent a room above the pub in Hope Falls. At this time of year, without the tourists, the place is a bit of a ghost town – not at all like the bustling and vibrant village I remember it being when I was a child. Every single room at The Smuggler's Inn was available and I was able to take my pick. I chose the one at the end of the corridor, farthest away from the bar and the other empty rooms, overlooking the harbour with a wonderful view of the sea. It's quiet. Peaceful. Private. Just what I needed.

My boss in London was shocked when I said that I wanted to quit. I didn't tell him the real reason why. I haven't told anyone that I'm ill; I don't see the point. I don't need or want their sympathy. People give away *sorrys* like sweets at Halloween and swallowing too many can make a person feel sick. People are grief vampires. They just want to suck on your sorrow, feed on your fear and feast on your failures. It makes them feel better about themselves. What I need is to make the most of the time I have left, and that's what I'm doing, by returning to where my story started: Hope Falls.

Being here feels like being a tourist of my own past. I was born here and it feels as though the place has been calling me back.

Or maybe it's *her*.

Now that I know I'm dying, I find myself wanting to visit my mother's grave and talk to her in a way I never did when she was alive. I never knew my father – she wouldn't even tell me his name – so she was all I had. I've spent years hating her for leaving me, and now I miss her more than I ever did before. I'm stuck somewhere between hate and forgiveness and I don't pretend to understand it. Some people leave a mark on your life, others leave a stain.

My mother left me when I needed her the most.

What a fucking unforgivable thing to do.

I try not to think about the past too much. Mining my memories only seems to result in disappointing nuggets of regrets and mistakes. I've taken a few too many wrong turns but it's never too late to try to steer your life back on track. It took a couple of months to make all the necessary arrangements, but once I was ready it all happened pretty fast. In the last few weeks I have quit my job, sold my flat in London, given away almost all my belongings – even my precious books; can't take them with me once I'm dead – then I packed a single suitcase and moved here with Sunday. According to Thanatos, I had just enough time to make some changes to my life, so that's what I'm doing. Today is the first day of the end of my life, and I plan to make it a good one.

I shower and dress – putting on my normal uniform of a white shirt, tweed jacket and skinny jeans because some things never change – then I polish my shoes until they shine before tying the laces in perfect bows. I put on my glasses, examine my reflection, turn my head from side to side, and see that my braids are perfectly symmetrical. I'm ready.

It's still a smidgen too early, so I walk into the village with Sunday by my side. We make our way along the coast path, where the sea is wild and rough and loud today. There is something calming about being surrounded by something more powerful than you, and being this close to the ocean makes me feel alive. Huge waves, taller than me, crash against the mighty granite walls of the harbour, and I see a storm on the horizon. I stop at the Driftwood Café on the corner, where I am the only customer, and order two cups of coffee. The place looks like it was last decorated in the seventies, and it's crammed full of carved pumpkins and Halloween knickknacks.

"I like the decorations," I say sincerely. Halloween has always been my favourite holiday.

"I like your tattoo," replies the old woman standing behind the counter as she gives me my change. She has a thick Cornish accent that reminds me of my childhood. I thank her and stare at the swallow on my hand – a reminder that some birds fly far from home but return eventually. Swallows leave these shores because they have to, and because they learned over time to come back to the place they are born only when it is safe to do so. I can relate in more ways than one.

"You seem to be the only place in Hope Falls ready for Halloween," I say, admiring the assortment of pumpkins.

The café owner grins. "Most folks in the village make a point of only celebrating the Day of the Dead. It's a local tradition. But at my age every holiday is worth celebrating," she says with a twinkle in her eye.

I tell my face to smile and take my coffee. Then I hotfoot it out of there and walk along the cobbled streets, past the pretty pastel-coloured terraced houses, and make my way towards the little cottage with the blue door at the end of the lane. If it weren't for the old-fashioned police station sign you would never know that's what it was. My steps seem as unsure of themselves as I am now that I'm here, so I stop for a moment to enjoy the view while I still can. Sunday sits down by my side as though doing the same. I take a deep breath. Then I take one last look around Hope Falls as it is now, wanting to enjoy this last moment of freedom. Nothing will be the same once they know who I am and what I have done.

I compose my thoughts.

Forget my feelings.

And step inside the police station.

It's time to confess.

22

HARRISON

I confess that what Sergeant Carter says about my wife knocks me for six.

I manage to keep it together until he leaves my house.

Then I fall apart.

I make myself drink some coffee – I need something to steady my nerves – but then I see Eden standing in the corner of the kitchen staring at me and drop my cup. My wife isn't really there – it's just my imagination – but the white porcelain has smashed into a hundred tiny pieces and there is spilled coffee all over the floor. I stand and stare at it as though I don't know what to do. I am too used to other people clearing up my mess.

And what a mess this is.

The police think my wife has killed herself.

My mind pivots from my wife to my PA. I need to call her, get her to cancel my meetings and rearrange my day. This could not have come at a worse time for the company. I should be in London, not *here*, but I'm guessing it would look bad if I left Hope Falls now. That's probably not what a grieving husband would do.

I step on a shard of porcelain and my foot bleeds onto the floor. *Fuck.* I need to keep my shit together. The boy cop asked a lot of questions before he left and I'm worried I shouldn't have answered them. But I am not a suspect. There is no suggestion that a crime has taken place. They think Eden killed herself and it would be strange if I didn't cooperate. But I do *feel* strange. A little dizzy. Discombobulated. As though none of this is real. Not that I could ever say that out loud.

I am not the kind of man who gets broken, even when I lose everything I love most. I know this about myself because I've had practice. We all just play the parts life gives us but I seem to have forgotten my lines. I don't have a script for this. There is no preprepared media-friendly statement that someone else has written for me to read. I'm struggling to remember how to be the man people expect me to be, the person they all think I am: Harrison Woolf, CEO. Fearless. Powerful. Honest.

Then I sink down onto the floor because right now I am none of those things.

I need to understand what happened. But I can't think straight, the walls are closing in. I have to know the truth. But it feels like I can't breathe.

Is my wife really dead?

I have a word with myself – several in fact – then pull myself up. I shower and shave and put on my favourite suit; it feels like my armour and I need it today. Then I see my wife's wedding and engagement rings left abandoned on the bedside table. As soon as I have composed myself I head to the police station in the village. Sergeant Carter said if I thought of anything that might help them find out what happened to Eden I should tell him straight away. So that's what I'll do.

Even though I would rather nobody ever finds out what she did, I do want them to find her.

23

BIRDY

I finally found you," I say, stepping inside the police station.

"It's *you*," Carter replies, his face a pretty picture of shock.

It's been a while since we last met. I'm impressed he remembers me.

Carter is alone and sitting behind a desk that looks too big for him. He is listening to what looks like an old Walkman with his feet up on the desk. I notice how neat and tidy it is, just like the man himself. His uniform is pristine and his hair looks as though he just combed it. His expression is one of surprise and something else I can't quite put my finger on. The first and last time I saw him was six months ago, but he looks different. Tired. Older. Hopefully none the wiser. I remember how we stood side by side standing over my grandmother's grave, while he told me why she was known as the woman who died twice. Then he walked me home and we had sex. He would have stayed the night if I hadn't asked him to leave. I'm guessing he didn't expect to see me again after that, which might explain his expression. His face looks like he just drank a pint of piss.

"You remember me, then?" I ask, stepping inside the station and closing the door behind me. Carter pulls off his headphones and removes his feet from the desk. He stares at me, then at Sunday, as though he might be afraid of us both, which is just silly. I'm aware that I am an acquired taste, but my dog is a sheep in wolf's clothing. I give Carter a moment to get over the shock of seeing me, and take in my surroundings. The station used to be a fisherman's cottage and it still looks like one.

"Of course I remember you," Carter says eventually, as though his pause button has been released. He sounds unsure and I raise an eyebrow. "Mrs Bird's granddaughter," he adds as though trying to prove it.

He can't even remember my name.

Carter's cheeks turn a surprisingly vibrant shade of red – he clearly remembers some of the things we did that night – and I feel a tad sorry for him. He's a good ten years younger than me, perhaps not the sharpest knife in the drawer, and I'm aware that he didn't know what – or who – he was getting himself into when he knocked on my door that night. I don't understand why he looks so guilty when he's got no reason to be. It isn't as though he could have called me even if he had wanted to; I never gave him my number. Maybe I hurt his feelings and he's still upset about it, even if the silly twit can't remember my name.

"You can call me Birdy," I say, putting one of the coffees I just bought on his desk. He stares at it. Then at me. He doesn't touch the drink. He looks horribly young to me today, almost childlike.

I wonder if I look dreadfully old to him.

Carter squirms in his seat. "I'm afraid things are a little busy around here today—"

"In Hope Falls?"

"Strangely, yes."

"Did someone steal a fishing net?" I thought that was funny but he doesn't laugh. "Look, I'm sorry to burst in here out of the blue, but I wanted to talk to you—"

"And normally I would love to catch up with . . ."

"An old friend?" I suggest, trying to help him out.

"Exactly. It's just that now is not a good time. I'm very—"

"Busy? In this sleepy village where you said nothing ever happens?"

"A woman is missing," he says as though trying to impress me.

"It's almost always the husband," I remind him. Then I take a sip of my coffee and perch on the edge of Carter's desk. He looks appalled and stares at me as though I might be dangerously stupid. Dangerous, yes. Stupid, never.

"Sorry, but I don't have time to catch up today," he says, standing and stepping away from the desk I am sitting on. He grabs his coat from the stand. "There is a new detective in town – they picked one hell of a first day – and I'm heading out to meet them now. So you'll have to excuse me—"

"Before you go, there is something I need to confess," I tell him, and his eyes dart to my stomach. "I'm not *pregnant* if that's what you're thinking," I say, unable to hide the horror of such a thought from my voice. He breathes a visible sigh of relief and I can't help feeling insulted. Carter's patience has clearly expired and he heads towards the door.

"I don't have time for this, whatever *this* is—"

"It was you who put the idea in my head," I say.

"What idea? Could we perhaps do this another time? I can't be late meeting the new detective."

"That's what I'm trying to tell you. You already have."

It takes so long for the penny to drop I'm surprised he passed the entrance exam.

His mouth forms a perfect O and opens and closes like a goldfish.

I almost feel sorry for him.

Almost.

"You can still call me Birdy, but officially it's DCI Olivia Bird. I'm your new boss."

24

CARTER

"*You're* the new detective in Hope Falls?" I ask.

She can't be. This must be a mistake. Anything but the truth.

"Well, Hope Falls and some neighbouring towns and villages, but I'll be based here."

I stop and stare at her but I don't answer. I take in the long plaited dark hair, tweed jacket, white shirt and skinny jeans. The red leather satchel on her shoulder looks more like something a child would take to school, and along with all the rings on her fingers, the tattoo on her hand, the great big bloody wolf by her side, this woman does not look like a detective. Let alone a senior one. Despite advertising for a senior detective for *six months* and finding nobody suitable, my bosses refused to promote me. Even though I've been here for years. And now, instead of giving me the job I deserve, they send *her*? This isn't happening. She cannot be my new boss and I can't seem to find the right words. Then a few wrong ones rush out all at once, tripping over themselves.

"Is this a joke?"

It sounds ruder out loud than it did in my head, but the corners of her mouth turn upwards into what passes as a smile.

"I know, it's madness," she says. "I've heard they let women vote these days too, and as if that weren't bad enough, now there's a *female* DCI in Hope Falls. What is the world coming to?"

"But that would mean that you're my—"

"Boss. Yes. I am your new boss. Sorry about that. I'm hoping it won't be too much of a problem for you. And just so you know, I actually have very strict rules about not sleeping with people I work with. Especially those who are under me, so to speak, but I wasn't your boss when we did what we did, so I'm hoping we can just put all of that behind us. Start again. Reset. What do you reckon?"

"I . . . don't know what to say."

"Well, 'Congratulations' might have been nice. Or, 'Welcome to Hope Falls.' Or, 'I'm thrilled I get to work with someone so experienced who can probably teach me more about being a detective in one day than I will have learned sitting around here for the last few years.'" I don't respond well to sarcasm and in this situation I can't seem to form a response at all. I've slept with my boss. I've seen her naked. I'm picturing that and all the things we did and I realize I'm just staring at her. "Do you need switching off and on again?" she asks.

"What?"

"Never mind. Perhaps you could tell me why today is so busy?"

"A woman is missing. Another suspected suicide."

"Why do you say another? How many have there been?"

"The waterfall at the top of the cliff is a popular suicide spot. We get a lot of jumpers, especially at this time of year," I say. Then I remember that my new boss's mother killed herself – that's why she left Hope Falls when she was a child – and it's probably not what she wants to be reminded of on her first day. I'm making a terrible second first impression.

My mind races ahead to all the reasons why her being here is bad. Then my mind wanders back to that night when I met her at Spyglass. I fancied Birdy the first time I saw her. She has a certain quality, a quirky uniqueness that I can't quite put my finger on. I doubt I would have done what I did if I'd thought I'd ever see her again, but she said she wasn't coming back and invited me in. How was I supposed to say no? I've never had sex like that before or since. I remember kissing her. I remember fucking her. I remember the taste of her—

"Carter?"

"Sorry, what?"

"I asked you a question and you're just staring into space. Have you had a stroke?"

"I don't think so. What do I call you now?"

"Birdy. I told you that already. Try to keep up."

"Seems a little informal."

"I find things tend to be less formal when you've seen a person naked." I can feel my cheeks burning. "Was there a witness to this suspected suicide?" she asks.

"A dog walker saw a woman running up the coast path to the cliff—"

"Did they see her jump off it?" I shake my head. "Have you found a body?" I start to shake my head again. "Use your words, Carter."

"No."

"How long ago was the woman reported missing?"

"She wasn't."

"So you haven't found a body and nobody has been reported missing. But you think there has been a suicide because . . ."

"I just formally interviewed the husband and I have reason to suspect—"

"You did what? I get that you're bored, but you can't just invent crimes to investigate."

"There have been some strange goings-on up at their house the last couple of days—"

"*Strange goings-on* don't stand up in court. On what grounds did you interview the husband of a woman who has *not* been reported missing because you *think* she might have committed suicide?"

I hate the way she is looking at me right now. I hate that she is here at all. When I got the call to say a new detective was starting today, I imagined a man. Someone I could look up to and learn from. She doesn't even look like a detective, and even her dog is staring at me as though I am an idiot. I'm not.

"The husband came here voluntarily. Said he had something to tell me."

"Is there a transcript?" she asks.

"No."

"You didn't record it?"

"Yes, but on tape. I was just listening back to it when you walked in."

"Tape?"

"Yes. We still use cassettes here. You can borrow my Walkman if you'd like to listen."

"Have I accidently time travelled? Is this the eighties?"

"My predecessor liked doing things the old way. He said, *If it's not broke, don't fix it.*"

"I'm more of an *if it's not broke, break it* woman when it comes to getting the job done. Sounds like I arrived in Hope Falls just in time." She reaches inside her jacket pocket and takes out a small leather notebook. Then she takes out a pen and clicks the top of it.

"What is the husband's name?" she asks.

"Harrison Woolf."

"And his missing wife?"

"Eden Fox."

She writes down their names. Proper old school. But then she is older than me.

By far the oldest and sexiest woman I've ever slept with.

And the scariest.

"Earth to Carter!"

"What?"

"Quit picturing me naked," she says, and I feel my cheeks burn. "I'm your boss now, you're going to have to get used to it." Her words feel like a slap. "I don't have time to listen to a *tape* but I want to know what the husband had to say. Transcribe the interview, or find an app to do it for you, then email it to me. I'll be in my office."

I look around the station that consists of just this one room. And just one desk. Mine.

"Your office?" I ask.

"Yes. Also known as The Smuggler's Inn."

"You're going to the *pub*. Now. This morning?"

"Well, I can't work here. This place is depressing."

"I thought you said you were never coming back to Hope Falls."

She takes a step closer and for a moment I think she is going to kiss me. Her face is so close to mine our lips are almost touching.

She smiles. "I changed my mind."

25

Interviewer: Sergeant Luke Carter (LC)
Interviewee: Harrison Woolf (HW)
Date: 31st October, 2025
Location: Hope Falls police station

LC: Thank you for coming in. I just want to state for the record again that you are under no obligation to be here.
HW: I need to know what happened to my wife.
LC: I understand. You said you had something to show me?
HW: Yes.
LC: For the tape, Mr Woolf has taken two rings from his pocket.
HW: Her wedding ring and engagement ring. Eden left them behind. She always does when she goes running. Have you found her yet?
LC: I'm afraid not.
HW: The crazy woman outside my house yesterday, who showed up again at the gallery claiming to be Eden, then broke into our home and stole her car. Have you found her?
LC: No. But we have found the car.
HW: Where?
LC: Abandoned about a mile from Hope Falls in Blackmoor National

Park. I'm just trying to establish the facts and understand how all of this fits together.

HW: Well, if you had arrested that woman in the first place maybe none of this would have—

LC: I'm sorry to ask, but was there any possibility of an affair?

HW: An affair?

LC: Yes.

HW: Who? Me? Or my wife? Do you mean me with that woman? Or do you mean my wife and someone else? Why do you think she committed suicide if nobody has found her? Did anyone actually see her jump? Shouldn't you be out looking for her?

LC: The coastguard is searching now, but due to the tides here it can sometimes take a long time for . . .

HW: A body to wash up? Is that what you're trying to say? Jesus fucking Christ. I can't believe this is happening.

LC: As you say, we don't know for sure what has happened yet. Is it possible your wife might have just left?

HW: Left me, you mean?

LC: Could she have gone to visit someone without telling you? Is there a friend who might know where Eden is? Someone who would know her real state of mind?

HW: Are you saying I don't know my wife? She was fine. She was happy until the other woman showed up.

LC: Do you have any children?

HW: A daughter.

LC: What is her name?

HW: My daughter doesn't have anything to do with this. She's never even been to Hope Falls.

LC: She doesn't live with you?

HW: She's eighteen.

LC: I'd like to speak to her.

HW: I already told you . . .

LC: Her name and contact details would be very helpful.

HW: Fine. Gabriella. What? Why are you staring at me like that?

LC: The woman claiming to be your wife last night also said she had a daughter called Gabriella.

HW: Well, she was clearly deluded about many things. She pretended to be my wife, so why not pretend to be the mother of my child too?

LC: Is there anyone else who might have had a grudge against you or your wife?

HW: Why are you asking about grudges if you think she committed suicide?

LC: Am I right in thinking you still have a flat in London as well as your home here in Hope Falls?

HW: I don't think it's illegal yet to own two properties.

LC: No, but I imagine it must be expensive. Did your wife have life insurance?

HW: I think I'm going to leave now. If you have anything else to say to me you can do it via my solicitor.

26

BIRDY

I stop reading the transcript and close my laptop because my drink has arrived. I rather like my new "office". The Smuggler's Inn is one of the oldest pubs in the country. I only know this because there is a sign on the wall behind the bar that says ONE OF THE OLDEST PUBS IN THE COUNTRY and yet they do not know how to mix a mojito. The pub is indeed very old, but it has been redecorated recently – I can still smell the paint – and the new soft furnishings are tasteful if a little twee. There is another framed print behind the bar that says STRANGERS ARE FRIENDS YOU HAVE NOT YET MET.

What a crock of shit that is.

Friends are strangers in waiting if you ask me.

Aside from the signage I like the place, with its old-fashioned bar, open fire and low ceilings with wooden beams. I also like that I'm the only person here.

I take a sip of my drink and text Carter:

SEE ME IN MY OFFICE.

"You called?" he says, walking into the pub five minutes later.

"Technically I texted, but thank you for coming so quickly."

He stares at Sunday and I'm starting to think Carter does not like dogs.

"I thought you didn't drink?" he says, eyeing my cocktail.

"What a good memory you have, and you're right, I don't. I know, a teetotal detective, whatever next? This is a virgin mojito, or at least an impression of one. I'd offer to buy you a cocktail but you have work to do. I'm only halfway through the transcript of your interview with the husband, and I needed to ask you something. What's all this about a woman pretending to be Eden Fox yesterday?"

"That's what I was trying to tell you. Last night I was called to Spyglass—"

"You mean my grandmother's old house?"

"Yes. Harrison Woolf and Eden Fox live in the house your family used to own." He pauses to let that news sink in then asks, "Did you ever meet them? They must have bought the house from you."

"No. It was a probate case, so I had very little to do with it. The solicitors and the estate agent dealt with everything. They hired a house clearance company, put the place on the market and it all happened very fast. Sad how quickly an entire lifetime can be tidied away."

"Well, if it's any comfort, they did a lovely job renovating the place," he says.

"You've been inside?"

"A few times. Yesterday evening Harrison Woolf dialled 999 to report that another woman was claiming to be his wife, and trying to break into their home."

"Was she?"

"Yes. I saw her when I responded to the call, and again when I apprehended her later last night at the art gallery in the village. She insisted that she was Eden Fox, and that the woman inside the gallery was an impostor pretending to be her husband's wife."

"How do you know she wasn't?"

He stares at me as though I might be a few sandwiches short of a picnic.

"Because I had already met the real Eden – half the village had – and then there was Harrison. Why would a husband lie about who his wife was? I interviewed this other woman and she seemed a bit crazy and possibly dangerous."

"Crazy *and* dangerous. But you let her go?"

"Not in so many words."

"How many words does it take to explain she got away from you twice? And the woman who Harrison claims *was* his wife. You said you met her?"

"Everyone who met the real Eden Fox liked her. She made a real effort from the moment they moved here to be friendly to people in the village. She would often visit the bakery, or the butchers, supporting local businesses, which always goes down well in a place like this. And we all saw her at her exhibition last night; the whole village was there."

"The whole village went to an art exhibition? Do people here not have Netflix?"

"I think people here are perhaps more community-minded than people in the city."

"Is that so? Fascinating insight. When did *you* first meet her?"

"Who?"

"Eden."

He shrugs. "At the gallery last night."

I wait for him to say more but he doesn't. "Then that's where I want you to go now. I need you to speak to the owner of the gallery while I finish reading the transcript of your chat with the husband. Find out how the exhibition came about, whose idea it was."

"Why?" he asks.

"Yours is not to reason why, your job is to just do what I tell you."

"Fine. Guess I'll go interview the black widow."

"Why do you call her that?"

"Everyone in the village calls her that, behind her back at least. Diana has had three husbands and outlived them all – she paid for the gallery with the inheritance – and rumour has it she's on the lookout for husband number four. Apparently she keeps the ashes of her last husband on the mantelpiece in her flat, and puts a teaspoon of his ashes in her tea once a day. She drinks him so she can keep him with her always."

Blimey.

"Well, if she offers you a cup of tea say no," I tell him. He just stares at me. "What are you waiting for? Off you fuck."

Carter shakes his pretty head then leaves the pub.

I can understand if his nose is a little out of joint about me being his boss. And I appreciate it might be awkward, for him, that we slept together. But what I'm most curious about is why he just said what he said. I know Carter didn't meet Eden Fox for the first time at the exhibition; they met before that.

What I don't know is why he lied.

27

Interviewer: Sergeant Luke Carter (LC)

Interviewee: Harrison Woolf (HW)

Date: 31st October, 2025

Location: Hope Falls police station

Cont.

HW: I'm sorry. I didn't mean to snap. Today is just . . . a lot. I still can't believe any of this is happening.

LC: I understand. If I could just have the contact details for your daughter—

HW: You don't understand.

LC: So explain it to me.

HW: Our daughter is eighteen but she's still just a child. She doesn't know anything about any of this and can't help you, but I'll give you a number for where she lives now if you insist on it.

LC: Thank you. It would also be useful if I could speak to some of your wife's friends. Do you have numbers for them too? They might be able to shed some light on how she was feeling.

HW: Haven't I done that already? I told you, Eden was feeling fine. Happiest she's been for years.

LC: Sometimes it can be hard to tell those who we are closest to how we are really feeling. You are completely right, we don't know for sure what has happened to Eden yet, but we do know that she is missing. Is there a friend you can think of that she might have confided in or gone to stay with?

HW: My wife doesn't have any friends.

LC: Really? She seemed very friendly when I met her. And very sociable at the art gallery last night.

HW: That was her wanting to make friends. This move, this place, it was all meant to be a fresh start for us. We got married when she was still very young, and taking care of our daughter took over her whole life for a long time. She always put Gabriella first.

LC: Were there other parents at your daughter's school that she was friendly and still in touch with?

HW: Our daughter was homeschooled. Eden didn't have time for friends and until recently didn't seem to want any. I can't explain it any other way. It's just how she was. Is. She has always been happy in her own company. I often have to travel for work, but Eden spent the last ten years at home with Gabby. That's just how our lives were.

LC: May I ask what you do for a living?

HW: I'd rather not say.

LC: Can I ask why?

HW: You can ask what you want, but my work isn't relevant.

LC: It might be.

HW: You think my wife jumped off a cliff because of my job? I've had the same job for years, and it paid for the life she wanted.

LC: The name of the company, if you don't mind?

HW: I do mind, but fine, if it helps find her. I'm the CEO of a pharmaceutical and tech company in London called Thanatos.

28

BIRDY

I stop reading the transcript and shut my laptop.

The walls of the pub fold in on me, the floor seems to tilt, and I grab the sticky wooden table for balance. I close my eyes and the world is dark. Sunday whimpers, somehow knowing that something is wrong. My head fills with a sound I can only describe as storm clouds colliding with each other, and I reach inside my satchel for some pills. I take two to take the edge off, and wash them down with the remains of my virgin mojito. Until recently, I had never even heard of Thanatos. Now I'm reading a transcript of an interview with the man who runs the company.

A company that claims to have predicted the day I will die.

It's hard to explain why I wanted to be here at the end. I'm sure most people would think it is crazy to start a new job at a time like this, and they might be right. All I know is it felt like Hope Falls was calling me home. I haven't told anyone that I'm dying, or when; I don't know if the date Thanatos predicted will really be my last or if it will turn out to be nonsense. But Harrison Woolf must know if he is the CEO of the company. I think he knows more than he is letting on about a lot of things. All of which are somehow linked; my grandmother's house, Thanatos, Hope Falls, Eden Fox . . . I'm sure of it.

I open my laptop again and google Harrison Woolf. A few results come up, but I know none of them are the man I'm looking for. I search Harrison Woolf and Thanatos, but again, nothing. No social media. No LinkedIn profile. Not a bean. The guy is a ghost online – a lot like me – which can only mean two things in my experience. Either he values his privacy or he has something to hide. Or both. I close the laptop again and slip it inside my satchel. The internet might not be able to tell me what I want to know, but I bet someone else can.

"I wonder if you might be able to do me a favour?" I say to the pretty barmaid sitting behind the bar. With her long red hair and big green eyes, she reminds me of someone, but I can't remember who. Maddy was here when I first arrived at The Smuggler's Inn, and said I could have any room upstairs I wanted given the place is empty. Sunday – who is an excellent judge of character – liked her straight away, and so did I. She's thirtysomething, beautiful, bookish, and has an emotional intelligence that is hard to find in people these days. I can't help thinking she should be doing more with her life than working in an empty pub.

"Do you mind keeping an eye on my dog if I leave him here for a while?" I ask.

"Sure," she says. "Not like I'm rushed off my feet doing anything else."

"Be good," I tell Sunday, and he tilts his head as though butter wouldn't melt.

Then I send a text.

MEET ME OUTSIDE MY OFFICE.

Quickly followed by another.

PLEASE.

Then a third.

AND HURRY UP.

I am aware that the last text I sent Carter was a smidgen rude, but I think it is important to start any working relationship the way you mean to go on. He pulls up outside the pub in his silly little police car a few minutes later. The thing is spotless, as though he just had it professionally cleaned. I'm sure it didn't look like this earlier; I can even see an air freshener shaped like a tree dangling from the mirror.

"What took you so long?" I ask through the open window.

"Are you joking?"

"I rarely joke. And I'm not getting in this tin can. I'll meet you up there," I say, taking the Vespa keys out of my pocket.

"Meet me where?"

"Spyglass, of course. Do try to keep up."

"You didn't say . . . Never mind. You know that Spyglass is just at the top of the hill?"

"I do know that. I used to own the place, remember? Albeit briefly."

"What I meant is that we could walk there just as quickly."

"We could but we're not going to."

"I've already questioned Harrison Woolf—"

"Yes, but you didn't ask the right questions. Think about it, Carter. Use that brain of yours. From what I know so far, we have a woman claiming she is the real Eden Fox who has now disappeared. And a woman who you say was the real Eden Fox, who has *also* disappeared. One of them was lying, we don't know why yet, but we do know that the common factor in all this is the husband." I climb onto the scooter. "Meet you there."

"Let me do the talking," I say a few minutes later as we crunch along the gravel driveway towards the front door at Spyglass. I notice the bird-shaped knocker has been replaced with a shiny fox head one, and wonder what else the new owners have changed about the place. I feel a little out of sorts and off-balance again just as I'm about to knock on the door, but I do my best to hide it. I don't know whether it is my health, this situation, or this house causing me to wobble. But I do believe Hope Falls called me back here for a reason. When nobody comes to answer the door straight away I knock again.

A man in his early fifties eventually opens it. He doesn't look surprised – or happy – to see me. But people rarely smile when they find police officers on their doorstep. I know it's Harrison Woolf without needing to ask – he looks exactly how I expected him to. I take in the expensive-looking suit, the black shirt and tie, the neat salt-and-pepper hair, the clean-shaven, chiselled chin. He looks well put together, confident, calm. Not exactly how you would expect a man who just possibly lost his wife to look.

"Hello, Mr Woolf. I'm DCI Olivia Bird. I believe you've already had the misfortune of meeting my colleague, Carter, and I wanted to apologize for his conduct earlier today."

Carter shoots me some serious side-eye, but I ignore him and his hurt feelings and continue with my prepared speech. "It was completely unacceptable for Sergeant Carter to question you the way that he did. I wanted to reassure you that now I am here, nothing like that will happen again. I understand what a difficult time this must be, and going forward we will be putting all of our efforts into finding out what happened to your wife."

"Thank you," Harrison says, already starting to close the door.

"Would it be okay if we came in for a moment?"

"I'm actually right in the middle of an important Zoom call for work . . ."

On the day his wife might have committed suicide.

"That's okay," I tell him, sidestepping my way into the house. "It's a bit chilly out today, we can wait inside until you're ready."

He does a terrible job of hiding his irritation and I watch him wrestle with how to respond. Eventually he bites his tongue and says, "Of course. Come on in."

We follow him through to an impressive kitchen at the back of the house. It didn't look like this when my grandmother owned the place. Everything is stylish and spotless now, so devoid of personality it's almost unrecognizable. Harrison's laptop is on the granite kitchen counter facing away from us, so I can't see who he was talking to, but he wasn't lying about a Zoom.

"Everything okay?" asks a female voice coming from his computer.

"I have to go," is all he says to the screen before closing his laptop. Then he looks up and fixes his eyes on me. "Have you found her?"

If he means his wife there is very little emotion in his voice.

"Not yet. Please take a seat," I tell him, sitting down at his kitchen table without waiting to be invited. "Can you make us a cup of tea, Carter?"

Carter pulls a face, as though I just asked him to wipe my arse, but reaches for the fancy kettle anyway. Harrison glares at me before sitting down. He looks reluctant. Defiant. Guilty. I notice how Carter seems to know exactly where to find everything; mugs, tea, sugar, spoons, but decide to focus my attention on the other man in the room. Harrison Woolf.

"I wonder if we could start again?" I ask, and Harrison stares at me. "Sometimes it helps to go back to the beginning. How long have you been married?"

His face does something strange, as though I asked a difficult question.

"Your colleague already asked me that—"

"He doesn't have any thoughts of his own so tends to borrow mine," I say, and Carter shakes his head. "If you don't mind just answering some questions again."

"I presumed you were here because you had something to tell me—"

"This won't take long, and it might help us find Eden. I know that's what we all want. You and your wife lived in London until recently, is that right?"

"Yes."

"So why the move to Hope Falls?"

"Eden always dreamed of living by the sea. She had this strange obsession with the ocean, nothing made her happier than staring at it and painting it. This house came on the market and seemed perfect. She was happy here."

Past tense.

"And, despite the move to Cornwall, you still work for a company in London?"

"Yes."

"A company called Thanatos? Is that right?"

He stares at me and his reaction is surprisingly hard to read. A curious mix of shock, contempt and defiance, with a side order of simmering rage. I get the impression Mr Woolf is normally the person asking the questions, not answering them. He soon recovers, his handsome features resetting to neutral.

"Yes. I'm the CEO."

"And what kind of company is Thanatos?"

"Is that relevant?"

"Might be."

He folds his arms across his chest. "Pharma tech."

"Sorry, you might need to explain that—"

"It's a little complicated."

"Enlighten me."

Harrison shifts in his seat. "We deal with high-end pharmaceutical research and scientific technology."

"What does that mean? AI?"

He sighs, visibly losing patience. "Artificial intelligence is a key part of any scientific endeavour these days, but Thanatos is a future-thinking company focused on research and studying human frailty, with an emphasis on comfort when there is no cure."

It sounds like a company motto he memorized. I think on his words for a moment, trying to translate them into something I can understand, but it doesn't work. And it doesn't matter. As CEO of the company, I doubt he gets involved in individual client cases. I don't think I'm going to learn anything new about Thanatos today, and I'm not going to bring up my diagnosis in front of Carter. This is just about seeing how far I can bend the man before he snaps. I stare at him and he stares at me and we wait to see who can stay silent the longest.

I win.

Harrison leans forwards, puts his elbows on the table, steeples his fingers. "I understand why you are asking about my job. But I loved my wife, and I've already told you everything I know. I have experienced grief before, and the only cure for heartbreak is hard work. You might think my commitment to my work is strange or suspicious at a time like this, but it's just my way of coping with what may or may not have happened."

The man can read my mind.

Like most people, Harrison Woolf seems like a contradiction of himself.

Confident but scared.

Wise but foolish.

One of my former colleagues at the Met Police once described me as a human lie detector. I liked that, and I wish it were the case, but I can't always tell when someone is lying. I've caught and interviewed some of the biggest, cleverest and most dangerous criminals during my time as a detective in London. I thought I'd seen and heard it all, because I have. But the thing that surprises me most so far about Harrison Woolf is that I believe every word he said just now is true.

Carter places a mug of tea in front of Harrison and another in front of me. Neither of us touches them. He doesn't even look at his, just stares at me with an unnerving intensity.

"I was told that you found your wife's phone," I say, and Harrison nods. "Would you mind if I took a look? It might help shed some light on her whereabouts and state of mind these last few days."

His jaw clenches but he nods. "Of course."

"And would it be possible for me to take a quick look at *your* phone too?"

He stares at me again but doesn't answer. I'm about to politely explain that I can ask his phone company for records any time I want, and that they can send me *everything*, even deleted texts, but then he reaches inside his pocket and puts an iPhone on the table. Unlike mine, it looks brand-new. Him handing it over like that without any further protest surprises me, and I am rarely surprised. I quickly scroll through his final messages with his wife.

Thurs, 30 Oct at 15:05

Leaving London now, will be home soon.

Thurs, 30 Oct at 17:10

Is everything ready for the exhibition?

Thurs, 30 Oct at 23:56

I'm so proud of you tonight. Love you x

She didn't reply to any of his messages and I think that looks suspicious. He said they came back here together after the exhibition, so why not just tell her? Why would you text someone that you loved them if you were with them? Wouldn't you just say it to their face? Unless he knew his wife was going to disappear and wanted it to look as though everything had been fine between them before she did.

"Thank you for that," I say, giving the phone back to him. "Would it be okay if we just took a quick look around the house?"

"Happy to help in any way. I don't have anything to hide," Harrison replies.

And there it is: his first lie.

29

CARTER

The husband is lying. It's obvious. DCI Olivia Bird is meant to be a shit hot detective, so I don't know how she can't see it. Having insulted me on the doorstep, then belittled me by asking me to *make the tea* like some kind of errand boy, my new boss does me the honour of asking me to accompany her while she searches the house. As though I didn't do it properly the first time. As though I haven't single-handedly been in charge of law and order in Hope Falls for four whole years before she turned up. I follow her as she walks around Spyglass. The house looks a little different from the last time we were here together – having sex downstairs – and I know she must be remembering that too as we walk through the rooms where we did it. But being back at Spyglass now feels strange for lots of reasons. Not just because of her. The elderly staircase creaks and groans with every step as we head upstairs.

"You do know I searched the place already?" I remind her quietly when we reach the top. DCI Bird – I can't call her *Birdy*; regardless of what she says it doesn't feel right now – asked Harrison to remain downstairs and I'm glad. I don't like him and I don't trust him. Even if I can't explain why.

"Given the house used to belong to my grandmother, I just

wanted to see what they did when they renovated it," she replies, heading straight for the master bedroom.

"Really?"

"No. Jesus, Carter. The gene pool in this village needs bloody lifeguards."

"What—"

"Forget it."

I'm starting to think DCI Bird is batshit. She might be too many flavours of crazy for most people's taste buds, but I'm still attracted to her. Even more so since I looked her up; she has a seriously impressive track record as a detective. One of the best in London from what I've read. She's supersmart, successful and hot too. I follow her around the room, watching everything she does, trying to guess what might be going on inside her head.

"Tell me what you see," she says, staring at the bed.

It sounds like a trick question, but I'll play along.

"A bedroom."

She rolls her eyes. "What's unusual about it?"

Nothing.

I shrug. "It all looks very neat and tidy to me . . ."

Then I spot an old Walkman on the bedside table, and I freeze because it is not a common household object and it looks just like mine. The exact same model. But it can't be mine, can it?

"Exactly," she whispers, thinking I am seeing whatever she is seeing. "The bed has been made and nothing is out of place. Would you make the bed if your wife was missing, possibly dead? And I think he has changed the sheets." She picks up a pillow and smells it. "Did you notice what looked like bedding in the washing machine downstairs?" I did not. "Does Harrison look like the kind of man who normally does housework to you?" I shake my head. "So why would he do that? You have to learn to look for the strange inside the normal."

I hope she isn't going to patronize me like this on a regular basis.

So what if he changed the sheets?

I'm starting to think my new boss doesn't trust me to tie my own shoelaces.

She pulls on some plastic gloves with a dramatic *thwack*, then takes a small evidence bag from a pocket inside her jacket. I watch transfixed as she swipes a hairbrush from the dressing table and seals it inside the bag. I follow her into the modern marble-and-granite en suite, where she looks at the two electric toothbrushes standing side by side, then at all the expensive-looking toiletries on display. I'm trying to see what she sees but everything looks as it should to me. Until Bird opens the medicine cabinet and I watch her scan the labels on pill bottles like some kind of robot. She slips some tablets into her jacket pocket.

"Shouldn't we bag that as evidence too if—"

She spins around almost as though she had forgotten I was here, stands right in front of me and puts a finger over my lips. She's so close I can smell her perfume. She leans closer still, until her lips are practically touching my ear, then whispers.

"Do you think we could use our silent voices for the rest of the search? I need quiet to do my job. Thank you in advance."

She does what appears to be a thorough search of every room after that, and I follow her without saying another word. I'm not entirely sure what she's looking for but don't want to make a fool of myself by asking any more questions. Back downstairs she returns to the small library at the back of the house. A galaxy of dust particles floats in a beam of light from the window, as though recently disturbed, but there is nobody in the room. Bird folds her arms before quietly saying, "A crime has been committed here."

"It has?" I ask, bewildered as to what I've missed. I look around but draw a blank.

"What do you see?" she asks, staring at the bookcases.

I hesitate, not wanting to make a tit of myself, but she's waiting for an answer.

"A lot of books?"

"*Anything* about this room look different to you?"

I take in the original parquet flooring and very old-looking bookcases, then shrug. "It looks like the only room in the house that they haven't completely renovated . . ."

"Because . . ."

"Because . . . maybe they ran out of money?"

"The car parked outside is worth more than your house. These aren't the kind of people who run out of money. These are people with more money than sense. As the former owner of Spyglass, I know that this old wonky house came with an ancient legal covenant which stated that these bookcases were not to be refurbished or removed, having been installed by some badass carpenter."

"The bookcases are still here."

"I can see that, thank you. But they have been painted. In complete contradiction to the legal documents they signed when they purchased the property."

"They painted the bookcases. That's a crime?"

DCI Bird doesn't reply. She seems lost in her own thoughts again.

"Maybe we should arrest Harrison for painting some bookcases?" I say. I'm joking, of course, but perhaps she can't tell. Londoners seem to have a strange sense of humour, and by strange I mean nonexistent.

"Did you say something?" she asks.

"I said maybe we should arrest Harrison—"

She shakes her head. "Not yet."

30

HARRISON

I'm not ready to face them again yet. I know the female detective doesn't believe me, and I feel numb as she walks around my house, already weary of their *boy cop, bad cop* routine. She asked me to wait in the kitchen while they went upstairs but now I wonder if I should have insisted on following them; it isn't as though they have a warrant. Maybe I should have said no but I was worried how that might look. I don't know what's *normal* in this situation, but given they think my wife might have committed suicide, it feels very strange for them to be trespassing on my grief like this.

Unless of course that *isn't* what they think.

I'm sure Carter suspects me of something, even if his new boss doesn't. I wish I knew what to do, but this isn't the sort of situation life prepares you for. So I pace around the kitchen, wondering how bad it would look if I poured myself a glass of scotch, listening to the sound of creaking footsteps up above, wondering what they are doing up there, what they are thinking and what they might find. My patience expires when they come back downstairs and – instead of coming to the kitchen, thanking me for my time and fucking off – they disappear into the library. I can hear them speaking in hushed voices and the longer it goes on the angrier I feel. I've reached an age where I seem to find most people deeply irritating, and nothing irritates me more than people who waste my time. It's pretty obvious Eden isn't in the library, this isn't a game of bloody Cluedo, and the police have already taken up too much of my day. I've got work to do.

"Did you want to borrow a book?" I say as I walk into the room, and they both spin around as though I have interrupted them.

"No, but would you mind if we take your wife's hairbrush?" the female detective asks, holding up a brush inside a clear plastic bag.

"Anything I can do to help," I reply from the doorway, trying to sound calm.

"Thank you. You've been very helpful," the detective replies with a wonky smile.

I'm sure she wants the hairbrush for a DNA test, but I think it looks better not to ask why. Less . . . guilty. The pressure of trying to act how I should is starting to get to me. I think I'm sweating. The male officer doesn't say anything, doesn't even look at me. He thinks I did something to my wife. Or he thinks I made her do something to herself. I'm not sure what Olivia Bird is thinking; she's harder to read.

I'm thinking I want them to leave.

Nobody except me understands how important my work is right now. It can't wait, regardless of what has or hasn't happened to Eden. Thanatos is at a crucial stage in its evolution. My whole career has been leading up to this moment. My whole life. After years of endless research, personal sacrifice and hard bloody work, I have finally found a big investor who also believes that people have a right to know their date of death. I can't slow this deal down now, and I can't tell the investors that my wife has disappeared. Nothing must get in the way of this deal, so if the police think my behaviour is strange then so be it. There are bigger things at play here. It's literally a matter of life and death.

In Greek mythology Thanatos was a god of death, the son of

darkness and the brother of sleep. He appeared to people when the time allotted to them by fate was up, and carried them to the next world. I borrowed his name for my company for obvious reasons, and I hoped Thanatos would be my legacy. The trials are over, the licence almost approved, and the new investors believe that Thanatos should no longer be an invitation-only service with participants carefully selected beforehand. Thanatos will no longer be free either. They want it to be available to everyone – everyone who can afford it at least – and if I sell my company now, I'll make a fortune. As I should, given all the sacrifices I have had to make.

Unlike a lot of scientists, I do not have a god complex.

But I do have a problem with the way God does things.

Time is money and money is time. We should all know how much we have and be able to budget accordingly. Thanatos is what I wanted to be remembered for. I dreamed it would change people's lives, and deaths, forever. That I'd be like Alexander Fleming, Edward Jenner and Marie Curie, but that *my* scientific discovery would be bigger than all of theirs and the world would remember my name.

Now I'm not so sure.

The detective and the sergeant finally take a hint and start to leave. I'm not too worried about him; it's her I need to keep an eye on.

I recognized Olivia Bird as soon as I opened the front door.

She was one of the clinical trial volunteers a few months ago, but unlike all the others, she turned up uninvited at the private clinic in London using her dead grandmother's name. Many of our clients are approaching one hundred years of age. Centenarians were one of our main targets for clinical trials for lots of reasons. Plus, I find the closer a person is to death the more they wonder about it.

When Olivia Bird turned up at the clinic, she did not look one hundred years old. And according to our records, the client was already dead. The team immediately raised the alarm that DCI Bird had applied using her grandmother's invitation, and it was *me* who had to decide what to do about her. I remember watching her on a screen as she was interviewed by one of our "doctors". Our client-facing staff are all out-of-work actors, none of them have any medical training, and they are carefully selected and auditioned. We pay them more than they can earn on-screen and we make them sign an NDA. I confess that the casting process was fun. I tell them what to do, what to say and how to say it, like a director in their ear. They aren't making movies anymore, but we tell them they are making history, and playing a lead role in changing the world. I shovel the shit and they spread it.

Some people – people like Olivia Bird – might question the ethics of what we do. As a rule, I have never allowed anyone working in law enforcement to be part of the programme. They tend not to understand that sometimes you have to break the rules to fix things. Luckily, she still hasn't asked the right questions, just more of the wrong ones. Strange, given her IQ. Distracted by her diagnosis I suspect. Caught in the no-man's-land between searching for the meaning of life and accepting that life has no meaning.

I couldn't let anyone get in the way of our clinical trials; the success of Thanatos matters too much to let that happen. So Thanatos started watching Olivia Bird from the moment she called the number on her grandmother's letter. When she clicked to accept our terms and conditions at the bottom of the online questionnaire, we started listening to her too, via her laptop, though I doubt she was aware. People never read the small print. And when she walked into the clinic on Harley Street, I watched her every minute she was in the building and dealt with her case myself. With the help of AI, a person's DNA and our bespoke algorithms, we predict when a person will die. But it was *me* who had to decide whether to tell Olivia Bird the truth.

As soon as she left the building I deleted all records of her from the database. For a long time I never thought I would see Olivia Bird again, but here she is. In my home. In Hope Falls. Back where she started. And that's okay, we all go back where we came from eventually, it's nature's way.

We're all born with an expiration date, we just don't know it.

31

CARTER

I just don't know what to make of any of this.

"You're unusually quiet," DCI Bird says when we get back to the station. As if she knows me. As though she cares.

"Am I?"

"Yes, it's nice. Easier to think."

"Glad to be of assistance. Why did you take the hairbrush?"

"In case we need it for a DNA match at some point. I think Harrison Woolf is the kind of shifty bastard who might get rid of evidence so I thought, best to get it now. I don't trust that fucker. I'm sure he's hiding something. You mentioned that there was some CCTV footage of the woman claiming to be the real Eden Fox. Can I see it?"

"It's not great quality – there's only one camera in the village – but I'll load it up," I say, sitting down at my desk as she stands behind me. Too close as always. So close I can smell her. The computer is painfully slow, and the silence while we wait feels uncomfortable, but she seems to prefer it when I say nothing at all and I'm starting to think it might be best, for both of us, if I keep schtum. Twenty-four hours ago everything about my life was exactly how I wanted it to be. Routine. Quiet. Content. Since the call came in last night about a random woman trespassing at Spyglass, everything feels wrong. A former one-night stand coming back to haunt me six months later and declaring she's my new boss is the final straw.

I am not in the habit of having one-night stands. I rarely leave Hope Falls, and it's not the sort of thing you do in a place like this where everybody knows you and everything about you. Especially when you're the local policeman. People here trust me. They respect me. They don't think I'm that kind of guy, and I'm not. Unless a stranger comes to town.

Me sleeping with someone I shouldn't has caused no end of problems.

"I looked you up," I tell Bird, unsure whether it is the right thing to say.

"What do you mean?"

"I wanted to see who they chose over me, so I looked you up and I get why you got the job. You joined the force when you were twenty, moved up the ranks pretty fast. You've had the highest number of arrests and convictions in London every year for the past five years and you turned down the George Medal."

"Nobody should get a medal just for doing their job."

"I couldn't find anything about your personal life. No social media accounts. I couldn't even find a photo of you online."

"Your point?"

"It's just a little strange in this day and age. As is you being here. Why would you take this job?"

"Gosh, let me try to answer the barrage of questions in order. There is nothing personal about me online because I'm not an idiot. I value my privacy, as should any sane individual. I'm here because I want to be, I fancied a change. Any other queries or could we perhaps focus on the job? You sound like a stalker, by the way, looking me up like that," she says as a grainy image appears on the screen. It eventually shows an eerie shape of a woman walking along the main lane in the village.

"Is that it?" Bird asks, clearly unimpressed.

"Afraid so."

"I can't tell shit from that. That could be anyone. It could be me."

Strange thing for her to say.

"The husband was lying to us just now. He's our best lead so far," she adds.

If she can tell that he is lying can she tell that I am too?

"I'm going back to my office," she says, heading for the door.

"The pub?" I ask, incredulous.

"I think better with company."

"I could come with you—"

"I meant my dog. Did you talk to the art gallery owner?"

"Yes."

"Great, send me a transcript, then join me. We'll call it a working lunch," she says then leaves the station, closing the door behind her.

Bird thinks she's so clever, and she is, but she still doesn't know how well I knew Eden Fox. Nobody does, thank god. Eden came to visit me at the station a few weeks ago. She told me someone had been outside Spyglass watching her and she thought she should report it. That was the first time we met, but not the last.

I liked her. She had a lot of questions about the village, and seemed fascinated by the poster on the noticeboard advertising the annual Day of the Dead festival in Hope Falls. She spotted it when putting up a poster about her exhibition, and I remember I laughed when our little festival seemed to shock her – I suppose it does sound a bit strange if you're not from around here – but then I explained that it was a local tradition celebrated by all the towns and villages within Blackmoor National Park.

Every year, on the day after Halloween – the first of November – the villagers gather at The Smuggler's Inn for a few drinks before a procession from the church cemetery through the village all the way to Blackwater Bay. We call it the Day of the Dead, paint our faces like skeletons and carry flaming torches through the streets. It might sound strange to outsiders but it's a lot of fun. When I told Eden about it, *she* seemed like a lot of fun. Said we could go together, because nobody would know it was us if we were wearing fancy dress. She was flirting with me, despite being married, and I confess I might have flirted back. I noticed how lonely Eden Fox was the first time we met. She seemed starved of affection and I found myself wanting to give it to her. She wore a polka-dot dress with buttons all the way down the front that day in the station, and her long blonde hair shone in the light. I liked the way she spoke, the way she smiled, the way she smelled. Normally I couldn't care less about art, but I sat and I listened to her talk about her paintings and I thought I'd probably like the way she tasted.

Then I saw the bruises on her arms.

I think he did that to her. The husband. How else could it have happened?

From the moment I met Eden Fox I imagined saving her. From him and whatever else caused the sadness she tried to hide behind a smile. That wasn't all I fantasized about. I imagined her coming back to the station scared that someone was still watching her, sitting on my desk, undoing all those buttons down the front of her dress and opening her legs nice and wide. Soft white flesh. Matching underwear. She was so lovely. So lonely. So hungry for it. So grateful. She wanted me inside her, right there and then, but it didn't happen. It was just a fantasy. A daydream . . .

I dreamed of fucking Eden Fox.

And I dreamed of saving her.

Now she's gone.

32

Interviewer: Sergeant Luke Carter (LC)
Interviewee: Diana Harris (DH)
Date: 31st October, 2025
Location: Saltwater Gallery, Hope Falls

LC: Thank you for your time and for closing the gallery.

DH: I just can't believe it. Last night she was standing right where you are. It was the best event we've had here for years.

LC: Tell me about Eden Fox.

DH: You met her too. She was just a lovely human being, and so talented. Are you sure that she—

LC: How did you meet her?

DH: Well, I didn't technically meet her until yesterday. Until the actual exhibition. But we spoke on the phone.

LC: Who called who?

DH: She emailed in the first instance. Said she was moving to the area and would I be interested in selling one or two of her paintings. I confess when I get emails like that my heart sinks. Everyone thinks they are an artist these days, just like everyone thinks they have a book in them, and most of the time when people get in touch like that the work on offer is mediocre at best. But this was different. She sent me a link to some of her paintings and I fell in love instantly. They were all of the sea, and there was something very unique and special about them. That's all we sell: art about the sea. Paintings, prints, pottery, greetings cards—

LC: What happened after that first email from Eden?

DH: We had a very pleasant phone call and I offered to take all her paintings. I knew I could sell them when the tourists came back.

LC: The tourists aren't back yet, and you don't normally do events out of season. How did the exhibition come about? Was it your idea?

DH: No. It was his.

LC: Who?

DH: The husband. He came in to the gallery one day – dressed in a very nice suit, tailored, expensive. He had a good head of hair and nice-looking hands, short clean fingernails. You can tell a lot about a man from his hands.

LC: Good to know. And Mr Woolf talked to you about his wife?

DH: He said how thrilled they both were that I was going to be selling her work. Told me that she'd had a really difficult time looking after their daughter and how much me believing in her art had meant to her. He asked if I might host an exhibition, something to make her feel good about herself, said he'd pay for the drinks and to invite the whole village, but not to tell his wife that he was behind it all. He wanted her to think it was my idea. Build her confidence. Apparently she was a bit of a recluse, he said she rarely left the house, though I have to admit she didn't come across like that last night. I thought it was very sweet for a husband to want to do that for his wife and I was pleased to help. Now this has happened. She seemed so happy last night, but do you think it was all too much for her? The attention and people looking at her work? Is this my fault?

LC: No, of course not. So you never met Eden Fox in real life until last night?

DH: No, but we spoke on the phone—

LC: And you're sure it was Eden Fox you were speaking to?

DH: Who else would it have been? We only spoke once, I mainly dealt with the husband. Harrison delivered the paintings, along with all the wine for the event. He's very generous and equally charming. A real gentleman. That poor man, he must be devastated. Do you think it's too soon to take him a casserole? I'm sorry, where are my manners, I didn't offer you a drink. Would you like a cup of tea?

LC: No.

33

CARTER

I head to The Smuggler's Inn looking for my new boss. I'm guessing she has read the transcript by now. I am greeted at the door by DCI Bird's wolf, and stand perfectly still while it stares at me. Big dogs make me nervous and I wish she would keep him on a lead.

"Don't worry, he's harmless," she says from a table in the corner.

"If you say so."

"I was talking to the dog."

Funny.

She invites me to join her, which I do, and the wolf dog sits down on the floor beside us, watching me. Bird looks up and does the same.

"Sunday."

"What?"

"You were about to ask his name."

"Was I?"

"The transcript of your interview with the owner of the art gallery was interesting. What do you make of her?"

"What do you mean?"

"Well, she was one of the last people to see Eden Fox before she went missing. Harrison said that he and Eden stayed late at the gallery and had a drink with Diana after everyone else left. The husband was lying about something. Was Diana lying too?"

"Diana Harris has outlived three husbands and might well be on the lookout for a fourth. She's guilty of having a crush on Harrison, but I don't think she's a suspect."

Bird tilts her head, taps her finger on the top of her laptop like she's sending Morse code, and stares at me in a way I find super disconcerting. The laptop is old and battered and covered in childish stickers. One says KEEP CALM AND FUCK OFF. She smiles and it only makes me feel more discombobulated.

"Everyone is a suspect until they're not, Carter. That's rule number two."

"What was rule number one?"

"Remember to eat. Nothing good is ever achieved on an empty stomach. Do you fancy a cheeseburger? They're really tasty. My treat," Bird says, as though I am a child.

I know they're good. I live in this village and I've eaten more burgers in this pub than she has. I want to say no but I say yes because I am hungry and I never turn down free food. Especially the best burgers in all of Cornwall. Bird waves at the barmaid who is behind the bar, and my heart sinks again. I already know that this is going to be awkward in more ways than one. Maddy looks up from her book, tucks her long red hair behind her ears and grins when she sees me sitting at the table.

"Hello, Lulu," she says to me.

This. Isn't. Happening.

My name is *Luke* Carter. I don't know why Maddy insists on calling me Lulu. Bird's face lights up like a Christmas tree and I feel my cheeks burn.

"Hello, Maddy," I reply.

Bird looks from one of us to the other with a smile bigger than I thought her face was capable of. It's not what she thinks but I can't be bothered to correct her.

"Can *Lulu* and I get two of the Smuggler's Ultimate Burgers, please?" she asks, but it turns out that's just the beginning of her food order. "On one of the burgers, can I have *no* lettuce, *no* tomato and onions, but *only* if they are fried. Any relish should be on the side and not touching anything else, ideally in individual ramekins. All I want on the plate is the burger, the cheese, which I hope will be melted, and the bun. I'd like the burger cooked medium to well. I don't like it overcooked but I don't want to see any blood. No salt on my fries either. Thank you. And can I get two milkshakes? One strawberry and one . . ."

She stares at me expectantly. "Oh, I'm fine with water, thanks."

"Have a milkshake. They're good," she insists.

"Fine. Chocolate."

"One strawberry and one chocolate," she says, putting down the menu. Maddy raises an eyebrow before smirking at me then disappearing back behind the bar.

"So . . . Lulu?" Bird says when she is gone.

"It's just a nickname. It's short for Luke," I say.

"Is it?"

"Why didn't you give him a harder time?" I ask, trying to change the subject.

"Who?" she says, polishing the cutlery with her napkin as though she thinks it isn't clean enough.

"Harrison Woolf. If you're so sure he's lying, why were you so nice to him?"

"Because sometimes you have to be nice to people to get what you want from them."

"Even people you suspect committed a crime?"

"Sometimes less is more when questioning a suspect. Wait. Watch. And above all else, listen. People are afraid of silence and will fill it with all sorts of things they didn't mean to say. And if they don't, then what a person doesn't say can be far more informative than what they do. Besides, what crime are you suggesting he committed? We still haven't found either of the women claiming to be Eden Fox."

"Well, there's gaslighting. Could be something like that. Could he have talked her into harming herself and jumping off a cliff? Maybe she was having an affair and he found out and—"

"Who on earth would she have an affair with *here*?"

"I'm just saying—"

"It's good to consider all the options but we need to stick to the facts and not jump to conclusions."

The term seems inappropriate given the circumstances, and I wish she would stop speaking to me as if I'm an idiot. Perhaps she has forgotten that Hope Falls has one of the lowest crime rates in the country, unlike London, thanks to me knowing how to do my job. I'm grateful for the distraction when our food arrives. I watch as she dismantles her already deconstructed burger to check it is how she ordered it. Then she cuts it into precise quarters before taking an enormous bite.

"I don't understand why we aren't speaking to the daughter," I say, before eating my burger like a normal person. "Harrison has made it clear that he doesn't want us to, which I think is strange and suspicious."

"Not really," she says, taking another bite.

"Why isn't it?"

"A simple Google search of the number Mr Woolf gave you yesterday is why." She hastily taps something into her laptop with one hand – the fingers on her other covered in grease and ketchup – then turns the screen to face me before popping some fries in her mouth. For someone so small she seems to have a huge appetite.

I see a website for something called The Manor.

"What is it? A luxury hotel?" I ask.

"Not quite. The Manor is where Gabriella Woolf lives. It's a very expensive and exclusive residential care facility for young adults who cannot take care of themselves. Either due to illness, serious injury, learning difficulties or mental health issues."

"Which category does the daughter fall into?"

"She was in an accident. Hasn't spoken a word for ten years. They say she is basically a child trapped inside a young woman's body. I don't think she can be a suspect, and I don't want you to give Harrison Woolf any more excuses to file a complaint."

"I think we should at least find out if the daughter is still there."

"I think you should quit while you're behind," she says, popping a final bite of burger into her mouth.

"You think you don't need me, but Hope Falls is not the same as London."

"Well, there's something we can agree on—"

"I know the area. I know the people. The locals here respect me and that counts for something even if you don't think so."

She doesn't answer. Instead she sucks each of her sticky fingers in turn, then takes what looks like a wet wipe from her bag and thoroughly cleans her hands. I've barely touched my food yet but she has cleared her whole plate. Even the dollop of ketchup is gone, as though she squeezed out the perfect amount. I take another bite but the wolf dog keeps staring in my direction and drooling as though he'd like to eat my burger, or possibly me.

"You do know it's illegal for a dog not to wear a collar?" I say, wishing he was tied to something. Preferably outside. Far away.

"He doesn't like wearing one. You can arrest me if you like."

"What if he got lost?"

"He won't, but if he did I'd find him. Sunday is smarter than most people."

She gives me a look that suggests she thinks the dog is smarter than me too, then she sucks the straw in her milkshake and returns her attention to her laptop as though I'm not here. I put down my burger; I'm not sure I can eat any more. I seem to have lost my appetite.

The barmaid comes to collect our plates and frowns when she sees that I barely touched my food. "What's wrong, Lulu?" she asks, placing a hand on my shoulder. "Not like you to leave food on your plate. He normally inhales it," she says, smiling at Bird, who suddenly seems more interested in me than whatever she was reading on the screen.

"We're trying to work if you don't mind, Maddy," I say.

"It's fine, tell me more about Sergeant Lulu," Bird says, closing the laptop.

Maddy laughs. "*Sergeant*, I still can't get used to people calling him that."

I glare up at her. "Thank you, Maddy. Always so good to see you. We really do need to get back to work now," I add, desperate to shut this down.

"Don't you be getting all high-and-mighty with me, Luke Carter. I've seen you naked," Maddy says, then she ruffles my hair. "Sorry, pet. Didn't mean to embarrass you. Luke is a man of many talents," she says to Bird.

"Thank you—"

"All of them unproven." Maddy chuckles to herself and walks away.

Bird laughs too. "You're right, the locals definitely respect you. You never mentioned that you had a girlfriend."

"She's not my girlfriend."

"She said she's seen you naked—"

"She means when we were kids. She's my *big sister*, not my girlfriend. She used to change my nappies, for god's sake."

I look up and it's the first time I've ever seen Bird look confused.

"Your *sister*?"

"Our parents used to be the landlords of this pub and it was our home when we were kids. Our folks never owned it, just ran the place, so when the brewery bought the freehold during the tourist boom a couple of years ago, Mum and Dad lost their home as well as their livelihood. Maddy still likes working here. I think it's her way of staying close to them."

"What happened to them?"

"They left. Couldn't afford to stay. The price of properties in Cornwall has gone through the roof because of people buying holiday homes. Mum and Dad couldn't afford to live in the village they were born in. The stress of it all was too much for them. They're gone."

"They died?"

"Worse. They moved to Spain."

Bird smiles, so I don't ruin the moment by telling her that Mum has been diagnosed with cancer or that I think the stress of losing the pub is what caused it. I'm sure she doesn't need to know my whole sorry life story.

"Carter, I know we might not have got off to the best start. And I'm sorry if this is strange, me being here; I know how badly you wanted this job. I probably haven't been very sensitive about that, but I do respect you. And, just to prove it, I have something very important that I need you to do."

34

HARRISON

It's so important that I do the right thing now.

I close the door, wishing I knew what that was. Then I stand perfectly still until I hear the officers drive away. Him in his ridiculous toy police car. Her on a red bloody scooter. Tweedle Dumb and Tweedle Dangerous. I double-lock the door and close all the curtains and blinds. The police looked in every room before they left, almost as though they thought Eden was here somewhere. Hiding. Or hidden. I find the intrusion deeply irritating, and retrace their footsteps, hurrying from room to room, trying to see our home through their eyes and wondering what they saw. I linger in the bedroom and stare at the bed. Maybe I shouldn't have been so quick to change the sheets, but I had to. I wanted to get rid of the smell of her from every room.

Having already gone willingly to the police station to answer their stupid bloody questions, I thought they'd have the decency to leave me alone. Guess I thought wrong.

Now that they're gone I start to relax, until I remember something.

Something I forgot about.

Something they missed.

I hurry downstairs, grateful in some ways that they asked me to wait in the kitchen because I know they didn't check the bin. I open the lid and stare at the black velvet dress all too visible on top. Eden loved this dress. I still remember the first time she wore it – our anniversary several years ago – I'll always remember the last. It's the kind of dress that makes you want to undress a woman when you see her wearing it. I pull it out of the bin, take it to the fireplace in the lounge and burn it.

While the flames lick and hiss and spit, I look around the room to check that I haven't missed anything else. There are a lot of pictures of Gabriella in here. Snapshots of our daughter from every stage of her life, from when she was a little girl, to more recently. There is one of me and her taken before the accident, before our lives got turned upside down. It's my favourite one of her, and us. There are no pictures of Eden in this room. No pictures of Gabriella's mother at all anymore.

I removed every single one.

Once the fire has burned itself out, I return to the little library at the back of the house. I stand and stare at the ancient bookcases containing stories I'll never read written by people I've never met. I have never understood the appeal of fiction. I don't have *time* for other people's stories; I'd rather live my own. Maybe when people know how little time they have left they'll use it more wisely. Thanatos means that I am more aware than most that life is short and time is precious. The thought leads me to thinking about my daughter again. I miss her. I should never have agreed to put her in that institution, because that's what The Manor is. Regardless of the fancy exterior and extortionate fees, and the "home away from home" description in the glossy brochure, my little girl is in a luxury prison. I'll never forgive myself for going along with it.

And I'll never forgive Eden.

My wife and I rarely argued, but we did disagree about Gabriella.

And we had conflicting views about this library too.

Seeing all these bookcases reminded me of my mother, who is someone I'd rather forget. My father died when I was ten, and my mother had little interest in me after that. She said I reminded her of him. She spent her time drinking cheap wine, reading cheap books and filling the house with stories that were happier than her own. She never worked – even when we were broke and had to choose between eating or heating the house – but she still spent money on novels. I don't have a problem with books, but you can't eat them. I spent a lot of my childhood feeling hungry. And cold. And alone. Navigating her moods was terrifying. As was her temper. Nothing I did was ever good enough for her and she made sure I knew it. She didn't abuse me with her fists, just her words. And her hate. So I grew up and I got out and I wrote my own story. One without her in it.

The last thing she said to me the day I left home was,

You'll never amount to anything.

It was the greatest gift she ever gave me; the determination to prove her wrong. And I did. I got into university on a scholarship because I was the best in my class. I was the smartest kid on that degree course too, but also the poorest. I taught myself how to blend in, but I never felt like I belonged in the world my studies or my work took me to. Everyone else was more confident, better connected. Their world always seemed out of reach to me even when I was supposedly one of them. My mother created my demons and I've never outrun them.

I spent my teenage years wishing she had died instead of my dad.

Then I grew impatient wondering when she would.

And I think that was the spark. The lightning-bolt moment. My eureka.

It was my burning desire to know when my mother would die, and how much longer I had to endure her hate, that led me into science and eventually to Thanatos. I studied hard, I worked even harder, and I launched an entire company to discover how to accurately predict the day a person will die.

My mother's date of death was the first I got right.

My daughter's date of death was the first I hoped was wrong.

After Gabriella's accident, the fear of losing her consumed me. I became so obsessed with how much longer I had left with my daughter, I spent even less time with her, too busy trying to crack the code. I created Thanatos to spite my mother and save my daughter, but in the process I lost so much precious time. Time I can never get back. Seeing anything that reminds me of my mother triggers me, including those old bookcases in our new home. So one evening when Eden was out for one of her runs, and despite the ancient covenants that came with the house saying this room should not be touched, I came in here with a sledgehammer.

I decided to remove the books before I started smashing the shelves, and that's when I found the small fake panel hiding a lever. A lever that I pulled. There was a creak and what sounded like a sigh, as though the bookcases had been holding their breath, and then I saw that they had come slightly apart in the middle. There was a centimetre-wide gap between them from floor to ceiling. I carefully slid my fingers inside the gap, and when I applied the tiniest amount of pressure, the bookcases slid apart to reveal a door behind them. I told myself that the door couldn't possibly lead anywhere; this part of the house was literally built into the cliff it was perched on.

But I was wrong.

35

CARTER

I was right about DCI Bird not taking me seriously. When she said there was something important she wanted me to do, I didn't think she meant walking her bloody dog.

"Are you serious?"

"Almost always," she replies without looking up from her laptop.

I stare at the wolf who stares back at me, as though he knows what is going on.

"Right. Well, does he need a lead?"

"No, he's very well trained. Sunday will come when you call him. Just whistle like this if he strays too far." She whistles two distinct notes, one high, one low, and the dog sits up, tilts his head and stares at her adoringly.

I do not.

I don't know what *my* face is doing, but I suspect it's more of a glare.

"Where do you want me to walk him?" I ask.

"Up to you. Maybe take him to the beach? He loves the sea and the sand."

"Fine."

"And behave yourself."

"You said he was well trained?"

"I meant you."

The dog and I walk out of the pub, and along the harbour wall, where I take the coast path that leads through the sand dunes to Blackwater Bay. It's only a ten-minute walk from the village, and I could do with some fresh air myself. In tourist season this beach is packed, but at this time of year it is normally deserted, because Blackwater Bay can only be reached on foot. I watch Sunday run ahead as soon as he sees the beach, ears flapping, tail wagging, bounding along the sand with the variety of carefree joy I have forgotten. Watching him makes me smile, which surprises me so much I have to look away. I take out my phone and try to catch up on all the things I haven't been keeping up to date with since DCI Bird arrived.

A short while later, the sound of Sunday barking makes me look up. The sky has darkened while I've been looking down. Storm clouds have drifted in from the Atlantic, the wind has picked up and the tide has rolled out, waves crashing and churning in the distance. I can't see Sunday. I call his name but he doesn't come. I can't whistle – I didn't want to confess to there being something else I can't do in front of the new boss – but now I think I might have lost her bloody dog.

All I can see is a vast empty beach, all I can hear is the ocean. Then I spot Sunday in the sea, too far from the shore and possibly out of his depth. Like me. Well trained, my arse, the husky is clearly suicidal. Maybe that's what happens if you live with someone like Bird. The thought quickly mutates into guilt. Then fear.

If something happens to her dog she'll kill me.

"Sunday!"

What a stupid bloody name for a dog.

I run towards the water, shouting his name over and over, like someone with days-of-the-week Tourette's. But I don't care if I sound like an idiot, nobody else is here and it looks like the tide is taking the dog further out. I just need to get him back even if it means going in myself. I start taking off my coat and anything else that will weigh me down in the water, but then the strangest thing happens. I hear a distinct whistle. Two notes. Just like Bird did in the pub, and the dog swims out of the sea and runs along the beach as though this was all a game. I'm the only person here and I can't whistle. I spin around, but with the sea and the wind filling my ears, it's hard to pinpoint where the sound came from. Until I see something out of the corner of my eye. A figure dressed in black on the other side of the bay. It's not Bird. I can't see their face, but from their height and build, I *think* it's a man.

I start walking towards them, but when they see me coming they run.

What the fuck?

I chase after him. I might not have been top of my class at the police academy, but I was always the fastest when it came to fitness tests. It doesn't take me long to shorten the gap. I sprint along the sandy beach, knowing they can't outrun me, getting closer every second. He briefly vanishes in the sand dunes, but I soon spot him again, and the chase continues. I almost fall clambering over the slippery rocks at the bottom of the cliff, and when I look up I can't see him anywhere. The dog is by my side, wagging his tail as though he thought the chase was a game, but there is nobody else here. I search in all the obvious places, but they've gone, even though there was nowhere for them to go. As if they just disappeared.

I stop and try to catch my breath.

Confused and disorientated.

I might be mistaken, I think I *must* be, but the person I saw who whistled to save the dog and then vanished looked a lot like Harrison Woolf.

36

BIRDY

Carter and his sister do not look at all alike. They are so different I'm finding it hard to believe they are related, and I use the time while Carter is gone to ask her a few questions.

Maddy is sitting behind the permanently empty bar of The Smuggler's Inn. She's twirling a strand of her long red hair around the finger of one hand and holding what looks like a romance novel in the other. I sit myself down on a barstool opposite her, and notice that my shoes could do with a polish. When Maddy doesn't look up straight away I clear my throat. She turns the page of her book, so engrossed in the story she hasn't noticed me. Or is pretending not to.

"I didn't know Carter was your brother," is my cunning opening line. She finally looks up from her paperback and smiles.

"You didn't ask."

"Don't ask, don't get?"

"More like don't ask, don't tell around here."

There is mischief in her eyes, and it makes me wonder if she knows I've slept with her brother. From what Carter said earlier, it sounds as though they've always been close.

"He said that your parents used to run this pub."

"That's right. For over thirty years."

"Must have been a fun childhood."

"Sometimes. We lived upstairs, and the place was so busy during the summer that Mum and Dad rarely had much time for us. It used to be busy in winter too back then," she says, looking around the empty pub now. "But that was before half the houses in the village became holiday homes. We didn't have a lot of money but we had a lot of love, and it broke my mother's heart when the old witch who owned the freehold decided to sell this pub."

"Why didn't your parents try to buy it?"

"They did try, and for a fair price too, using every penny of their savings. Owning this place had always been their dream, so we could keep it in the family. But they were outbid by the brewery and that was that. Luke and I were devasted too; this place was our home. There used to be marks on this wall showing our heights every year when we were kids, but the new owners painted over our lives and turned our home into a gastro pub. Profit was more important to them than people."

"I'm sorry, that must have been hard."

She shrugs. "Life is hard. It was worse for my brother. Luke was born here, it was the only home he'd ever known. He was in his early twenties when Mum and Dad ran off to Spain – just a big kid really – and family has always been important to him. There's a bit of an age gap between me and him – seven years – so it felt like it was up to me to keep an eye on him when they left. I like to think I did a good job. He completed his police training, stayed in Hope Falls when most people his age couldn't wait to get away, then he took over running the police station when Nick retired. He's doing pretty well for a twenty-eight-year-old."

"Carter is twenty-eight?"

I had told myself he was a baby-faced thirtysomething.

She nods. "I know. He looks even younger. It's the sea air!"

"Tell me about Carter. What was he like when he was a boy?"

"I don't think he'd like me—"

"I won't tell him if you won't. Don't ask, don't tell, like you said."

She grins. "Well, in some ways my brother never really grew up. He spent a lot of his childhood in this pub, dreaming about smugglers and inventing stories about secret tunnels in the cellar. He was convinced there were tunnels dug into the cliffs all the way from here to Blackwater Bay. If there are, he never found them, but despite all the lies he told as a child he grew into an honest man. A good man. The whole village loves him."

"That's nice."

"He is."

As though on cue Carter bursts through the door of the pub closely followed by Sunday.

"Everything okay?" I ask.

Carter shakes his head. "No. There's a body on the beach."

37

CARTER

"Sorry, it sounded like you said there was a body on the beach?" Bird says.

I nod, but they both stare at me as though they don't understand. As if I'm speaking a foreign language.

DCI Bird surprises me by looking surprised; she never has before.

Maddy doesn't behave how I would have expected her to either. She stands perfectly still behind the bar and gives me the look she used as kids when I was about to get us both in trouble. She almost looks . . . guilty.

Were they talking about me when I walked in?

I bloody hope not.

"Is it her? Is it Eden?" Maddy asks. Her normally rosy cheeks are pale, and my fearless sister looks afraid.

Does she know what I did?

"He can't tell you that," Bird interrupts. "Where is the body now?"

"On the beach. Like I just said—"

"What? You just left it there—"

"No, of course not. I—"

"Bloody hell."

"I haven't even seen it yet. I got a call from HQ to say a swimmer found a body on the beach, that's all I know so far."

"Well, don't just stand there, Carter. Let's go. What are you waiting for?"

38

BIRDY

I can't wait for Carter to catch up with this latest development. A body being found on your first day in a new job is never a good start. I hurry out of The Smuggler's Inn and am about to climb onto my scooter.

"No need for that," says Carter. "It will be quicker to walk."

I reluctantly follow him, already worried about how much time has passed since the body was discovered, how much evidence might have already been compromised and how many people might have seen things they should not have seen.

"Were you questioning Maddy just now?" Carter asks.

"Would it be a problem if I was?"

"She's my sister, not a suspect."

I find his reaction interesting but park that thought for now.

The sky has turned dark and inky, and the wind kisses my cheeks as the impending storm settles over Hope Falls. It's noticeably colder than it was earlier and a dew-like mist coats my skin as we walk along the harbour wall. Carter – with his freakishly long legs – walks considerably faster than I do, and I soon get warm practically running to keep up with him. I'm not as fit as I used to be. Going to the gym has been the last thing on my list of things to do since I found out I was dying. It's hard to live in the moment when you know all your best moments are behind you.

I follow Carter onto a narrow coast path winding through sand-banks covered in long grass, wondering how much bloody further we need to go.

"Are you sure it wouldn't be faster to drive?"

"Why? Worried about getting your shoes dirty?" he says over his shoulder.

Sarcastic little shit.

"You'll go far one day, Carter. And when you do I hope you stay there."

"The beach is only accessible on foot, I'm afraid," he reminds me, and I'm about to make another witty comeback when I trip on a rock. Carter catches me before I fall, then holds me a little longer than necessary. I am not imagining the chemistry between us but I am choosing to ignore it. I'm forty. And now that I know he's only twenty-eight, I feel like Mrs Robinson.

"Thank you," I say, when he finally lets go.

"No problem," he replies, his cheeks blushing like I suspect mine are too.

The coast path winds its way around a corner, so that when I look back, Hope Falls can no longer be seen. As though it has vanished or was never there. All that is visible from this part of the path are the ocean and the cliffs, including the section that Eden Fox may or may not have jumped from. We are travelling in the opposite direction, away from where she would have jumped, but the tides are a law unto themselves, and I suppose it is possible they might have carried her this far.

"How much further?" I ask.

"Just over this next hill," Carter says as we approach a part of the path that looks so steep this *hill* ought to be reclassified as a mountain. But the view when we reach the top is stunning. Forgotten memories of being here as a child ripple through my mind. A vast white sandy bay stretches in front of us, surrounded by a turquoise-coloured sea. I pause for a moment, trying to get my breath back. I can see what looks like the wreck of a small wooden fishing boat, broken bits of wood scattered on the sand. Eventually nature always takes back what she loans us. And what we steal. It's only ever a matter of time.

"Blackwater Bay, isn't she stunning," Carter says, waiting for me. "Do you need a minute to catch your breath?"

"Not at all. I'm fine," I lie.

"Okay," he says, but walks a little more slowly and stays by my side. "This concealed cove used to be used for smuggling. A hundred years ago, boats carrying stolen goods would sail to this spot, hidden out of sight from the village. Whatever they were carrying – gold, guns, alcohol, money – would be carried through the sand dunes under the cover of darkness to The Smuggler's Inn. There are stories about secret tunnels in the cliffs that lead from the pub all the way up the hill to Spyglass."

"Ever find any when you were a kid?"

"What?"

"Tunnels."

"No, but not for lack of trying," he says.

I'm not sure I believe him.

"They were just made-up stories that local people told for fun."

Doesn't sound like my kind of fun.

In fact, I've thought of a new slogan for the place:

Hope Falls – Where Fun Comes to Die.

We start heading downhill into the bay and as we turn a corner I spot a woman in the distance standing over what I'm guessing is the body. She's on the other side of the beach. Carter runs ahead down the uneven coast path – which has crumbled away completely in places – and I can feel myself eroding too, getting closer to oblivion. I do my best to keep up with him, while also doing my best not to slip or trip or break my bloody neck. He reaches the woman long before I do, and they appear to be whispering when I finally catch up.

"This is Diana Harris. She found the body," Carter says. The name immediately rings a bell. The art gallery owner who likes a spoonful of her dead husband's ashes in her tea. Allegedly. And one of the last people to see Eden Fox before she disappeared.

My first impressions of Diana Harris having read the transcript of Carter's interview don't quite match the woman I am now meeting in real life. I imagined her to be middle-aged, tall, thin, heavily made-up, well-groomed and well-dressed. In reality, she is shorter than me – which is saying something – looks like she has a healthy appetite and is makeup-free. She is still wearing a swimming cap on her head, Crocs on her feet and what looks like a fancy dressing gown with the word DRYROBE on the front.

"I was swimming, like I do every day after lunch. I didn't see the body until I got out of the water. Must have washed up on the shore when I was in the sea. Strange though, because the tide is going out," she says, her words rushing out of her like they couldn't wait to escape. She glances at the body, which is lying face down a few metres away, and I follow her stare. It's clearly a woman, but without getting closer and rolling her over it isn't possible to identify her from here. "Sorry I moved her, I know I shouldn't have."

"Then why did you?"

"I was just trying to help – I have a certificate in first aid – but she's a bit beyond that. Aren't you going to ask me if it's her? Eden Fox? Because I honestly can't tell and I doubt you'll be able to either."

What an odd thing to say.

If it is Eden, she's only been in the water for a few hours. Her body shouldn't have decomposed so badly that nobody would recognize her. I ask Carter to take a witness statement, and to do it further away from the body, while I take a closer look. I should really wait for the forensics team to arrive but my curiosity gets the better of me.

I gently roll the body over and take a step back. Time stops, rewinds, and I am a little girl again, standing on the beach staring at the body of my dead mother. For a second it is her face that I see.

But it is not my mother.

The woman's skin has a greyish tinge to it and her long blonde hair is plastered to her head. Her feet are bare, but the rest of her is clothed, fairly nondescript blue jeans and a T-shirt. Her hair is the same colour and length as the missing woman's, and she looks roughly the same height, but her face is unrecognizable because she doesn't have one. All that remains is a broken and bloody mess of skin and bone. I search for any ID or a phone inside her pockets but find nothing.

"I think her head must have hit the rocks when she jumped," says Mrs Harris from a few feet away, shouting to be heard over the roar of the ocean. "Smashed her skull to bits. I rolled her over to stop the seagulls eating what was left of her face. I doubt you'll even be able to identify her with dental records, I can't see any teeth left, can you?"

Carter comes to stand by my side and looks down at the body. Then he turns around, doubles over and vomits on the sand. I leave him to pull himself together while I walk Mrs Harris away from the scene and ask her a few more questions.

"You said you come to Blackwater Bay to swim at the same time every day. Do you normally see anyone else here?"

She shakes her head. "Not at this time of year, except for the Day of the Dead. There is a torchlit procession that starts in the village and ends here in Blackwater Bay on the first of November every year. Then we burn a boat on the beach, there's a big bonfire, everyone throws their torches on top. It's always a great night, so there are a lot of people on this beach then, but otherwise not a soul."

I remember the annual celebration from when I was a child. The costumes, the torches, the boat on fire, the fireworks. Mum would let me stay up late and take me every year. The festival and the parade were just a thing everyone in the village went to. I never gave much thought to why we did it. It was just something that I took for granted and thought was normal, until I moved away.

"Why burn a boat?" I ask, unable to remember the reason but soon regretting the question.

"Because in 1878 a ship called *Serendipity* ran aground in this bay. It was thought to be a smuggler's ship," she continues. "But the ship was found abandoned and nobody ever came to claim it. When the locals investigated the empty boat they found a table set for dinner. The candles were all lit, the food on the plates was still warm but untouched and there was wine in the goblets. It was as though the whole crew were about to sit down for a meal but then *vanished*," she says, staring at me intensely. "Hope Falls is full of lost souls . . ."

I think about my mother again.

"And the festival is our way of making sure they aren't forgotten. But most days at this time of year the beach is the same as it was back in 1878. Empty."

"And was that the case today? Or can you remember seeing anyone?" I ask.

She frowns as though it might be a difficult question, looks at Carter still bent over double in the distance, then back at me. "Yes. Him."

39

CARTER

"She says she saw you," DCI Bird informs me after sending Diana Harris away.

"I'm fine, thanks for asking," I reply, wiping my mouth with an embroidered hanky from my pocket. I can't believe I was sick, I'm so embarrassed. I've seen dead bodies before, but not like this – with their faces bashed in – and never someone I might know.

"She said you were running away from the scene."

"Then I'm guessing she saw me running back to the village, with *your* dog, having got a call from dispatch about a body being found. They didn't know which beach when they first called me and there's more than one near Hope Falls. Diana dialled 999. It goes through to a switchboard at Devon and Cornwall Police HQ, and I guess whoever took the call doesn't know one Cornish beach from the next."

"She said she called after you, when she saw you earlier."

"Well, I didn't hear her. If I called your name from a distance right now with the sea and the wind I doubt you'd hear me either. I didn't see her. I didn't see the body. But I did see someone else."

"Who?"

"I don't know. A man."

"What man?"

"I chased him but he vanished."

"Vanished *where*?" Bird looks around at the vast sandy beach, the rocks and the cliffs. She looks at me as though she doesn't believe me, as though she suspects *me* of something, and I hate her for it. I wish we'd never met. It's my fault she's here. My fault she applied for what should have been my job. My fault she's ruining my—

"How are you feeling?" she asks then, with a tiny dose of something like compassion.

"I've been better."

"This can't be the first dead body you've seen?"

"Do you think it's her?"

"Do you?" she asks but I just shake my head. "You must have an opinion, you met the woman."

"She still had a face when I met her."

"What does your gut say?"

"My gut says I'm going to throw up again."

Her face darkens, any trace of patience gone. "There's the reason you didn't get promoted. You're not ready to do my job, you don't have what it takes. You need to show some initiative. Trust your instincts. Follow your gut."

"It could be a coincidence."

"There is no such thing. Is. It. Her?"

Her words sting so much I'm scared I might cry.

"It's possible," I say. "Sorry, I think I might be sick again—"

"For fuck's sake. It's just a body."

"How can you say that?"

"Because that's the only way to survive this job. To unsee what we have to see. A body is brilliant but weak. A miracle but also a failure in waiting. A body is a walking, talking, life support machine that will inevitably fail you, and when it stops working you will stop living. Eventually, dictated by your popularity, you will be forgotten.

In most cases, so devastatingly forgotten it will be as though you never were. A body is the prison that gives you a life sentence and determines your death. That's all a body is."

"Were you always this cheerful?"

"I'm going to head back to the village, talk to the husband again before someone else tells him about this. Do you think you can manage to stay with the body and keep the seagulls away? And can you call HQ and get a team out here?"

I should tell her that I think I saw Harrison on the beach just before the body was found. But I don't. Instead, all I say is, "Yes, boss."

"Thanks. As first days go, I'll be honest, it's not been great," she replies, already walking away.

She keeps behaving as though all of this is my fault.

But I can't really complain about that because it is.

Eden Fox came to the police station a few days ago to tell me she was scared, that she thought someone had been watching her. She was trembling when she told me. I feel so guilty because, looking back now, I think it was a cry for help. But I had other things on my mind. There was a bottle of whiskey at the station, a gift I'd never opened, but I opened it then and poured some into a mug – just a little something to calm her nerves – then poured myself some too. I tried to reassure her that Hope Falls was a safe place, where people could be trusted, but I guess that was a lie.

Because before I even knew what I was doing, I kissed her.

Now she's dead.

40

HARRISON

My wife is dead and there is only one person to blame.

I crawl through the tunnel. It is centuries old and has collapsed in places, so sometimes the only way through is on my hands and knees, with the headlamp in my black beanie barely lighting the way. Sergeant Carter saw me on the beach, I know he did, but I don't know for sure if he knew it was me. I was on the other side of the bay when he spotted me, and the only reason I recognized him from that distance was his uniform. It was stupid of me to let myself be seen – the beach is normally empty – and the only reason I was there was because of *her*. If anyone asks why I was on the beach I will say I was looking for my wife.

The truer the lie the easier it is to believe.

There was a tracker inside the phone I left in Eden's car, and it led me right to her – or at least what was left of her – on the beach. Everything I have researched about tides suggested she would be dragged miles away after plummeting off that cliff, or so far out to sea she'd never be seen again. Trust Eden to wash up like a bad penny on the nearest beach. I would have expected the phone to die underwater in the sea, but when I found it wrapped in a plastic bag inside her pocket I understood how it survived. I'm glad it did, otherwise I would have had no way of knowing if the body on the beach was really Eden. The clothes she wore did not look familiar to me, and the woman was unrecognizable. Her face was so badly smashed in even I wouldn't have been able to identify her. I didn't linger, I barely looked at her at all to be honest, it wasn't pretty. I just had to get the phone back – worried it could be traced to me – but I left her where she was.

With the seagulls.

Even if Tweedle Dumb did see me it doesn't prove anything other than I left the house. No law against that, and it isn't as though there's a rulebook for what to do if your wife disappears. The only rule that matters now is "don't get caught". When I finally crawl out of the tunnel at Spyglass, I close the secret door behind me, push the bookcases back into position and collapse onto the library floor.

I feel ill with guilt and regret and shame.

And dirty.

I pull off all my clothes and burn them. They are soiled with mud and sand and sweat and seawater. And blood. The sooner I get back to looking like myself, the sooner I'll start to feel like me too. Harrison Woolf, CEO, doesn't wear joggers and crawl through dark, damp tunnels. I watch everything I was wearing burn, and remind myself why I am doing all of this: for *her*. What I really need now is time, but time takes pity on no one. You get what you're given, end of story.

I feel exhausted when I finally head upstairs. The bathroom that Eden recently decorated is modern and classy, all granite and marble, with a powerful rain shower to wash away my guilt. She had good taste, I'll give her that. I'm shocked by the sight of myself in the bathroom mirror. I have aged since we bought this house, I barely recognize myself and I do not like what I see. I remember something my wife used to say and for the first time it makes sense to me.

Your biggest enemy is always the person you see in the mirror.

She was right. I am my own worst enemy but I am also my best friend.

If anyone calls again today I won't answer the phone.

If anyone comes to the house I won't open the door.

I just need to keep a low profile for the next day or so.

And try not to say or do anything stupid.

I step into the shower and turn up the temperature of the water until it is so hot it scalds my skin. It feels good to feel something. My body and mind have felt numb since it happened and I need to stay focused. The police are going to start getting suspicious if I keep making mistakes. I stay in the shower for so long that a thick fog of steam has filled the bathroom by the time I step out. I grab a towel and wrap it around myself, then stop when I look at the mirror again. Not because of my reflection – the glass has misted up too much to see one. Instead I stare at the word that has appeared in the steam:

LIAR

41

BIRDY

More than one person in Hope Falls is lying. What I don't know is why.

COME SEE ME IN MY OFFICE BEFORE YOU GO HOME.

I send the text to Carter and hope he comes to The Smuggler's Inn soon. It's late and I want to go to bed. He's been avoiding me since the beach earlier, but I don't feel bad about what I said. If he wants to do my job one day then he needs to wise up.

It's been one hell of a first day and it's almost midnight. The pub is in semidarkness. Maddy locked up and left hours ago, and I suspect most people in Hope Falls are asleep. I wish I was, but there is still so much to do. I left Carter to it at Blackwater Bay. A tent was put up around the body to prevent any lookie-loos from seeing more than they should, and the forensics team are on the case. Things are definitely slower here than they are in London, and we won't get confirmation of it being Eden Fox until at least tomorrow. Sunday is already snoring on the floor beneath the pub table and I don't blame him, I'm tired too. Exhausted. I close my laptop, then close my tired eyes just for a second.

"Sleeping on the job, boss?" Carter says, startling me.

I didn't hear him come in.

"I thought your sister locked the doors when she went home. How did you—"

"I have a key. I used to live here, remember?"

Years ago.

It seems odd that the locks were never changed. I can't put my finger on it, but it often feels like Carter is keeping something from me.

"Where have you been all night?" I ask. "I told you to come here when you were done, and I thought the forensics team left hours ago."

"They did."

I frown. "Then where the fuck were you?"

"I drove to the coroner's office to give them the hairbrush we took from Spyglass. Just in case they need extra help trying to match the DNA of the missing woman with the victim. Given that—"

"Her face was smashed in. Good thinking. But I didn't ask you to do that."

"You said I needed to be more assertive. That I should—"

"Fake it till you fuck it."

"Something like that."

"Most coroners I know don't work this late, so what else have you been up to?"

"I was at the station," he says, the tone of his voice suggesting he thinks that's where I should have been too. "Someone had to do all the paperwork. No joy with the husband then?"

"No," I say, hoping he didn't get any silly ideas about trying to question Harrison by himself again. "I went up to the house three times. Harrison isn't answering the door or his phone, but his car is still in the driveway. He's the kind of man that won't think twice about filing a police harassment complaint, so you just leave him to me. Until we know the identity of the woman on the beach for sure I think we need to tread carefully. I'll try again tomorrow."

"What about the daughter?"

The pain starts small. Just like always.

"I told you already. She's in a secure facility—"

"According to Harrison. Shouldn't we verify that for ourselves? At least *try* to talk to her?" he asks but I can't answer. The pain spreads and it hurts so bad I feel sick. I realize that with everything going on I've forgotten to take my medication. I need Carter to leave. Now.

Nobody can see me like this.

"I'm going to bed. You should go home and get some rest too," I say.

"What? Why did you summon me here if you just wanted to—"

I try to stand up and a new wave of pain floods through my body. I grip the table and squeeze my eyes closed, hoping it passes quickly but it doesn't. The pain only gets worse and I feel as though I can't breathe. I am such a fool. I forgot to take my pills and I haven't eaten since lunchtime; after seeing a faceless corpse on the beach I didn't have much of an appetite. I try to move but it hurts too much. I used to have a high threshold for pain – the physical *and* emotional varieties – but I am not who I was and I'll never be who I wanted to be. Everything I ever was or might have been will be gone soon.

The thought only seems to make it hurt more.

"Are you okay?" Carter asks.

"I'm fine," I lie. "Just a little lightheaded, I forgot to eat."

"You don't look fine," he says, taking a step closer.

I feel dizzy and the pain is so intense I close my eyes again. It's far worse than normal. The painkillers will fix this, I hope, but they are in my bag in my room. Sunday starts to whimper. My dog knows me better than anyone and he knows when something is wrong. Dogs are so much smarter than humans in so many ways.

"You're scaring me a little bit. Please tell me what to do," Carter says.

"There are some pills in my room. They're in a bag under the bed—"

I'm expecting him to go and get the bag, but instead, he picks me up in his arms and carries me up the stairs towards my bedroom at the end of the corridor. I don't know how he knew which room was mine. Maybe Maddy told him. He sets me down gently on the bed then grabs the bag and hands it to me. There are several different bottles of pills inside. I'd rather Carter didn't see what I'm taking so I ask him to get me a glass of water from the sink in the bathroom. I pop two tablets in my mouth and swallow them.

"Just give me a minute," I say, curling into a ball and closing my eyes again.

When I open them, Sunday is sitting at my feet, and Carter is sitting on the bed beside me. His face a picture of genuine concern.

"You going to tell me what just happened?" he asks gently.

"I get migraines," I lie. "Sometimes they're really bad."

He nods and I'm surprised he believed me so easily.

"I'm okay now, honest. You should go home."

"I'm not leaving until I'm sure you're okay. I'm going to go get myself a drink from the bar. You want one?"

"Are you allowed to just help yourself?"

"No. But I don't think you're well enough to arrest me so—"

"I'm fine. You don't need to stay."

"I want to. Just until I know you're all right."

Carter disappears from the room. He's clearly very at home in the pub – which I suppose makes sense given he used to live here – and I hear him walk along the corridor and down the stairs. The pills quickly start to do their job, and by the time he returns I am feeling much more like myself. Carter still looks concerned, but is carrying two packets in his teeth, while holding a pint for himself and what looks like a cocktail for me in his hands.

"Dinner is served," he says, giving me a packet of cheese and onion crisps. "Along with a virgin mojito. My sister says they're your favourite, but I won't be offended if you don't like my attempt at making one," he adds, putting the glass down on the bedside table. "You feeling any better, boss?"

He stares at me with his big brown eyes and I remember the first time we met. I'm very aware that Carter has a crush on me. I think about him too. I should charge him rent for all the time he spends living inside my head when I'm alone in bed at night, but it would be a bad idea to sleep together again now. So I surprise myself when I lean in and kiss him. I know it's a stupid thing to do for so many reasons. I think it was the way he wanted to help me when he could see that I was in pain. I've been on my own for so long, I had forgotten what it was like to feel as though someone else cared.

"Are you sure about this?" he asks as I start tugging at his uniform. But I am sure. I need to feel something tonight. I need to feel loved even if it isn't real.

"It isn't as though we haven't done it before," I tell him.

"Yes, but that was months ago and you weren't my boss then."

"Then pretend I'm a stranger before I change my mind."

Carter doesn't need telling twice. He pulls his shirt off over his head, and I can't help being impressed by the sight of his toned body. Beneath the uniform it's clear that Carter works out and takes very good care of himself. He gently guides Sunday out of the bedroom.

"I can't have him watching."

I laugh and remove my remaining clothes, then Carter pulls me close. He kisses my mouth, my neck, my breasts, while his hand slips inside my knickers. His mouth takes over from his fingers, and I watch his head move between my legs while his tongue teases and pleases me. The pleasure after the pain is almost too intense, so I lean back and close my eyes. He comes up for air and I reach for his boxers. I want them off and him inside me. He moves slowly at first, as though scared he might hurt me. So gentle. So good. Then he finds his rhythm and the bed rocks with each thrust, banging against the wall. Luckily, there are no other guests. We lay on our backs side by side afterwards, sweating and breathless, then something else unexpected happens.

Carter holds my hand.

He pulls me close and I don't push him away.

Instead, I do something I never do and invite him to stay the night.

42

CARTER

1st November

I want nothing more than to stay the night but I have too much to do. So I creep out of the pub at around 4:00 AM. I managed not to wake her when I left the bedroom, but Sunday – who was asleep downstairs – looked thoroughly unimpressed with me. Like he knows I slept with his mum.

DCI Bird talks in her sleep.

She said things that didn't make sense but made me worry.

I wonder if she knows.

My opinion of her has changed since she almost collapsed last night. Seeing her like that – vulnerable – made me want to protect her. She isn't as tough as she pretends to be, and I like that I get to see a side of her nobody else does. Curiosity got the better of me this morning. I looked inside her bag to see what other pills she was taking and it looked like she had robbed a chemist. I recognized one of the drug names – it's the same pills my mum takes, and they are not for migraines. She isn't who I thought she was but that's okay. I am not the man she thinks I am either.

I want to prove to her that I'm not as useless as she thinks.

And I've had an idea for how to do that.

Show some initiative.

Trust your instincts.

Follow your gut.

That's what she said I should do so that's what I'm doing.

It takes over an hour to navigate my way to The Manor. Blackmoor National Park borders Hope Falls but the park is vast, over fifty miles of knotted single-track lanes, and The Manor is not easy to find. It doesn't appear on any map. The sun is just starting to rise when I arrive at the gated property surrounded by miles of nothing. Nothing except wild and rugged countryside. It looks like a posh prison. I press the buzzer and tell them who I am and why I am here before they ask. There was something about the way Harrison Woolf reacted when we spoke about his daughter that has been bothering me ever since. Bird says Gabriella can't be involved because she's locked up here, but I want to see for myself.

The gates open and I drive down a long, winding, tree-lined driveway. There is an impressive – and slightly intimidating – building when I reach the end. It reminds me of *Downton Abbey* and I'm half expecting to be greeted by a butler. I park the squad car right outside the giant front doors – no doubt ruining the view – and hurry up the steps. The doors open before I reach them to reveal a small woman dressed in white. Her name badge says INGRID.

"Can I help you?" she asks, sounding like she'd rather not. She has a clipped European accent, and a face as unfriendly as a closed door.

"I'm sorry to turn up so early like this, but I need to speak to one of your residents."

"It's six AM. Everyone is asleep. The day team haven't even arrived for their shifts yet."

"I'm afraid it's a police matter and it's urgent. I'm looking for Gabriella Woolf."

Ingrid raises an eyebrow. "She's very popular all of a sudden. You'd best follow me."

She leads me through a grand entrance hall, up an impressive spiral staircase and along a maze of corridors. We stop outside a door and she takes out a giant set of keys that once again make me think of a prison. The oversized and sturdy door looks exactly like all the others we have passed, but the sign on the front confirms I am in the right place.

Room Thirteen
GABRIELLA WOOLF

"You lock her in?" I ask.

"For her own safety," Ingrid says, then adds, "And ours."

While she jangles her keys trying to find the right one, I wonder what to expect on the other side of the door. All I know about Gabriella is that she is eighteen and lives here. I do not know why. As the door opens I start to doubt myself. Coming here was going against a direct order from a superior officer. Maybe it wasn't the right thing to do. The woman dressed in white finally opens the door and it's too late to turn back now.

"Wait here while I wake her," she says, disappearing inside.

I nod, remaining in the corridor. I look both ways and now the place reminds me of *The Shining*. The woman reappears sooner than I was expecting and makes me jump.

"She was already awake. You can come in."

I step inside what could best be described as an extravagant hotel suite. There is a beautifully decorated lounge with expensive-looking furniture and huge windows offering spectacular views of the grounds and the shadowy moors in the distance. I can see a door leading to what looks like a designer bedroom, and everything about the place screams wealth and luxury. This is *not* a prison. It is not what I was expecting at all, and neither is Gabriella Woolf. In front of one of the enormous windows, a stunning young woman with pale skin and long black hair is sitting in front of an easel holding a paintbrush in her hand. She doesn't turn to look at me as I enter the room, instead she carries on painting as though I'm not here.

"Can she hear me?" I ask Ingrid.

"Oh yes. Nothing wrong with her ears. Gabriella hadn't spoken a word for years before she joined us, but she's making good progress since she moved in."

"Hello, Gabriella. My name is Sergeant Luke Carter. I'm a policeman and I wondered if I could ask you a few questions."

She doesn't react at all, just stares at the canvas as though she didn't hear a word. The watercolour painting is of Spyglass and it's very good, the sort of work a professional artist might produce. I look around the room and see there are dozens more just like it.

"How long has she been here?" I ask Ingrid.

"Not sure, I'm not her primary care assistant. Six months or so, I think?"

"And why is she here?"

"Her parents felt like this was the best place for her."

"But . . . what's wrong with her?" I ask, given it looks like nothing is.

"Gabriella had a condition called selective mutism, but unlike the name suggests there was no choice involved. She didn't choose not to speak, she couldn't. It's a severe and complex childhood anxiety disorder. Sometimes when a child experiences a trauma at a young age, they retreat inside themselves. Gabriella was in a serious accident at the age of eight; she basically spent ten years locked inside her own mind. Her parents decided to care for her at home after the accident, which in my view was a mistake. She needed professional care to rehabilitate her mind as well as her body. That said, Gabriella has made excellent progress since she moved in here. She goes for supervised walks around the grounds, she's eating three meals a day so is at a nice healthy weight, she enjoys painting and reading, and thanks to Mary, one of our specialist carers, she's started to communicate."

That gets my attention. I stop staring at Gabriella and turn back to Ingrid.

"She can talk again?"

"She . . . whispers."

"What?"

"Sometimes she whispers. What she says doesn't always make sense, and she tends to only do it when Mary is here, but I've heard it with my own ears. Mary records her to keep track of her progress."

"How often does she . . ."

"Whisper? Not often. It's normally an emotional response that triggers it. We're all hopeful that one day, Gabriella might talk again and be able to have a normal life. She's fit and healthy in every other way, and as you can see, she's a wonderful artist."

"Like her mother," I say, but the woman shrugs. "Can I ask her some questions?"

"Feel free to try, but I don't think she can help you."

I walk over to Gabriella and she is even more beautiful close-up.

"That's a really good painting," I say. My words sound patronizing but they are true, she is very talented. "Did it take long?"

She doesn't even look up.

Ingrid stands behind us, as though on guard, and I know I need to be careful what I say. I notice that Gabriella has painted the word *home* in tiny letters at the bottom of the canvas.

"I met your father the other day and he mentioned you," I tell her.

Again, no visible response.

"I met your mother too."

She doesn't even blink, just carries on painting as though I'm not here.

"Oh, look," says Ingrid, staring out of the window. "There's Mary now, just arriving for her shift. You might have more luck talking to her?"

It seems unlikely and I fear this trip was a complete waste of time.

I peer out of the window where Ingrid is pointing, and see another woman dressed in a white uniform crossing the gravel driveway and heading towards the main door.

But I recognize this woman and her name isn't Mary.

It's Eden Fox.

43

BIRDY

I wake up, look in the mirror, and barely recognize myself.

The first thing I think of every day now is how many days I have left. Thanks to Thanatos, it's like I have a death clock ticking inside my mind. It's impossible not to worry. All I can think about is what happens to who I love when I am not here to love them anymore. Like my dog. I've written a will, made some plans, but that doesn't make me worry less. People rarely do what they should, they do what they want instead, because humans are a selfish species. I know I should focus on the present, make the most of the time I have left, but like so many things in life that is harder to do than it is to say. How can a person live in the now when, every single second, now becomes then?

The present is only ever the past in the making.

I heard Carter leave in the middle of the night, but I kept my eyes closed and pretended to be asleep. Once I was sure he was gone and saw him walking down the lane outside the pub, I whistled for Sunday. My most loyal friend – my *only* friend – came running up the stairs, leapt onto the bed, and made a very good replacement. I am normally okay being alone but right now I don't want to be. The physical and emotional pain was too much yesterday; it's getting harder to hide. The thoughts that trespass in my head are too loud for me to sleep or dream, and even when I do, my dreams turn into nightmares. I'm not scared of dying, I'm just scared of what it means.

Soon I'll be nothing more than a memory.

Pretty soon after then I won't even be that.

Everyone who remembered me will be gone too.

I didn't intend to sleep with Carter again, and I know I shouldn't have, but maybe I just wanted to trick myself into thinking that someone somewhere might miss me when I am gone. That I didn't completely waste my life. That it wasn't all for nothing. When the sun starts to rise I decide to stop wasting what little time I have left. I get myself up, get myself dressed and get myself ready. It's going to be another long day.

I call Carter to tell him where to meet me but his phone goes straight to voicemail. I don't like leaving messages, and I don't see the point, his phone will show him that I called and that should be enough for him to know to call me back as soon as possible. It's still too early for Maddy to have opened the pub, so Sunday and I head out in search of breakfast. I see that the Driftwood Café overlooking the harbour is already open.

"We're closing soon," the old woman behind the counter hollers in a thick Cornish accent when I step inside. She's busy with something and doesn't even look up. Her eyes are too big for her face, and she radiates a no-nonsense vibe. Cath – if the name badge is to be believed – served me coffee yesterday, but has clearly forgotten me already. Just like everyone will soon. "We only open early doors at this time of year, to cook breakfast for the local fishermen before they head out for the day," she says, and now that she's mentioned it I did notice there were fewer boats in the harbour. "Oh, it's you," she says, finally looking up and seeing me. A sliver of a smile spreads across her face. "The woman with the bird tattoo on your hand."

Perhaps I'm not as forgettable as I feared.

"Do you want two coffees again? I can manage that before I lock up," she says.

"Just one would be great. I'm on my own today."

I don't know why I said that.

I'm on my own every sodding day.

I must look as shit as I feel because Cath seems to take pity on me.

"Had a falling-out with someone, have you? Don't you worry, love. There's plenty more fish in the sea, you might just need a better net."

Plenty of rubbish in the sea too.

"I've got a bit of leftover bacon and eggs if you'd like some? Perhaps a sausage for the dog?" Cath offers.

"Thank you. I forgot to eat yesterday after what happened."

She shrugs. "You mean the suicide?" I nod. "Can't let a thing like that ruin your appetite, it happens all the time. There are a lot of sad people in the world."

Her indifference shocks me. Maybe the world would be less sad if people cared a bit more. I think of Mum and blink away the tears that are threatening to fall. I don't know what is wrong with me today.

Everything.

"You all right, pet?" Cath asks, as though she can see inside my head.

No.

"Yes, sorry. I didn't sleep well."

"Not eating and not sleeping are a recipe for not feeling like yourself. Everything seems worse than it is when you're tired, and nothing good was achieved on an empty stomach." A woman after my own heart. "You sit yourself down and I'll make us both a cup of coffee – the good stuff – and get you some breakfast. Just let me lock up and get the dishwasher on first or I won't be home in time for *This Morning*," she says, waddling past me to flip the OPEN sign to CLOSED.

"Did you know her? The missing woman?" I ask, taking a seat in the booth nearest to the kitchen, while Cath makes me a plate.

"No, and I'm not one for gossip," she says, sounding like someone who lives for it. "But from what I've heard she was a wealthy woman who moved here from London, fancied herself as an artist."

"Nobody seems to know very much about her."

"Nobody knows anyone anymore, do they? Not really. People only care about the people they care about, and these days that's often themselves."

Cath sounds like an unexpected kindred spirit. She puts a plate of food down in front of me, and takes off her apron. "You eat what you can, pet. It's on the house."

"I'm happy to pay—"

She shakes her head. "Accept kindness when it's offered, it's in short supply."

I think I like being someone's good deed.

I thank her and eat, moving the bacon away from the eggs on my plate before I start so that they are not touching. I am not used to people being nice to me, and Cath has been kind for reasons I don't quite understand. As though she sees me. The *real* me. I suspect she misses having a busy café filled with people to chat to.

"The missing artist had an exhibition the other night. Did you go?" I ask.

She shakes her head. "I get up early every day to open this place for the fishermen, so I never go out late. Never go out at all these days, truth be told. Enjoy life while you can because you'll catch up with the likes of me sooner than you think. Old age sneaks up on us all like an unwelcome thief."

It will never catch up with me.

I silence the thought, along with all the others I'm too scared to think out loud.

"But I saw her yesterday morning just before she jumped," Cath says then.

"Eden Fox?"

"I watched her run up the hill. She had this lost look about her, like she didn't want to be here anymore. I see it all the time."

I wonder what this woman sees when she sees me.

"You're sure it was her?"

"Who else would it have been?"

"Did you see anyone else?"

"Not that I remember, but I would have been busy in the kitchen."

I thank Cath for breakfast and try to pay again but she refuses. She walks me to the door to unlock it, then points out a man on the cliff path. "Old Stu might have seen more than me. He was walking his dog, just like he always does in the morning."

After I leave I call Carter but his phone goes to voicemail again. No bother, Carter already sent me a transcript of his interview with "Old Stu" the dog walker yesterday. I didn't read it before, but I plan to now. When Sunday and I return to The Smuggler's Inn the doors are unlocked and Maddy is back behind the bar.

"You're up and out early," she says. "How was your breakfast at the café?"

Has she been spying on me?

"Lovely. It was the only place open when I woke up, I've always been an early bird," I reply, but she misses the reference to my name. "Not like your brother. Can't get hold of him at all so far today."

She frowns, looks a little defensive on his behalf. "That's not like him."

It's nice that she's so protective of her little brother, they're obviously very close. I hope they aren't so close that she knows about me sleeping with him. I feel embarrassed asking his sister the next question, but I just want to be sure I haven't made an even bigger mistake than the one I knew I was making. I thought Carter was single but I now realize I never checked. I force my face to smile.

“Is there a girlfriend who keeps him up all night and makes him late for work?” I ask.

Maddy smiles too, shakes her head of red curls, and I feel a rush of relief.

“No jealous girlfriends to worry about. Just his wife.”

44

CARTER

What the actual fuck.

I'm certain I just saw Eden Fox dressed as an employee at The Manor.

Not dead.

Not missing.

Very much alive and walking into the building.

My instinct is to run out of Gabriella's room and down the stairs and confront her as soon as she steps inside. But I hear DCI Bird's voice in my head. *Sometimes less is more when questioning a suspect. Wait. Watch. And above all else, listen.* I know more than Bird gives me credit for but she is a good detective, and I should try to learn from her.

"I'll go downstairs and tell Mary that you're here," says the woman dressed in white. I've already forgotten her name and glance again at her badge.

"No need, Ingrid. I have some more questions for you while we wait for her. Is it likely that Gabriella will ever leave this place? You said she's eighteen."

"It's possible, but she would still need full-time care. Her father is very successful at whatever he does but that means he is a busy man.

I get the impression that if he could care for her himself he would. He visits all the time, and I think he just wants what is best for his daughter."

"What *does* he do?" I ask, wondering if she knows more about the company that Harrison works for. I looked up Thanatos but couldn't find much online.

She looks puzzled. "I don't know, but whatever it is pays well. The fees here are not cheap."

"And Gabriella's mother? Do they not visit their daughter together?"

"I've never seen her parents here at the same time. It's normally only him."

I glance at Gabriella.

Eighteen. Elegant. Beautiful. Clearly talented.

"She doesn't *look* like she needs full-time care."

The girl stops painting and stares into space and I remember that she can hear me. I feel bad about how insensitive some of the things I have already said might have sounded.

"Gabriella's case is complex and unique. In her mind she is still a child, frozen in time when the accident occurred. Her most recent assessment was the same as the last, that she still has a mental age of eight, which is how old she was when the accident happened. For her, we think it might feel as though it happened yesterday, but she has never talked about it. Shuts down and clams up if anyone tries. She looks eighteen to us because she is, but she does not recognize pictures of herself how she looks now or even her own reflection – we had to remove all the mirrors from her room because she was scared there was someone else there – but she has frequently demonstrated that she recognizes herself in photos of when she was eight or younger. In extreme cases of trauma some people remain trapped in that moment for days, weeks, months or even years. Sometimes forever. Gabriella can barely speak. She can't work or support herself financially. She'll eat if food is put in front of her but has never prepared a meal. Although she is making progress – whispering the odd word here and there – it would be like leaving an eight-year-old child home alone."

All the while we are talking I keep checking the door, waiting for Eden – or Mary, as this woman calls her – to walk through it.

"And tell me more about Mary. It sounds as though the two of them are close?"

"Mary hasn't been working with us for very long, but she's wonderful at her job and very popular with the residents. Especially Gabriella. I don't know much about Mary's personal life, she keeps herself to herself, but I know she started working here after her former employer died."

"Who was her former employer?"

"I don't remember the name. An elderly woman who needed a full-time, live-in carer, somewhere by the coast, I think. Mary had worked for her for years and was a little out of practice when it came to looking for a new job. She just turned up here one day with her CV. We were so short-staffed – we always are, staff turnover is high in this business; it's hard work for low pay and people rarely stay for long. So Mary was given a trial run on the spot and everyone adored her from the beginning. Especially Gabriella. The two of them have become quite close. I didn't believe Mary when she said Gabriella had started to communicate. It was only the odd word at first, none of it made much sense, and she wouldn't do it in front of anyone except Mary. So Mary started recording her on this old Walkman that she has, I think to prove she wasn't making it up." She looks towards Gabriella, then lowers her voice. "Honestly, the first time I heard the girl whispering it gave me goose bumps. I'm guessing her vocal cords are damaged after so many years of not being used, so the sound that comes out of her is a little bit *creepy*."

Gabriella drops her paintbrush. It clatters to the floor and I worry that she heard what Ingrid said. She doesn't move, just sits and stares at the canvas. I walk over to her and bend down to pick up the brush, and when I place it on the easel I see that she has added a few more details to her painting of Spyglass. There is now a fox on one side of the house and a wolf on the other. Her parents are Eden Fox and Harrison Woolf. It can't be a coincidence; DCI Bird says there is no such thing.

Gabriella turns her head to stare at the door. We all do when we hear the sound of footsteps approaching. Then her lips part and I hear the girl "whisper". That isn't what I'd call it. The eerie, broken sound that comes out of her mouth is so quiet it's barely audible, but the raspy words wheeze out of her body, and when I hear what she says it sends a chill through mine.

"Run rabbit, run rabbit, run, run, run."

The door opens and Eden Fox walks into the room.

It really is her. Her long blonde hair is tied back in a ponytail, and she is wearing a white uniform with a name badge that does indeed say MARY.

Eden stares at Gabriella.

Then she stares at me.

Then she runs.

45

Interviewer: Sergeant Luke Carter (LC)

Interviewee: Old Stu (OS)

Date: 31st October, 2025

Location: Hope Falls police station

LC: Can I get your name for the recording, please?

OS: You know my name.

LC: It's just for the tape.

OS: Stu.

LC: Your full name, sir.

OS: Old Stu.

LC: Got it. So you were walking your dog when you saw her?

OS: Yes. I told you that already. And I really ought to be heading home, Tilly will be wanting breakfast.

LC: Tilly?

OS: My dog.

LC: Right, of course. This won't take long. Tell me about the woman that you saw running up the hill on the coast path. What was she wearing? Where was she going? Did you recognize her?

OS: No, I didn't recognize her.

LC: You didn't see her at the art gallery the night before?

OS: What would I be doing going to an art gallery? And why would I be buying paintings of the sea when I can look out of my bleedin' window and see the real thing? Besides, Tilly doesn't like being left alone. Is this going to take much longer?

LC: I just need to know what you remember about what you saw.

OS: I remember everything. I'm old, not senile. And don't be backchatting to me, Luke Carter. I've known you since you were shitting your nappy. I saw a woman. She was running towards the suicide spot at the crack of dawn. She looked upset. When I walked back up the hill she was gone.

LC: But you didn't see her jump?

OS: No.

LC: In what way did she look upset?

OS: She'd been crying – nose as red as Rudolph's – and she was distracted.

LC: What makes you say that?

OS: Well, I said hello and she didn't say hello back. She didn't even look at me, just carried on running up that hill, like Kate bleedin' Bush. I thought it was rude at first, but my eyes aren't great these days, she might have been listening to music or something. Sometimes young'uns have those white things in their ears nowadays, don't they. Looks like they're talking to themselves when they're not. Perhaps she didn't hear me.

LC: Did she see you?

OS: I don't know. She seemed to be in a hurry.

LC: And, just to be clear, you didn't see her jump?

OS: How many times? I told you already. Are you not listening? I didn't see her jump, but she was running towards the waterfall when I passed her. And when I turned back, I couldn't see her on the coast path. As you know, that stretch of path is straight, you can see for miles, and I couldn't see her at all. It was like she just vanished. Make of that what you will. Can I go now?

LC: Soon. I just need to—

OS: Christ on a bike. If you want to know more about what happened, why don't you ask the other woman?

LC: Other woman?

OS: Is there an echo in here or do you have cloth ears? I told you there was another woman who ran up the hill after her. She is far more likely to have seen what happened than me. Why don't you go and bother her instead?

46

BIRDY

Whenever I think I've got my ducks in a row one of them fucking flies off.

It was like someone had punched me in the chest when Carter's sister said he was married. For a moment it felt like I couldn't breathe. I tried to hide it as best I could, made my excuses, then hurried up to my room. I feel like a fool. I try to distract myself by reading the transcript of Carter's interview with Old Stu the dog walker, but it feels like an additional kick in the tits. Why didn't Carter tell me that another woman was seen chasing Eden Fox up the hill?

Carter has been lying to me.

About himself and the investigation.

I can understand him not wanting me to know he was married – cheating little shit – but keeping important information from me when a woman is missing, suspected dead, is not okay. And it doesn't make sense.

Why would he do that?

I'm absofuckinglutely furious, but fury has always made me productive.

I need to speak to Old Stu myself.

It doesn't take me long to find out where he lives. Everyone seems to know everyone and everything about each other in this village. Or at least they think they do. I have always preferred keeping a low profile, but that's proving tricky in a place like this. I head up the hill until I reach a thatched cottage with a black door.

"Who is it?" shouts a voice inside when I ring the bell.

I don't answer. Instead I just wait. Eventually the door opens and a short, angry-looking man appears behind it. He has long white hair and bushy white eyebrows. *Gruff* is the first word that springs to mind.

"What do you want?" he growls.

Right now I'd settle for the truth.

Despite being in his seventies, Old Stu is dressed like a surfer dude. He is not what I was expecting, and is clearly not interested in talking to people unless he has to. I take out my badge. "What are you showing me that for? I already told Carter everything I know," he says, starting to close the door.

"I appreciate that, Mr—"

"Everyone calls me Old Stu."

"But your full name is Stu Cummins. Is that right?"

He narrows his eyes and raises one of his old-man brows. "How do you know that?"

"I know a lot of things. I wonder if I could come inside? It won't take long."

His fluffy white brows knit themselves into a frown, but I'm already through the door. The house smells of wet dog and burnt toast. I linger in the hallway, not wishing to intrude any more than I have to.

"I know you have spoken to Sergeant Carter, but I'd like to ask you a few questions myself. Sometimes people remember things differently once a little time has passed. Especially when a crime might have taken place."

"Are you suggesting I'm a few sandwiches short of a picnic?"

I smile. "Not at all. The same rules apply to everyone. Almost all witnesses are unreliable and they sometimes remember something they forgot to mention the first time or didn't think was relevant when we ask them again."

"Fine. Hope you don't mind dogs."

I like them far more than I like people, so no worries there.

As though on cue a sausage dog and a Labrador come into the hallway to sniff and greet me. A pug follows close behind and I wonder how many dogs there can be in such a tiny house. I politely refuse the half-hearted offer of tea, I just want to be sure of what this man did and didn't see. The answers he gives me are very similar to the answers he gave Carter, but what I'm most interested in is the other woman he thinks he saw.

"What other woman?" he asks, staring over my shoulder at the muted TV in the living room behind me. I get the impression I might be keeping him from his favourite show.

"When you spoke to Sergeant Carter you said you saw another woman, running up the hill after the first one."

"No, I never."

"You didn't see a second woman? Or you didn't tell him that you did?"

"You're making my head hurt speaking in riddles. I saw a woman, just the one, running up the hill towards the suicide spot. How many times do I have to tell you people the same thing? Carter has always been a scobberlotcher. Back in my day police officers wrote things down and remembered what you told them. Not anymore. Now there are two of you asking the same bloody questions and still getting everything I say wrong. Have you got cloth ears too?"

I leave feeling even more confused than before.

Did Old Stu forget what he saw?

Or did Carter make up what he said in the transcript?

47

CARTER

You couldn't make this up.

That's what I think when I see Eden Fox alive and well at The Manor.

I genuinely thought she was dead – that the body on the beach was her – and now I don't know what to think. I thought I knew the woman. I thought she had feelings for me, but now I feel like a fool. I kissed her and she kissed me back, but clearly it meant nothing to her. She lied to me – possibly about everything – and I need to know why.

I hurry out of the room and chase after the woman dressed in white who I know as Eden Fox, but who has been calling herself Mary here. I see her running down the grand spiral staircase and do my best to catch up, but she's fast. She turns a corner, runs across the entrance hall – almost losing her balance and skidding on the polished parquet floor – then through a door, slamming it closed behind her. By the time I catch up and yank it open I see that it leads to a large dining room. There are small tables immaculately set with white linen tablecloths, elaborately folded napkins, silverware and crystal glasses. Classical music plays softly in the background, and well-dressed young people are helping themselves to breakfast already. There is a huge, round table in the middle of the room covered in an abundance of delicious-looking food as though this were a luxury hotel and not an institution. They all stop and stare when they see my police uniform.

"Where did she go?" I ask nobody in particular.

"Who?" asks a random girl.

"Eden." My answer is met with blank faces. "*Mary*," I try instead, and someone points towards a set of glass doors leading to the formal gardens. I weave my way through the tables and chairs and out of the building. I stop and scan the grounds for any sign of her, then I hear a car engine in the distance. I sprint towards the car park just as a red Mini appears on the driveway. It's her. I block the car's path, thinking she'll slow down, but the car speeds up, hurtling towards me. I only just manage to dive out of the way in time.

Eden Fox won't come back to The Manor, not now that she knows I'm on to her, but her daughter is still here. Gabriella warned Eden to run. She's not as innocent or as broken as everyone else seems to think. I hurry back inside and run straight into the nurse dressed in white.

"I need to speak to Gabriella again."

She glares at me. "Absolutely not. I don't know what is going on here but I won't have our residents upset like this. That poor girl will need sedating, thanks to you."

"Then you can answer my questions. How long has Gabriella's mother been visiting her here and pretending to be an employee?"

"What *are* you talking about? That wasn't Gabriella's mother. That was Mary, and she wasn't *pretending* to be one of the staff, she works here."

"That woman was Eden Fox," I insist.

"No, she wasn't. Come with me to the office and I'll show you Mary Kendall's staff file. We do checks on all of our employees, for obvious reasons, and we keep detailed records. I have no idea why she ran away from you – that's her business – but she isn't who you think she is. I am telling you that you are mistaken, and your mistake has caused a vulnerable young woman a great deal of stress. Follow me."

I do follow Ingrid to the office, feeling more like a chastised school boy with every step. But I'm getting used to women telling me off and telling me I am wrong about everything. A symphony of tiny violins starts playing inside my head, but I can't seem to silence them. I thought Eden had feelings for me, but clearly she doesn't. I thought she was dead but she isn't. And I was convinced that Harrison Woolf was protecting his daughter, and that Gabriella had something to do with all of this, but I guess I was wrong about that too.

Old Stu thought he saw a second woman following Eden Fox up the hill. He sometimes – quite often actually – gets confused, so I didn't tell Bird. And if he did see someone, I thought I knew who it was, but Gabriella hasn't left this place, and Eden Fox is alive.

So who was the dead woman on the beach?

And what else am I wrong about?

I think I've made a terrible mistake.

48

HARRISON

My life is a series of mistakes stitched together into something resembling success. I know that, even if nobody else does. Other people only see the version of me I let them see.

Ten years ago, when Eden called me to say that Gabriella was missing, I thought calling the police was the right thing to do. Surely most parents would think the same. But that was a mistake too. *Everything* I did that day was an error of judgement. A miscalculation. A major fuckup. I think when your life unravels you can normally look back and pinpoint the moment you took a wrong turn. There's almost always a crossroads with RIGHT clearly signposted for one direction and WRONG would mean heading the opposite way. But wrong can sometimes feel so damn right; that's why so many people feel lost.

I was driving to the city when it happened, heading back to work. Things were just as busy for me then as they are now. I should have been able to trust Eden to look after our little girl. Gabriella's mother was always too distracted to properly care for our child, her head was elsewhere, and I should have done more to make sure she was being properly looked after. There were so many warning signs but I didn't pay attention. I was still desperately trying to get funding to start the company; Thanatos didn't even have a name back then, I was working crazy hours and I was distracted. But a parent's number-one job is to keep their child safe, and we both failed. They were already at the hospital by the time I got there, and as soon as I saw my broken little girl I cried.

You should be able to trust a mother to take care of her daughter.

She didn't.

But it wasn't her fault.

It was mine.

We gave Gabriella the bike for her eighth birthday. It was my idea. Gabby loved it just like I knew she would, spent hours riding up and down the street outside our home, it made her happy. But then she wanted me to take off the training wheels because she'd seen other kids her age without them. I said no. I wanted to keep her safe. I wanted to teach her to ride without them myself, and I didn't have time that day. If I'd said yes, I wonder if things might not have played out the way they did. If I'd said no to work that day, instead of no to my daughter, maybe our lives would have been different.

Eden was inconsolable. Gabriella's mother blamed herself, for all of it, but it was *my* fault. Trusting Eden in the first place was my biggest mistake. One I have paid for every day since, and will regret for the rest of my life. I know how long I have left with my regrets, and everything I am doing now is for her: my daughter.

I have locked all the doors and windows at Spyglass, and closed all the curtains and blinds. I want to hide from the world and pretend I haven't done what I've done. So I'm sitting in the dark, in a house I did not want to live in, wondering how it came to this. I have invested everything I have to build Thanatos, to make something of my life, and change the lives of others. And now I fear I might lose it all, everything I have worked so hard for, and the sacrifices I have made along the way will have been for nothing.

All because of one mistake:

A kiss between two people who should have known better.

Jealousy gives birth to monsters, and that is what I have become.

I guess we're all just a bad roll of the dice from sliding back down to the bottom of the ladder we spent our whole lives trying to climb. And I don't see a way to pull myself back up this time.

My phone rings, vibrating silently on the bed. I've been screening my calls for hours, but when I see the display says THE MANOR, I answer immediately. Some primal instinct takes over and I become the man the rest of the world believes I am. The man I used to be.

"Harrison Woolf speaking."

The voice on the other end of the line sounds small and afraid. Their words are too fast, tripping over themselves; my mind can't seem to keep up or translate them fast enough.

"What do you mean the police interviewed Gabriella?" I shout into the phone. "They can't do that and you should never have let them. She's a child, for god's sake." The voice on the other end of the line contradicts me and I am not in the mood. "You and I both know she is only eighteen in years. I said strictly no visitors. That means *none*. I bet Sergeant Carter didn't even have a warrant and you just let him in? Remind me how much I am paying you to take care of my daughter?"

The voice keeps apologizing.

"I don't want to hear any more—

"Just have the doctor call me—

"I'll deal with this matter myself," I say and hang up, rage rushing through me.

Tweedle fucking Dumb went to The Manor and tried to question my little girl. The police couldn't do their job ten years ago and they can't be trusted this time either.

I'm doing this my way from now on.

49

Interviewer: DCI Olivia Bird (OB)
Interviewee: Maddy Carter (MC)
Date: 1st November, 2025
Location: The Smuggler's Inn

OB: Thank you for speaking to me on the record.

MC: No bother. Not exactly rushed off my feet, am I.

OB: It's nothing to worry about, we're interviewing a lot of people in the village, so just standard procedure really. But, for the record, where were you yesterday morning when Eden Fox was last seen alive?

MC: Me? Blimey! Surely you don't think I had something to do with it?

OB: Like I said, nothing to worry about. We're asking everyone.

MC: Well, I was probably still in bed. From what I heard she jumped first thing, shortly after dawn. I don't open the pub until midmorning. Pretty pointless opening at all this time of year, and pubs close late, so I have a lie-in most days.

OB: Did you go to Eden's art exhibition the night before?

MC: Not on your nelly. I was working, but even if I hadn't been, art isn't exactly my cup of tea. Most folks went to the gallery that night for a free glass of warm white wine. I've got all the free drinks I could ever want right here.

OB: Tell me about Old Stu.

MC: Not much to tell. He likes his dogs, he likes to surf, he likes to walk along the coast path every morning at sunrise.

OB: How do you know that if you never get up early?

MC: I work behind the bar in a village pub. I know most things about most people.

OB: Do you know if Old Stu likes to make things up?

MC: The clue is in the name. He's old. Sometimes his memory might play tricks on him. He gets confused. He doesn't mean any harm.

OB: And your brother, where might he have been first thing yesterday morning?

MC: Why are you asking me? Why not just ask him?

OB: All routine questions and standard procedure.

MC: My brother is a hardworking, honest, decent man. And he was born to be a policeman.

OB: That's debatable.

MC: Sorry?

OB: Your brother didn't even show up for work today.

MC: Then there must be something wrong. That's not like him.

OB: I'm just doing my job—

MC: You mean his job? That promotion should have been Carter's. Why does Hope Falls need a senior detective from London? What happened here yesterday was just another suicide. Seems to me you just want to justify your existence by going around asking people questions that don't need asking.

OB: There's no need to get upset.

MC: Hope Falls is our home, always has been, always will be. Other folks come and go, but the people who live in this village stick together. My brother only has good things to say about you, he trusts you, thinks you can teach him a thing or two. Me, I'm not so sure.

OB: Really. What do you think about me?

MC: I like your dog.

OB: Thanks.

MC: I think Hope Falls and my brother were perfectly all right without you. We don't need someone like you here. No offence.

OB: Some taken.

50

BIRDY

I can't decide whether questioning Carter's sister was a good idea or not; it was definitely more confrontational than I expected. Maddy helped establish that Old Stu is not a reliable witness, and made me feel as popular as a fart in a lift, but I'm not sure I'm any closer to finding out what really happened to Eden Fox. I feel like everyone in this village is keeping secrets. And I'm starting to wonder if coming to Hope Falls was a huge mistake.

I have spent the last couple of hours checking files and paperwork in what this place laughingly calls a police station to see if there is anything else Carter is lying about. I'm normally a pretty good judge of character, but it turns out the man I shared my bed with last night is married *and* he might be lying about this case. I never pegged Carter for a Casanova. It's not like me to make such an error of judgement. I don't know whether it's the stress of everything I have going on, or whether I'm just too ill to think straight; the drugs I'm taking do ease my pain but they also slow my mind. I need to catch up. I need to know what Carter knows and if there is anything else he and the other residents of Hope Falls aren't telling me.

I go through Carter's desk before trying – and failing – to log in to the computer. The cursor winks as though mocking me. I fucking hate computers. And the internet. And almost all technology. I think I should have been born a hundred years earlier. Jessica Fletcher didn't have to deal with all this shit. The blue door of the police station bursts open, but it isn't Carter – he's still AWOL – instead it is a red-faced Harrison Woolf. He might not have killed anyone, but he looks as though he could be about to. He reminds me of a gremlin who has been fed after midnight.

"Where is he?" Harrison asks, voice raised, practically spitting the words.

"You might need to be a little more specific—"

"Where is Sergeant Carter? That piece of shit has been to interview Gabriella. I told him she has nothing to do with this. I told him she wasn't to be disturbed. You gave me your word that she would be left out of this, and now I'm getting phone calls from The Manor telling me my little girl has been interrogated."

She's eighteen. Not a little girl, I think but don't say anything. In my experience parents rarely want to hear the truth about their children.

"I intend to make a formal complaint about Sergeant Carter, and I want that incompetent, irresponsible shit-for-brains fired."

"Okay. Calm down. Breathe—"

"Don't patronize me. He had no right. This never should have happened."

"I agree with you. I didn't know that's what he was doing. I can only apologize, and promise I will deal with him myself when I next see him. I'm not that happy with him either right now. Is Gabriella okay?" Carter should not have gone to The Manor. I specifically told him not to, I don't know what he was thinking. No wonder Harrison is furious.

"Of course she is not okay. None of this is," he says, towering over me and standing too close. "I already answered all your bloody questions. Twice. I let you and him come into my home and treat me as though I've done something wrong. *I'm* the victim here. If the police had done their fucking job in the first place none of this would be happening. Carter has crossed a line. And you let him. This is your fault. You should have kept your sidekick in line. You should have done your job."

I've grown rather weary of people thinking they can speak to me like this. People who think their time is more important than mine. People who think everything is everyone else's fault. People who lie.

I can't stand it anymore.

"You need to calm the fuck down," I say firmly, and Harrison's face turns an even brighter shade of red. He looks like he might explode, like the kid at Willy Wonka's chocolate factory. "Seeing as you're here, perhaps we could talk about *your* job again," I say, and he blinks as though he doesn't understand. "Thanatos. Is it real?"

He frowns. "You're asking if my job is real?"

"Is *Thanatos* real. Can your company really predict the day a person will die?"

I have to know.

The frown stretches into something else. Pity perhaps. No, not pity. Something like disdain. He stares at me then slowly shakes his head as though I am the lowest of the low for asking a question like that at a time like this.

Then he says, "This is about *my daughter*."

I feel myself snap, crackle and pop.

"Oh, I'm sorry, I thought this was about your wife. The reason Carter felt the need to question your daughter is because your wife is missing."

"I know that my wife is—"

"Do you? I thought you might have forgotten. Let me remind you. Your wife was last seen at a suicide spot. A body was found on the beach yesterday and you seem to be the only person in the village who isn't talking about it. You haven't even asked me who it is. You haven't been answering your door or your phone, when most people in your situation would be desperate for news about a missing loved one. I think that is strange. Suspicious even. And it makes me wonder if the reason you haven't asked who the dead woman we found on the beach was is because you already know. You coming in here screaming and shouting about your daughter looks a lot like deflecting to me. Your way of trying to divert this investigation from the truth. And it makes you look guilty."

He stares at me and I know I've gone too far.

"If you found my wife why haven't you asked me to identify her?"

"There isn't enough left of the woman we found to identify."

His face drains of colour and I regret my words as soon as I've said them, but before either of us can say anything else the door opens again and Carter walks in.

We both stare at him and he stares back.

"Everything okay?" he asks, as though butter wouldn't melt.

"No, Carter. Everything is not okay. You've been AWOL all bloody day. I'd ask where you have been, but in case you're too much of an idiot to guess, I know. You disobeyed a direct order. You're off the case – and you're suspended."

51

CARTER

I can't believe I'm suspended. Losing the job I love is the worst thing that could ever happen to me. I leave the station in a depressed daze and go for a walk along the coast path. I need to clear my head. I find myself standing at the waterfall, at the top of the cliffs, peering down at the waves crashing on the rocks below. The exact spot where I *thought* Eden had jumped. Now I don't know what to think. All we found yesterday morning was an abandoned sweater, but today I spot something in the dirt. Something small and shiny. Something we might have missed. I bend down to pick it up, and see that it is a silver key chain. With the name EDEN engraved on it. Just like the one the woman I tried to arrest showed me.

When the sun starts to set, I begin walking back towards Hope Falls. I hesitate when I pass The Smuggler's Inn. I could really do with a drink – I know there's nothing good at my house – but my sister has always been able to read me like a book she's read too many times before, and I can't handle her judging me right now. Plus, with DCI Bird renting one of the rooms upstairs and calling the place *her office*, she's bound to be there, and I don't want to run into her again anytime soon either. It's the Day of the Dead festival, so the pub will be packed with people drinking before the parade tonight, and full of more faces I don't want to see, so I head home. The last place on earth I want to be.

I bought the cottage a year ago with a tiny deposit and a huge mortgage. My parents aren't the kind of people who could ever help their kids financially – they can barely support themselves – I expect all they'll leave behind when they die are debts and regrets. But I worked hard, I saved hard, and when most of my mates were having fun I made sacrifices so that I could afford my own house in Hope Falls. The place that has always been my home. Property prices here have rocketed thanks to rich Londoners buying holiday lets, and it wasn't easy, but I did it. I moved in just before January and I was so proud of myself. A tad too much perhaps.

I went to the pub along with everyone else in the village that New Year's Eve. I celebrated a little bit too hard. So hard that in the morning I couldn't remember half of the night before. The room was still spinning and I could barely see straight, but I could see Jane in my bed. Even if I couldn't remember how she got there.

Jane was in the year below me at school. She was a nice enough girl, but not someone I was especially interested in or attracted to. But somehow there she was, naked beneath the sheets, her head on my pillow, her underwear on my floor. Jane left my flat on New Year's Day, left me her number too, but I didn't call. I felt bad about it for a while then forgot it ever happened. Until she came back two months later and told me she was pregnant.

Jane wanted to keep the baby. I supported her decision because it was the right thing to do. She wanted to move in together, and I said yes because it was the right thing to do. Then she wanted to get married, so we did, because it was the right thing to do.

I was raised to always do the right thing.

But now almost everything about my life feels wrong.

So I've become a bit less risk-averse when it comes to morality. I didn't tell DCI Bird I was married because in almost every way it feels like I'm not. It's a marriage of inconvenience. That's all it ever was. And although I care about the mother of my child, I do not love her. I never did. I don't even wear a wedding ring – I told Jane I couldn't afford two when we got married, but that wasn't the real reason. Doing the right thing has got me into all sorts of trouble. I'm trapped by a moral compass that often seems to send me in the wrong direction, and this feels like a dead end.

Harrison Woolf looked delighted when I was suspended. I'd give anything to wipe that smug smile off his face. I'm desperate to tell Bird what I've discovered and show her what I've found, but when she took me off the case she looked so disappointed in me. She refused to listen to a word I had to say, suspended me until further notice and sent me home. All because I went to The Manor. If she gets this angry about me questioning someone she told me not to, thank god she doesn't know I'm married after we slept together again last night. I'm quite certain she'd tear me a new one if she did.

I've never been suspended before. I don't know if I'll still get paid, and I don't know if I can afford my next mortgage payment if I don't. Before I reach the house I call an old pal of mine who works at Devon and Cornwall Police HQ. When he doesn't answer I leave a message. "Hi, Dave, long time no speak, beers soon? DCI Bird took over my patch yesterday, and long story short, I've been suspended. Can she do that? Just want to know where I stand. Call me when you can, buddy. And don't tell anyone."

I slip my phone back in my pocket and try to compose my emotions and my face.

"Luke? Is that you?" Jane calls from the kitchen as soon as I walk through the front door. Our cottage is a tiny two-up, two-down terrace, so there's no avoiding each other.

"Who else would it be?" I reply, taking off my coat.

"You're late. You okay? Dinner is almost ready. I've just put her down, but you can say good night if you like."

She means our daughter and I do want to say good night. I quietly climb the stairs, avoiding the ones I know creak, and creep along the landing to the little nursery at the end of the hall. My baby girl is asleep in her cot, safe and sound, her mobile still spinning above her head, the night-light casting a pattern of stars on the wall. I might not love her mother, but I love Steren more than I knew it was possible to love another human being. I'd kill to protect my daughter. And for the first time I start to feel a little guilty about my actions today, interviewing Gabriella Woolf when I knew it might be the wrong thing to do. Harrison's rage may or may not have been justified, but I understand it now. I think little girls stay little girls forever in their fathers' hearts.

I head back downstairs and into the kitchen where Jane is standing at the cooker wearing an apron over her casual clothes. She dresses like it's Sunday every day of the week. I'm surprised to see she has opened a bottle of wine – she rarely drinks – and I decide not to spoil the mood by telling her I've just been suspended. Her brown hair is in a messy bun as always – she pays even less attention to her appearance since Steren was born – but it looks like she might have washed it at least. She's set the table too, which is strange, we normally eat our dinner on trays in front of the TV. My heart sinks when I see that she's set three places. I am not in the mood for company, and an extra plate normally means my mother-in-law is coming. I kiss Jane on the cheek out of habit.

"What's wrong with your face? Bad day?" she asks, giving me half a hug.

"Just tired," I reply, peering inside the oven to see what she is cooking.

"Well, you'd better wake yourself up. She'll be here soon."

"Who?"

"Your new boss."

I freeze. It had occurred to me that DCI Bird and Jane might meet at some point – in a village this size everyone knows everyone – but there hasn't been time to think that through since she arrived without any warning. Sleeping together again last night didn't help with bringing up the subject of my marriage. There's never been a good time to tell Bird the truth or try to explain. *Fuck.* She already knows.

"DCI Bird is coming here?" I ask, hoping I might have misunderstood.

"Yes. She was here earlier looking for you. Twice. Said that you weren't answering your phone and that she was worried. I guess I've been worried too. What with you sneaking in at 4:00 AM last night then sneaking back out again. You're working too hard, my love. I know you've been worried about having a new boss so I invited her for dinner."

"*You* invited *her* here?"

"Yes, I thought it would be nice. Why, what's wrong?" Jane asks.

Everything.

Before I can answer someone knocks on the front door.

52

BIRDY

The door opens and I enjoy the sight of Carter squirming in the distance as I enter his home. The usually empty pub was packed full of people – all with their faces painted like skeletons for the Day of the Dead parade – so in lots of ways it was a relief to get away. Carter's lovely, albeit *very* young wife takes my jacket and hangs it on the bottom banister of the stairs, on top of an already teetering pile of coats. I see the large and messy collection of wellies and walking shoes in the hallway, some caked in mud and sand, and it seems Carter's home is not as neat and tidy as the rest of his life.

Jane leads me through to the kitchen and I take it all in. The house has been decorated on a budget, but everything looks tasteful and carefully chosen. It's clean enough but not remotely tidy. There is evidence of a baby everywhere I look, from the photos on the wall to the baby bouncer in the corner, and blankets, toys and bottles strewn about the place. But it still looks nice. Feels welcoming. Like a real home. There's something rather lovely about the organized chaos of family life.

I bookmark that thought and take a seat at the table.

"I'm not the world's best cook, sorry in advance," Jane says.

Looking at her I'm not convinced she's the world's best anything.

World's best mother maybe? says a cruel voice inside my head.

Jane certainly seems to love her little girl. Carter's wife is not at all what I was expecting – but then I didn't even know he was married until a few hours ago. Jane looks exactly the same as she did earlier today, with her denim dungarees over a Breton top, and slippers shaped like animals that should only be worn by children. She's made no effort with her appearance from what I can tell, even though she was expecting me this time. She clearly doesn't see me as a threat or anything other than Carter's boss.

And why should she?

Wives should be able to trust their husbands.

I try to have kind thoughts – apparently it's scientifically proven to be better for your health – but it's hard. Jane is not the sort of girl I would have imagined Carter settling down with when he seems so overly ambitious in every other area of his life. She's a plain Jane if ever I saw one. "I hope you like homemade lasagna," she says.

Depends on the home and who's making it.

"That sounds delicious. Thank you so much for inviting me."

"Well, I thought it would be good to get to know Carter's boss. I know you're new to the area, and he said you're all alone, so I thought a bit of company might be nice."

I am alone.

Forty-something years on the planet and I seem to have very little to show for it. Jane didn't mean the words in a hurtful way, so I try not to let them hurt.

"Can I get you a drink?" she asks.

"Just water would be lovely."

"We have wine. I bought it especially—"

"DCI Bird doesn't drink alcohol," Carter interrupts, as though I can't answer for myself. It's the first thing he has said since I arrived.

"Water is fine for me, but you go ahead," I say.

"Oh . . ." Jane replies, as though I just said I drink only blood. "Well, never mind. You've arrived in Hope Falls at a fun time. Did you know about the Day of the Dead festival? The torchlit parade starts just down the lane later. I can't go this year because of the baby – obviously – but the two of you should check it out after dinner."

I'd rather eat my own liver.

"That sounds wonderful. Can't wait!"

Carter, who doesn't seem to know where to look or what to say, fills my glass from the kitchen tap. He must be wondering what I'm doing here and worrying about his lovely wife finding out he's been cheating on her. Why must men be so predictable and disappointing, even the good ones? I hear a baby crying somewhere and the sound makes me shiver. I look around, as though the child might be here in the kitchen, but then I see Jane checking what looks like a baby monitor. I guess they make them high tech these days, there is a video feed and everything.

"Excuse me for a moment, Steren doesn't normally fuss once she's been put down. I'm just going to double-check everything is okay, back in a minute," Jane says before leaving the kitchen and scurrying up the stairs. The room is thick with silence as soon as she is gone. It isn't just uncomfortable, it's excruciating.

"Please don't tell her," Carter whispers as soon as she is out of earshot.

"Which part would you rather I didn't tell your wife? That you had sex with your new boss, or that you lost your job today?"

"I thought I was just suspended?" I shake my head in disbelief. "I'll do anything you want if you don't tell her. Anything. I'll . . . walk your dog, clean your scooter, I'll buy you lunch every day, I'll do all the station paperwork for a year. Two years. How does that sound?"

"It sounds like you should go fuck yourself."

He looks like he might cry.

"I'm *begging* you," he whispers.

"Well, I'd rather you didn't. There's no need to start shitting kittens, I'm not here to tell your wife anything. But I will say you're an idiot for cheating on her. People would kill for what you have here. A real family."

"What happened was a mistake, it didn't mean anything—"

"Must you lower the bar every time you open your mouth?"

"I mean her, not you. She was a mistake," he says.

"Has a lifetime of sea air rotted your brain or something?"

"I got married in a hurry. I wasn't in love. We were drunk, we had sex—"

"And you thought your personality was sufficient birth control?"

I have no interest in his sob story. Carter's sister already filled me in on how a drunken night *minus* the sense he was born with *plus* a one-night stand *plus* a pregnancy *equalled* a shotgun wedding.

"I was trying to do the right thing," he says, looking very sorry for himself.

"For who?" I ask.

"My little girl. She's the best thing that ever happened to me and I'd do anything for her. So just tell me what I need to do to make this right."

There is something very likable about a man who cares more about his children than he does about himself.

"I met your daughter when I met your wife earlier. Steren is beautiful," I tell him and his face transforms with pride.

"Thank you."

"She has a very pretty name. Is it Cornish?"

He nods. "It means star, and she means the world to me. Tell me how to fix this. I can't lose my job, we need the money—"

"Calm down. You're not really suspended. I just said that to satisfy Harrison. He was so angry because of you I thought he might have a heart attack. One dead body on my first day is unfortunate, two would just be careless."

"So I'm *not* suspended?"

"Not yet. Tell me what happened when you interviewed Harrison's daughter. Was it a waste of time like I predicted?"

"Actually no." He reaches inside his pocket then puts a silver key chain on the kitchen table. It says *love you to the moon and back* and seems deeply inappropriate given his wife is upstairs. I frown, he flips it over, and now I read the name: *Eden.* He stares at me with a ta-da expression on his face.

"Am I missing something?" I ask.

"My fault, let's start with Gabriella," he says, then leaps up and grabs a slim folder from the kitchen counter, behaving like an excited schoolboy desperate to show me his homework. "Gabriella Woolf can't speak. She whispers things, but nothing she says makes any sense—"

"So you had something in common then?"

He ignores me. "Her main carer is someone called Mary, but Mary looks like this."

He puts what looks like a copy of an employment record on the kitchen table. It includes a picture of a blonde woman. I stare at it. And at him. Then start to say, "But I thought this was—"

"Eden Fox. I thought so too." Carter reaches for a pink laptop that I'm guessing belongs to his wife. The screen displays a recipe for "Easy Lasagna". Carter starts tapping on the keyboard and I see a search engine. He types in EDEN FOX and ARTIST and up pops a website full of paintings of the sea and a picture of her face. There is no doubt about it. Eden Fox and Mary are the same woman.

Oh. My. God.

I thought Carter was a nice-to-look-at waste of space. One of those junior police officers who is super keen but just not cut out for the job. Now I think I might have been wrong.

"Why on earth didn't you tell me this before?" I ask.

"You suspended me before I got the chance—"

"So Eden Fox isn't dead?"

He frowns. "No, I think the real Eden Fox *is* dead. I found her key chain on the cliff."

"What are you talking about?"

"I think *Mary* was pretending to be Eden Fox. I think the woman I arrested who said that her husband changed the locks when she was out for a run was the real Eden Fox and was telling the truth. I think Mary pretended to be her when she befriended people in the village. I think Mary was pretending to be her at the art gallery. I think Mary was pretending to be her husband's wife, and that Harrison went along with it."

"Let me get this straight. You think there was more than one wife?"

"Yes."

"And that Harrison and Mary pretended Mary was Eden?"

"Yes."

"If that's the case, where is the real Eden Fox?"

"They killed her. Or tricked her into killing herself. I think she's who we found on the beach and it's only a matter of time until the coroner confirms it," Carter says, looking exceedingly proud of himself. And I think maybe he should be.

"But . . . *why*?"

"I haven't figured that out yet," he says. "Perhaps we could brainstorm?"

I think Carter's version of a brainstorm would be more like a light drizzle, but he's on to something. I'm sure of it. Even if his theory is a smidgen far-fetched.

"You do know that what you're suggesting sounds batshit?" I ask and he nods. "But it's also good police work. You've shown initiative, you trusted your instincts and you followed your gut. Well done, Carter. Perhaps we'll make a detective out of you yet."

If he were a dog he'd be wagging his tail.

"Thanks, boss. What do we do now?"

I pause to think for a moment, remembering why I came to Hope

Falls. Most people might have used the time to say goodbye to loved ones, or kept themselves busy crossing things off their bucket lists. But I just want to do what I am best at while I still can: getting justice for people who can't get it for themselves. Putting wrongs right.

And there is something very wrong about all of this.

"Well, after what you found out at The Manor, we clearly need to find Mary. But before we do that, we need to take all of this to Harrison," I tell Carter.

"Really?"

"Yes. We need to question him again."

"In the morning?"

"No, right now. Tonight."

53

HARRISON

I have to deal with this situation tonight. Carter has caused more problems than I could ever have predicted. He seemed like a pushover when I first met him. Someone desperate to please but without the skill set to do so. But he's been asking too many of the right questions, which can sometimes result in the wrong answers. How dare he judge me. I know what he did and what he wanted to do. The boy cop is a hypocrite and a liability. I fear being suspended might not be enough to shut him up, but hopefully it will slow him down long enough for me to finish what I started.

As soon as I'm back inside the house I think I see Eden.

I hurry to the library, push the books to one side and pull the concealed lever. I slide the bookcases apart and open the secret door. She isn't there. A book falls to the floor, making me jump – a battered old copy of *Frankenstein* – so I pick it up and put it back on the shelf. I fear the stress and lack of sleep caused by this whole sordid affair is starting to get to me. I've heard strange rumours about the old woman who lived here before us. They say she died twice, that she came back to life and back to Spyglass *after* her family buried her. The story gave me the creeps. And now I'm scared Eden will reappear too, like a ghost, even though I know there is no such thing. Once you're dead, you're dead.

Onwards, as my wife liked to say whenever life took a wrong turn.

I'll leave tonight. That wasn't the original plan but it's for the best – there are too many eyes on me now – so I hurry out of the library and up to the bedroom and start packing two suitcases. One for me, one for her. Then I find the passports and the cash I stashed away for if things didn't go the way we hoped. A good plan B is the secret to success. I wish I had more time, but time is never on anyone's side and no amount of money can change that.

Mary sends me a text message on the phone I use only for her.

I told her not to contact me for a few days but clearly Carter turning up at The Manor has properly spooked her. To be fair, it's spooked me too. I quickly text her back to say STICK TO THE NEW PLAN and hope she does as I ask. There is still a way to steer this back on track if I can just quiet my mind and think.

I'm smarter than all of these people. I built Thanatos from nothing, so I can fix this. But now Mary, who has always seemed so calm and collected, has started sounding more and more like my real wife, which is far from ideal. I could do without any additional crazy right now. At least she isn't planning on coming back here, that really would be a disaster. My phone buzzes again and again, but I ignore it and keep packing. I regret that when I do eventually pick it up and read Mary's latest messages.

I NEED TO SEE YOU.

WHY WON'T YOU REPLY?

I CAN'T DO THIS ON MY OWN.

I'M COMING BACK TO HOPE FALLS.

I dial Mary's number but it goes straight to voicemail. She *cannot* come back here. Now that the police are asking too many questions, and now that Carter knows Mary is called Mary and works at The Manor, Mary must *never* be seen here ever again. Nobody was supposed to see Eden running up to the suicide spot, she was supposed to get there before dawn. Nobody was supposed to find her car abandoned in the national park. Nobody was supposed to suspect a thing. Eden was just meant to disappear and nobody was supposed to notice because everyone in Hope Falls thought Mary was my wife. Not a care assistant being paid to impersonate her. But now, with all this attention, the best thing to do is run.

They all believed that Mary was Eden, even Sergeant Carter. When he kissed her in the police station, it filled me with a variety of jealousy I had forgotten I could feel. But at least Mary told me the truth. She said it only lasted a few seconds before she politely pushed him away. It was that moment, him kissing her, which made me realize how I truly felt. Mary and I had hit it off as soon as we met at The Manor. She's clever and cunning and I find that so damn sexy. She's also a fantastic actress for someone who has worked in the care industry all her life. And, most important of all, she fixed my little girl. The only person who could. Seeing how Mary helped Gabriella made me see what a fool I had been staying with Eden all these years. I don't just want Mary to take care of my daughter anymore. I want her to take care of me. I think we should be a family. But we can't do that here now.

Carter has ruined everything.

He is as clumsy as a pig on ice, but he's smarter than I thought. Since the hillbilly spotted Mary at The Manor, I can tell he's not going to let this go, and he's not going to go away. So we have to. Before anyone gets any closer to the truth. Which also means Mary must never come back to Hope Falls. If she does and someone sees her, I could lose everything and everyone I've ever loved.

I'm never going to let that happen.

54

CARTER

I don't know how I let this happen. DCI Bird being in the same room as my wife was more than just uncomfortable. I am not looking forward to seeing Harrison Woolf again either. I know too much about him now, and I worry about him knowing too much about me. Sometimes it is better to fly under the radar of people who *think* they are powerful; they can be even more dangerous than powerful people. Dinner with my boss and my wife was a disaster, and I feel nothing but relief when Jane starts clearing our plates from the table.

"That was delicious, thank you," Bird lies.

"We're going out for a bit," I tell Jane.

"Are you two going to join the Day of the Dead parade?" she asks.

"Yes," Bird replies before I can answer. "Can't wait."

I'm glad she doesn't tell her we're working. I'm already in the doghouse for "working late" last night.

"The parade will be fun! I'm jealous I can't join you – I would if it weren't for the lil'un upstairs – it was lovely to meet you," Jane says.

"Likewise."

"Won't be late," I tell her as we head out the door.

The festival is well underway, and the torchlit procession through the village is approaching my house just as we leave. It's quite something to see and we join the crowd, weaving our way through a sea of people in fancy dress. As is tradition, the majority are wearing skeleton costumes with elaborate face paint or masks, but there are a few smugglers, and a couple of mermaids too. Most festival-goers look like they've had a drink or three already, and with almost all of them carrying a flaming torch, it looks like a scene from a horror film. When we pass The Smuggler's Inn I'm surprised to see the pub is in darkness. It's normally the busiest night of the year.

"Why is the pub closed so early?" Bird asks, shouting to be heard above the merry mob making their way along the street.

"Not sure. Might text Maddy, check she's okay," I reply, before sending a quick message to my sister.

"Maybe she's in the crowd, you'd never know," Bird says.

She's right – everyone is in costume and most people are wearing masks. When the rest of the procession snakes around the street towards the coast path, the two of us take the lane that leads up the hill to Spyglass instead. I feel anxious for so many reasons when we reach Harrison's house, and I stop on the lane a short distance away before going in. The lights are on. I'm sure he's inside.

"What's wrong?" Bird asks.

"That's Mary's car," I tell her, staring at the red Mini parked on the driveway.

"You're sure?"

"She almost ran me over with it earlier, so yes."

But now that we're here I'm feeling unsure about everything. What if my theories about all of this are as crazy as they sound?

Why would a man pretend that a woman was his wife if she wasn't?

"And seeing her car *here*, parked outside Spyglass . . ." I say.

"What? Spit it out."

"Well, your grandmother's carer – the one nobody ever saw – always parked a red Mini outside this house. That's how I knew someone was here taking care of old Mrs Bird."

"You think Mary used to be my grandmother's live-in carer and now works at The Manor looking after the new owner of Spyglass's daughter? That would be a bit of a mad coincidence."

"There's no such thing. You taught me that."

Before she can answer, the front door swings open and Diana Harris from the art gallery strolls out. The door closes behind her, and she smiles to herself as she walks towards us. We're standing in the shadows and she doesn't see us straight away.

"Oh my goodness, you scared me!" she says when she does. "Why are you here?"

"We could ask you the same question," I say.

"Have they confirmed the body was Eden? That poor man. I just dropped off one of my special homemade casseroles. Perhaps I should stay? Be on hand to offer him some comfort after you have broken the news? A man like that shouldn't be on his own at a time like this."

"That's very *thoughtful*, but we don't know for sure that the body is Eden yet."

Mrs Harris barely hides her disappointment.

"That lovely man has been through so much. I just wanted to let him know that I – we – are all here for him if there is anything he needs. Anything at all."

"We've got this, Mrs Harris, but thank you," Bird says. "You have a good night now." She waits until Diana takes the hint and has waddled away down the lane and out of earshot before adding, "That's right, off you fuck."

"Are you sure we should be doing this?" I whisper when we reach the front door with its fox-head knocker. I used to hate the fact that nothing ever happened in Hope Falls, now I wish it never had. I miss the quiet life. "What if I'm wrong? Harrison Woolf is a powerful man. He already tried to have me fired—"

"Tried and failed and poppycock. You can't be afraid of people like him. Nobody is above the law, I don't care how rich or successful they are. After what you've shown me tonight, I think we can safely say that Harrison has been lying from the start. Why a person lies is almost always more interesting than the lie itself. That's what we need to find out now. *Why.* This is the right thing to do and you did good, I'm proud of you," she says.

It feels like my favourite teacher gave me a gold star. It's also the first kind thing she has said to me, which might be why it sounds strange. Like when people take the time to learn a foreign language but mess up the accent.

"Thank you, DCI Bird. That means a lot to me."

"Call me Birdy, for god's sake, and don't start getting sentimental. Let's get the job done and arrest this fucker," she says, sounding far more like herself.

The door opens almost as soon as she knocks on it.

"I thought he was suspended," Harrison says when he sees us standing there. He looks at me as though I were a piece of shit on his handmade shoe.

"Can we come in?" Bird asks.

"This isn't a good time."

"I noticed the extra car on the driveway. Bit late for visitors."

They appear to have a silent staring contest, but Harrison is the first to look away.

"Perhaps it's best if you speak to my solicitor from now on," he says.

"I think it might be better, for you, if we came inside. We know that someone called Mary Kendall was impersonating your wife. We know she works as a care assistant at The Manor where your daughter lives. And we know you went along with it. Sergeant Carter has uncovered a sufficient amount of evidence to arrest you. We can talk inside the house or we can take you to the station, your call," Bird says and he stares at her without saying anything. As though he is buying some time. Thinking. Amending his plans.

"Have it your way," he says to her, then turns to me. "For the record, you're wrong. About everything. But you'd better come in."

A voice inside my head screams not to. Everything about this situation feels off. One minute Harrison is insisting we speak to his solicitor, then he just invites us into the house? This doesn't feel right. Or sensible. Or safe. But I don't know how to tell Bird that without sounding like a wimp. I think I've finally earned her respect; I don't want to lose it now. We follow Harrison down the dimly lit hall towards the kitchen at the back of the house, and I wonder why the lights are turned down so low. Spyglass feels cold and damp tonight, as if the heating has been switched off, as though nobody really lives here.

Bird walks ahead of me and I feel bad about all the lies I have told her. I used to hate this house, but now I realize I just hated the woman who owned it. Bird's grandmother, the woman who died twice, ruined my family's life when she decided to sell the pub. She owned both properties – Spyglass and The Smuggler's Inn had been in her family for over a century. Just the luck of being born rich rather than a result of any hard work on her part. There have always been rumours that the Bird family arrived in this village at the same time the *Serendipity* washed up on Blackwater Bay, and that all their wealth was a result of stolen gold. That woman never worked a day in her life, and her greed cost my family everything.

Nothing has been the same since.

When Mum was diagnosed with cancer, I was convinced she got ill as a result of the stress of losing her home and her business. Old Mrs Bird said she was forced to sell the pub to the brewery to pay for her live-in carer. She told my parents, via her solicitor, that she had run out of money, and that she had to sell Spyglass or the pub to pay for her care. She said that Spyglass was her home, so she could never sell it, but didn't seem to mind selling ours. I tried to talk to her myself, but she wouldn't even open the front door. She said she didn't have a choice about selling the pub. But life is all about choices. I guess sometimes so is death.

Old Mrs Bird made the wrong choice, then she died.

I hear a kettle boiling in the kitchen, and it sounds like screaming.

When I spot two suitcases at the bottom of the stairs the alarm bells inside my head only ring louder. Was Harrison just about to do a runner? My phone buzzes inside my pocket causing a temporary distraction. I wouldn't normally check it at a time like this, but the only person who tends to text me late at night is my wife, and since Steren was born I'm always anxious to know that my daughter is safe.

"Maybe turn your phone off if it is going to keep beeping and buzzing," Bird says with her usual disdain for technology. I switch it to silent before opening the message. It isn't Jane texting, and it isn't a number I recognize. I see a message from the coroner's office and my eyes can't read the words fast enough.

"It's the team trying to identify the body on the beach," I say.

They both stop and turn to stare at me.

"Well?" Harrison asks. "Is it my wife?"

I don't answer.

"Carter? Are you okay?" Bird asks.

Her patience soon expires when I still don't reply.

"For fuck's sake, Carter. Do you have the results or not?"

55

BIRDY

The results are inconclusive," Carter says, staring down at his screen.

"What does that mean?" Harrison asks.

"Let me see that," I say, taking the phone from Carter and reading the message. "According to the coroner's report, they cannot confirm that the victim was Eden. They have requested and are still waiting for dental records, but they say the DNA sample from the missing woman's hairbrush is not a match with the victim."

"Well, I guess there's no need for your little visit now," Harrison says, looking a bit too pleased with himself. "Thanks for popping in, but you can't arrest me for killing my wife if she isn't dead. And if they can't identify the body—"

"Just because they haven't yet doesn't mean they won't," Carter says.

"You just can't let it go, can you?" Harrison replies.

"There's still dental records."

"Good luck with that. She didn't have any teeth left."

"How do you know?" Carter asks.

That's a very good point but I've grown weary of this shit show.

"Where is Mary, Mr Woolf?" I ask, and they both turn to stare at me as though they had forgotten I was here.

"Forget about Mary. I think we should arrest him; he's practically confessed. Look at the suitcases in the hallway, he was about to do a runner," Carter says.

The two of them go at it again.

"You think you've got it all figured out, don't you?" Harrison responds with an unkind smile. "You don't know shit, you pathetic little prick. You should be more careful. You might be dead soon too. It happens to someone somewhere every day, every hour, every minute, every second."

"Perhaps you would like to continue this conversation at the station?"

"I'd rather slam my penis in a car door."

Why must men behave like men?

"Let's just all take a breath and take a step back," I say, trying to calm things down, but Harrison is having none of it.

"Look at you, *Sergeant Carter*, playing dress-up like the rest of the losers in this village tonight. Except your costume is a police uniform. Sergeant Cock-up would be a better fit. Wearing a badge doesn't make you an upstanding member of the community. How dare you come into my home, judging me. You're a hypocrite and you should learn to keep your dick in your pants. Walking around like you matter. You're nobody. You're nothing."

"And you're a gold-plated arsehole," Carter says. "If *you* won't tell us the truth about your wife, maybe we should arrest your freak of a daughter and question her again instead?" he says and Harrison launches himself at him. Carter is the younger and fitter of the two men and dodges out of the way. I put myself between them, trying to keep them apart, wondering what the fuck I am doing here and how it came to this.

"That's enough. Both of you. Harrison Woolf, I am arresting you for intimidating a police officer and withholding evidence from a police investigation. You do not have to say anything but it may harm your defence if you do not mention when questioned—"

"Is this a fucking joke?" Harrison roars.

"Do I look like I'm laughing?" I say, taking out my handcuffs. He stares at them, then at me, and regains his composure.

"You don't need those, I'm sorry," he says, sounding like a smaller version of himself. Defeated. Deflated. "There isn't anything I wouldn't do for my daughter."

It's exactly what Carter said about his own child earlier tonight.

The two men have more in common than I think either of them realize.

I catch Carter smiling. "Wait outside," I tell him.

"But—"

"But nothing. You almost jeopardized this entire investigation with your misconduct. Again. I'm calling it in and I'm calling for backup. Wait outside."

56

HARRISON

Carter goes outside but insists on standing on the bloody doorstep, as though guarding the front door, which he has refused to close. Every now and then he turns to look through the crack at us, as though he thinks I might be about to attack his boss. I've realized tonight, and too late, that the boy cop isn't as dumb as I thought.

And DCI Bird isn't as smart.

"You can't arrest me," I tell her. "Take these bloody cuffs off."

"No," she says calmly, but then she grimaces, as though she might be in pain, and I remember how ill she is.

Thanatos told her how little time she has left and this is how she chooses to spend it. In Hope fucking Falls. It isn't what I would have done in her situation. She's a beautiful woman. The clothes – the tweed jacket and sensible shoes don't do her any favours – but the plaited hair is a nice touch. I almost feel sorry for her as she paces up and down the hallway, trying to put the remaining pieces of the puzzle together. Trying to make them all fit.

They do not make a pretty picture.

Unlike the one of my daughter in the hall.

It's an old photo, I only just put it up. It hides where one of Eden used to be. Gabriella was eight when it was taken, just before her accident. I see the detective stop and stare at the picture as though she has just seen a ghost. Because she recognizes my little girl.

Just like I knew she would.

57

BIRDY

I knew coming back to Hope Falls might be challenging in all sorts of ways, but I could never have predicted how things have unfolded since I arrived. I've made a huge mistake coming here. I stare at the picture of Gabriella Woolf when she was a little girl. This picture was not on this wall the last time I was in this house.

I recognize her straight away.

The worst night of my life happened when I was a junior detective. I'd just been promoted and was having a few drinks with my colleagues to celebrate when I got the call. I was as obsessed with my work back then as I am now, but even hungrier for success. I wanted to be the youngest DCI in the country and I wanted to be the best. Most dreams come with expiration dates; if you don't chase them soon enough they'll be out of reach forever. I chased mine until I caught them. But everyone drops everything when a child goes missing. It's just what you do. Doesn't matter who you are, where you are or what time it is, everything stops until they are found.

She was only eight years old.

Every police officer in the area was alerted to her disappearance, but I was the first one on the scene. It's a common misconception that the initial forty-eight hours are the most critical when a child goes missing, but that's a lie. If it has taken that long to find them, chances are they are already dead. I drove faster than I should because time is the most important factor in finding a missing child alive. I knew I was over the limit, but not by much, and I felt sober enough to do what needed to be done. I couldn't bear the thought of something happening to that child because I wasn't there to do my job.

I remember getting the call that Gabriella was missing. I remember the rain, so heavy it seemed to be falling up as well as down. I remember how cold and dark it was that night, and thinking that no child should have been out alone. I remember how the siren sounded louder than normal, more urgent, the blue light on the top of my car casting an eerie glow on the shiny wet road ahead. It seemed to scream at the world to get the fuck out of my way.

I remember all of it.

My phone rang just as I turned into the street where Gabriella lived. I had to answer it because of who was calling. My eyes were off the road for a second, maybe two, no more than that. When I looked up I hit the brakes but I was too slow. And it was too late.

The bike was already under the car.

And Gabriella was there on the road in front of me.

She looked like a broken doll.

I guessed that the impact must have knocked her off the bike and tossed her into the air. I stared at the scene. I couldn't move. It felt like I couldn't breathe. Everything was silent and still except for the flashing blue light, as though time had actually stopped.

Gabriella was in a coma for months. I thought I'd killed her. I couldn't even visit the hospital she was in or tell her how sorry I was. Her father looked at me with nothing but hatred in his eyes when I tried to visit the ward, so I stayed away.

I never forgave myself. I didn't drive a car or drink alcohol ever again after that day. I became a recluse, transferred to a new police force and focused on the job I was lucky to keep. I lost my family, and my friends, because I couldn't stand the way they looked at me after what happened. It was the same way I looked at myself whenever I saw a mirror. Ten years ago I made the biggest mistake I'll ever make and I'm still paying for it.

I recognize the photo of Gabriella in the hallway.

There is no such thing as coincidence.

Harrison knows who I am and what I did ten years ago.

Me being here now is no accident.

And I think I might be in trouble.

58

CARTER

I know I'm in trouble, again, but I can't believe DCI Bird made me wait outside. Harrison is dangerous. I'm certain of that now. She shouldn't be alone with him.

But she's the boss.

From Spyglass, I can see the whole village down below. Blackmoor National Park is shrouded in darkness on one side, and a moon-stained Cornish coast on the other. The view from up here stretches all the way to Blackwater Bay, and it's beautiful. I can see a blanket of fog on the horizon, rolling in from the Atlantic as it often does. I can even see the bonfire on the beach, the final act of the Hope Falls Day of the Dead parade. I've missed the festival this year but I'm just glad today is almost over.

I can see my house from up here too, and I wish I was there instead of here. I long to be at home and in the warmth right now, with Jane and Steren. It's a simple life, but it's a good one. And my daughter is a miracle. I still can't believe we made a tiny, precious, perfect human, or that she's really ours. I love her so much it honestly hurts sometimes. I can't wait to see who she's going to be, and I'd do anything to keep her safe.

Anything.

It's quiet up here. Almost completely silent except for the sound of the sea in the distance. It's like a soothing lullaby, and despite the adrenaline rush just now I am very tired. I haven't really slept since DCI Bird showed up – and I'll be glad when this is all over and life can return to my version of normal. I look down at The Smuggler's Inn, my old family home in the middle of the village. There is something very odd about the lights being off and the pub being in darkness on festival night, and there is still no reply from Maddy, so I take my phone out to try her again.

It's even later than I thought – almost midnight – and I see that I've missed a call from Jane. It's too late to call back now, I don't want to wake the baby, and I kick myself for putting the phone on silent earlier. Nothing matters more than family. There is a message, as well as a missed call, but it's not from my wife. Or my sister. It's from my old pal at HQ, the one I got in contact with earlier to find out if DCI Bird could really suspend me. His reply isn't relevant anymore – given I'm not suspended – but something about the start of the message catches my eye and I open it.

CARTER! LONG TIME NO SPEAK! DCI OLIVIA BIRD CAN'T SUSPEND YOU.

SHE DOESN'T WORK FOR THE POLICE ANYMORE. TOOK EARLY RETIREMENT FROM HER JOB IN LONDON A FEW MONTHS AGO. HQ ARE STILL LOOKING FOR A DETECTIVE TO WORK IN YOUR PATCH, NO ONE EXCEPT YOU HAS EVEN APPLIED. NOBODY

WANTS THE JOB! YOU OK MATE?

I stare at the screen and read the message again.

Then I turn to stare at the house behind me.

I am definitely not okay.

59

BIRDY

2nd November

Nothing about this situation feels okay anymore.

Harrison sees me staring at the photo of Gabriella. Before he or I can say anything the alarm I set on my phone goes off.

It's midnight, which means it is now the second of November.

For a lot of people that means it is All Souls' Day. First comes Halloween, then the Day of the Dead, then All Souls' Day – a time to remember family members who have died.

It means something else to me this year.

I remember the letter I got from Thanatos. The one that set all of this in motion. It's not the sort of news anyone would forget.

Thank you for joining the Thanatos Family.

You'll find your date of death confirmed below.*

Olivia Bird – 2nd November 2025

We all have a right to know when our last day will be, and now you can live your best life every day until the day you die, and make any arrangements with peace of mind. Do be sure to contact us if you need any further information at the number below.

We wish you a Happy Deathday.

*Terms and conditions apply.

Today is my deathday and I'm terrified.

60

CARTER

I'm not scared of DCI Bird anymore. According to the text I just read, she isn't even my boss. I don't know what is going on here, but I hurry back inside Spyglass to find out. There is no sign of Bird or Harrison Woolf. Anywhere. They are not in the hallway where I left them. They are not in the kitchen. I run up the staircase two steps at a time but it's the same story. I don't understand. It's as though they've just . . . vanished.

The message from HQ said that DCI Bird never got the detective job in Hope Falls. That she didn't even apply for it. At first I thought that must be a mistake, but then I replayed the last few days in my mind. I remember getting a random call from someone I'd never heard of saying a new detective was starting the next day. When I asked who, they said it hadn't been formally announced yet, and that they needed to inform all the unsuccessful candidates – including me – before saying who had got the job. Standard procedure, they said. But the more I think about it, nothing about any of this has been standard.

When DCI Bird turned up out of the blue and told me she was my new boss I didn't question it. Anyone who works for the police knows that communication is not the force's strong point. And I'm so far down the food chain I rarely hear about anything until after it has happened. So it didn't surprise me one little bit that I hadn't been fully informed about who was taking over my patch. Everything I subsequently read about DCI Bird said she was a high-ranking and highly decorated detective in London before she came here. She didn't make *that* up. But was everything else she told me a lie?

And if so, why?

My heart is thudding so loudly I can hear it in my ears.

Then I hear something else.

The sound came from the back of the house, so I sprint downstairs to the little library. But it's empty. There is nobody here. It looks like a book just randomly fell off a shelf and landed on the floor. When I pick it up I see that it is *Frankenstein*. The same book old Mrs Bird was reading when she died. DCI Bird went on about this room when we were here before. Something to do with an ancient covenant and the floor-to-ceiling bookcases. I take a closer look and see a gap between them. I slide my fingers into it, and I'm gobsmacked when I discover I can push the bookcases apart.

I'm even more stunned when I see a secret door.

It looks like the entrance to a tunnel.

I get closer, cautious about who or what might be waiting for me. But I don't find out because as soon as I step inside I feel a sharp blow to my head. My vision blurs, I'm unsteady on my feet, and I fall to the floor.

Seconds later my world fades to black.

61

HARRISON

The future is looking a lot brighter all of a sudden.

I heave the suitcases into the trunk of the Mini. One is much heavier than the other, and I have to shove them hard to make them fit. Then I squeeze myself into the driver's seat, wishing I could take my own car to the airport instead. I can't because the police might be looking for it – and with cameras everywhere these days checking licence plates, they could find me in no time – but I'm going to miss my Porsche. Eden was upset when I bought what she called my midlife-crisis car without talking to her first, but I earned it. Along with everything else I own. I worked bloody hard for all of it, and I won't let the countless sacrifices I have made be for nothing.

I turn on the engine and pull out of the driveway. A few minutes later I'm on the winding country lanes that are like veins throughout Blackmoor National Park. There are no streetlights and it couldn't be any darker tonight. The car's headlamps struggle to light the way in the thick mist that seems to have descended over the whole area. What I wouldn't give for a decent stretch of road right now. I should be driving in the other direction, towards London Heathrow and my ticket out of here, but there is just one more thing I need to do.

Death comes for us all but we waste time wondering why instead of when. Finding out how young I might die made me question everything about the life I had lived. All the highs, the lows, the regrets. I have been addicted to ambition my whole life. Working, but not living, my eyes fixed on a lonely prize. Because that's all success really is, it's all it can ever be. There are winners in life, and there are losers. Nobody ever remembers the runner-up.

I thought my work was my greatest achievement, but then life held up a mirror and I finally saw all my mistakes. My wife was my biggest regret. My daughter was my best accomplishment, and yet I had let her down, over and over again. I don't know how I managed to miss seeing that for so long. I realized that all that really mattered to me was my daughter: everything else had always been about and for her.

And yet I'd let them lock her up in a glorified prison.

I had this moment of clarity where I finally understood I'd spent my whole life looking the wrong way. I'd wasted almost all the time I'd been given *working*. And for what? For who? To make a dead mother proud? My work had made me a wealthy man, but I might have had a richer life had I spent more time with my family and less time on my career, and understanding that too late made me miserable.

I tried all the normal things men my age do when faced with a midlife crisis. I bought an expensive car, but it didn't make me happy. I had an affair, not even my first, but it didn't make me happy. I thought about quitting my job, and that thought didn't make me very happy either, until I realized how much I could sell Thanatos for. If I could just gather enough evidence to prove my theories, there were bigger companies out there who would pay a fortune to provide a reliable date-of-death service. Because everybody wants to know when they are going to die, right?

Wrong.

Once I knew how little time I had left I wished I didn't.

And I didn't find out my end date from Thanatos. I died, without warning, when I had a heart attack while sitting at my desk working late, running a company that should have predicted it. Ain't irony a bitch. I was clinically dead for ten minutes. It was only luck that a colleague walked past my office door and saw me slumped over my keyboard. I was resuscitated, brought back to life, but I was never the same.

The doctors who treated me afterwards said if I didn't reduce my stress it was only a matter of time until it happened again, and that my chances of survival would be dramatically less. Eden begged me to quit my job and move out of London, but how could I abandon Thanatos? I'd accomplished big things after a somewhat small start in life, I was so close to achieving my dream, but the things I believed were important changed overnight.

I thought knowing how long we have to live would be a good thing.

But I was wrong.

Knowledge is power but there are some things it is better not to know. Besides, Thanatos failed to predict my date of death accurately, which was a bit disheartening after all those years of research. Each time I used my bespoke algorithm on myself I got a different end date. Every bloody time. Not that I shared that information with anyone else.

Thanatos had started life as a DNA-testing kit firm on the internet. People *paid* to give me their most personal information in exchange for a bullshit report about their genetic makeup and predisposition to certain illnesses. They literally paid *me* to send *them* a box full of swabs, sample pots and questionnaires, then diligently posted highly sensitive data back to an anonymous post office box. People being naive about the value of their own DNA funded the first stage of Thanatos.

Once I had enough free data from dim-witted participants, I launched an aggressive campaign to get the rest of what I needed to attract big investors. I targeted people I *knew* would die soon, using a combination of NHS health records – which should be private and protected but are only too easy to access – medical health insurance claims to target patients who were starting investigations but not yet diagnosed, combined with algorithms taken from supermarkets highlighting those with poor diets or a regular higher-than-average household spend on alcohol. Nothing is private these days. Everything you buy online is available for anyone to see if you know how. Every thought you think that you are dumb enough to share on social media is out there for people like me to take advantage of. I can't tell when a person is going to die just from looking at them, but with the combined efforts of AI and a few bespoke tests, it seemed there might be a way.

Until I failed to predict my own date of death correctly.

I would have figured it out eventually. I was so damn close to perfecting the algorithm, I'm sure of it. But then Olivia Bird walked into the clinic on Harley Street. Seeing her again after all these years, after what she did, resulted in a variety of rage I hadn't felt for a long time. I honestly don't know whether the date of death I gave her is correct, but in theory *today* is her end date. Nobody except me knows the algorithm sometimes gets it wrong. I guess she'll find out one way or the other soon. I do know that her visit to Thanatos that day turned my whole world upside down.

Everything I have and haven't done since has been to protect my daughter. I won't be around forever, and then both her parents will be gone. So I sold the company, tonight, just now, for that reason and ten billion others.

The world population is estimated to be ten billion by 2026. Human beings are already the most dangerous species on the planet. When people know they are dying anyway, and have nothing left to lose, they'll take the rest of the world down with them knowing they'll never have to pay the price. When you remove consequences, you get chaos. Even people you would never have thought capable of murder can turn into monsters when they think their time is up.

So I have reached the unhappy conclusion that Thanatos is a terrible idea, which is why I had to sell it.

Then kill it.

But I didn't kill my wife.

I *wanted* to murder Eden, but I didn't.

A world without consequences terrifies me. Imagine if a world leader with access to nuclear weapons knew they were dying and decided to take the rest of us with them? Or a mass murderer who knew they were going to die anyway going on a final killing spree. Because of *me*. Because of my invention. I don't want to be a part of that. I thought I was offering a cure, but now I fear I am just a symptom of the disease that killed humanity.

But the money I've made from selling the company now, before I'd planned to, is more than enough to take care of my daughter when I am gone. So at least I might have got one thing right.

"Siri, call The Manor," I say, still not slowing down even though I can barely see the road ahead thanks to the fog. The phone rings once. Twice. Three times. Why the fuck don't they answer? Why does *nobody* do their bloody jobs anymore? The planet seems to be populated with nothing but lazy, work-shy, entitled, two-for-one arseholes these days. All looking for a free ride. No wonder the world is fucking fucked.

"Hello, this is The Manor. How can I—"

"It's Harrison Woolf. I need you to pack up my daughter's things and get her ready. I'm coming to collect her."

"Sir, it's after midnight—"

"I don't need you to tell me the time, just do what I asked. I'll be there in an hour." I end the call and speed up.

Five minutes later when my phone rings I only answer because of the caller ID.

"Hello, Mr Woolf. I'm just calling you back from The Manor—"

"What now?"

"I'm afraid we're unable to locate your daughter."

"What are you talking about?"

"She's not in her room."

"It's after midnight. Where else would she be? You lock the bloody bedroom doors, she's not fucking Houdini. Go and look again."

I hang up and grip the steering wheel.

Then I feel a small, cold hand on my shoulder.

And a female voice whispers, "I love you to the moon and back."

62

CARTER

A voice whispers in the dark: "Carter, can you hear me?"

I'm dreaming about DCI Bird and not for the first time. In this dream she is telling me I did a good job and she is sorry. I don't know what she is sorry for or why she keeps asking if I can hear her. Of course I can hear her.

"Open your eyes if you can hear me," she says.

I've never had such a demanding boss. She even gives me orders in my sleep. I don't want to open my eyes, but when I do, I see I am not where I thought I was. Unless I'm still dreaming. But that wouldn't account for the pain or dizziness. I'm in what looks like a tunnel. Bird is on her knees beside me. She's taken off her jacket to put it beneath my head, and has rolled up the sleeves of her white shirt revealing a lot of tattoos. I have a curious urge to touch them.

"Where are we?" I ask.

"Spyglass. You were right about the secret tunnels. This one leads all the way to Blackwater Bay."

Everything starts coming back to me. Eden. Mary. Harrison. Her.

"Did you lie about being my boss?" I ask, sitting up too fast.

"Shh, take it easy. You're bleeding."

"Where is Harrison? Did he get away? Is he in the tunnels?"

"Try to relax. You've lost a lot of blood."

"What about Mary?"

"You don't need to worry about Mary. She lived and worked in this house for almost twenty years, caring for my grandmother. She dressed her, fed her, cooked for her, cleaned for her, washed her, cleared up her mess and her accidents, barely earning the minimum wage, and all on the promise of one day inheriting this place when her employer died. But it took longer than either of them expected for that day to finally come, and when it did, Mary wasn't too happy about my grandmother's will saying that Spyglass had been left to someone else after twenty years of servitude. Mary wanted what she believed was hers, and that's why she went to work at The Manor, to get closer to the family who now owned the house she thought was owed to her. Gabriella and Harrison had no idea about her true motivations until she had already befriended them."

"I don't understand—"

"I know and I'm sorry. I wish I could explain but I have to go now. I'm almost out of time and there is something I need to do."

"What are you talking about? You can't leave me here."

"You're going to be okay. Mary told me that I got trapped in this tunnel myself once, stumbled into it by accident from the library when I was a child and almost died. But then I followed a bird all the way to the ocean. A swallow! Turns out my mother stopped speaking to my grandmother because of that, even though it was just an accident. Apparently my mum even wrote in her will that if something were to happen to her, my grandmother should not be trusted to care for me. My family has never been good at forgiveness."

"Wait. What? When did Mary tell you that?"

"Just now. Before she left. Funny how life gives you the answers to questions you didn't know to ask. Follow the sound of the sea and you'll be fine."

DCI Bird does not sound like herself. I think they might have drugged her. But then she kisses me, so now I'm sure this is just a dream. The kiss is slow and gentle. I close my eyes and I kiss her back until she pulls away.

"I just needed a kiss for luck. Goodbye, Carter."

I open my eyes but she's gone. All I see is darkness.

And all I hear is the sound of a door closing.

63

BIRDY

When one door closes, another one slams in your face.

That's a lesson life taught me more than once. I close the secret door, lock it, then slide down to sit on the parquet floor in the library. It feels fitting that I am going to spend my final moments surrounded by books. I have always been happiest when hiding inside a story. I do not feel good, so I rest my head against the wooden panelling and close my eyes for a second.

Carter pounds his fist on the other side of the door. "Birdy?"

"Yes, Carter."

"What the fuck?"

"I told you to follow the sound of the sea. Why are you so bad at following orders?"

"You're not my boss. You're not my anything. It's dark in here, where is my phone?"

"I took it, you don't need it. Nobody needs those bloody things."

"Let me out!"

"Can't do that, sorry. I have a date with death."

"What? My head is bleeding."

"I know."

"Do you know who hit me? Was it Harrison? I knew he was dangerous."

"No, you silly sod. It was me."

64

BIRDY

Six months earlier

Feelings are like visitors, they come and they go, and sometimes they stay when uninvited. I sit in my little flat above the bookshop with Sunday at my feet and a blanket on my lap like I'm already fucking dead. Then I have a word with myself. It's been three days since I visited Thanatos. Two days since I opened the letter telling me my date of death. And one day since I fell apart. I can't eat, can't sleep, but I know I need to snap out of it. Ever since I discovered I had so little time left, there has been one person I knew I needed to see. I've thought about her so often over the years. Every day for always. And now I need to visit her before it is too late.

To say sorry.

To say goodbye.

Even though it has been years since I said hello.

Now I know exactly how little time I have left, I need to use it wisely, not sit around drowning in self-pity. The first thing I did, the same day I found out, was quit my job. I have spent most of my life working for the police. I think I'd like to spend whatever time I have left just being me. Whoever that is.

Now that I'm dying I wish I'd done a better job of living. I think I might leave London. Maybe I'll sell the flat above the bookshop, and take Sunday somewhere I've never been before. I certainly have no intention of going back to Hope Falls; that's the last place I'd want to spend my final days. I plan to sell my grandmother's house and put the money to good use. I might take a trip to Scotland; I hear it's very beautiful there. No more police work, no more stress, no more anything. Just me and my dog far away from it all for as long as life lets me.

But I have to see her first and I'm so scared.

It's the last thing I need to do before I leave it all behind.

Sadly, it's also the hardest thing.

Because how can you face a person knowing you destroyed their life?

The Manor looks like a luxury hotel surrounded by miles of nothing, but it's really an expensive and exclusive institution for rich young people who, for various reasons, cannot care for themselves. I could never afford something like this, but I guess the girl's father can. His job must pay pretty well. I'll never forgive myself for what happened to Gabriella. I have relived it over and over since, and spent the rest of my life trying to do the right thing to make up for the worst thing I ever did.

I still remember everything about that day as though it were yesterday, because it changed my life, and hers, forever. I had just been promoted and was on my way to becoming the UK's youngest DCI. I was on top of the world and then, because of the accident, I hit rock bottom. What I did ruined her life, so I ruined my own in a feeble attempt at justice. I didn't want to ease my guilt, I wanted to live inside it. I abstained from joy. Deprived myself of hope. And denied myself love. All because of what happened to Gabriella.

She's eighteen now. Her father can't stop me from seeing her.

I just want the chance to say sorry. For all of it.

I have to show my ID, along with the relevant paperwork to prove who I am, to be allowed into The Manor. I instantly hate the place. It reminds me of a prison. I am shown to Gabriella's room by a woman wearing a white uniform. Her name badge says MARY. She has very long blonde hair, and she seems kind. She says that Gabriella hasn't been here long, and to try to not be upset when I see her, which makes me feel even more anxious. I don't know what to expect. I don't know if I'm doing the right thing. I don't know how to feel about any of this. Lately I think I just don't know how to feel. Maybe feeling things is something people can learn to forget.

"You know that Gabriella can't speak?" Mary says and I nod. "She was in an induced coma for six months after the accident – by all accounts nobody thought she would survive – but here she is. The most important thing in cases like this is not giving up hope. Broken wings can still fly if given time to heal. She's a tough little girl, resilient, and she's in there somewhere, trapped inside herself. The doctors say her brain function is normal but she still hasn't spoken a word since the accident ten years ago. Not even a whisper. She's painting – just childlike pictures – but at least it's a way for her to express her feelings. When she's sad she paints a wolf. When she's scared she paints a fox. And when she's happy she paints a bird. We're all secretly confident that she might speak again one day, sometimes it just takes a trigger. There can be a person or an incident that unlocks what got locked."

Gabriella has been trapped inside herself for ten years.

Because of me.

My heart breaks a little bit more when Mary says that.

The guilt I feel is all-consuming. When we reach the door I have an almost overwhelming urge to run in the opposite direction, but Mary opens it before I can escape. I'm frozen to the spot and speechless myself when I see someone painting a picture by the window. The person I came to see isn't here. The eight-year-old girl I remember has transformed into an eighteen-year-old young woman.

I barely recognize her.

But it's clear when I walk into the room that she *does* recognize me, even after all these years of not speaking and no contact. She looks in my direction and the paintbrush falls to the floor. I feel devastated all over again. Dismantled. Destroyed. My face is wet with tears. I shouldn't have come here. But then, despite everything I've been told about her not speaking for ten years, Gabriella opens her mouth and whispers one word. It's so quiet I barely hear, but I didn't imagine it. Mary hears it too and gasps. It's a word I haven't heard for a very long time.

Gabriella stares at me and whispers the word again: "*Mummy.*"

I run to my daughter and hold her, wishing with all my broken heart that I had never let her go.

65

CARTER

2nd November

"You have to let me go," I say, but DCI Bird does not answer. It sounds like she is crying on the other side of the door. "Are you okay?" I ask.

Because I'm not. The tunnel is cold and dark. And my head hurts.

She still doesn't answer so I try a different question.

"Why did you hit me? Were you trying to protect me from something?" For a moment I think she might have gone, left me here, but then I hear her voice again.

"You can't protect people, not even the ones you love," she says. "Everyone thinks that dying is the worst thing that could happen to them, but they're wrong. The worst thing in the world is not *dying*. Something terrible happening to your child is worse than dying, but that's not the worst thing either. Something terrible happening to your child and it being your fault is the worst thing in the world."

"I don't understand—"

"Marriage is a myth. A lie handed down from generation to generation, because someone somewhere decided that two people living together was a good idea. That's what I think now. And we do it because we think we're supposed to. Because it's what everyone else does. But the truth is some people are better off alone. I was married once, and I think it bent our love out of shape. All the things I found charming about him at the start of our relationship were the things I couldn't stand about him in the end. The things we had in common became the things I most wanted to change about myself. Funny that. I think love is a filter that turns everything ugly about a person into something that appears beautiful."

"Fascinating stuff, but what has this got to do with anything?"

"Everything. Because once upon a time I was married to Harrison."

What the actual fuck?

She can't be serious. She carries on and I think she must be.

"We were married until an accident that happened when our little girl was eight. Gabriella got hurt and I blamed myself, he blamed me too. Something got broken that day, and I genuinely thought they would both be better off without me."

"Gabriella is *your* daughter?"

I picture the beautiful woman on the other side of the door, with her plaited hair and quirky clothes and amazing career as one of the best detectives in the country. Then I try to process what she just said but can't. Too many questions are now swirling around in my head.

"But that would mean that you knew who Harrison was this whole time?"

"Well done, Carter. I knew you'd get there in the end."

"But what about Eden—"

"*Eden* was just the hired help," she interrupts. "Harrison has always been a workaholic, and I was training to be a detective *and* trying to be a mother. So we got a nanny. Eden was only twenty-one when I interviewed her, but she seemed smart and reliable. I'm the one who hired her, so it was all my fault in more ways than one. I thought I could trust her, but she ruined my life and took everything I cared about from me. And I didn't even know it until six months ago! She made me believe that everything that happened was my fault.

"I only visited the hospital once after the accident. Harrison blamed me, and I felt like staying away was the right thing to do. When Gabriella finally went home, he invited Eden to move in with them to care for her, and I was so stupidly grateful that she did. She and Harrison got married a couple of years later – after he and I divorced – and Eden became Gabriella's stepmum. I never felt any resentment about that. At the time, I presumed their relationship began after she moved in. I was thankful that my daughter and my ex-husband had someone to care for them. Because I couldn't. I got it into my head that they deserved someone better than me, and that she was it. But that all changed when I found out the truth."

"I can't believe *you* were married to *Harrison*," I blurt out.

"Why is that the part that shocks you the most?"

"Because he's such an arrogant, rude, narcissistic arsehole."

"Well, I guess opposites attract." *No comment.* "He wasn't always the man he is now. Life changed him. We were happy in the beginning. And after that we were happy enough until Eden came along. We built a life together, a home, a child, a dog—"

"You had a dog with Harrison?"

"I've always had dogs. We had two together. Harrison loves dogs as much as I do, there you go, he wasn't all bad. Harrison isn't the villain in this story. For years I thought it was me, and that Eden was the hero. But I was wrong. She was a liar. She stole my family from me. She was my husband's wife – his second wife – and she deserved to die."

DCI Bird sounds like she's lost her mind.

I have so many questions, but I ask the one that is loudest.

"Birdy, did you kill Eden Fox?"

"No. I just wish that I did."

66

BIRDY

I wish I could go back and do things differently,” I tell him.

“I wish you would open this door,” Carter says from inside the tunnel.

“Do you think our paths are already mapped out for us no matter what we do? Or if someone *knew* when they were going to die, do you think there could be a way to change it?”

“I’m not sure I understand. Perhaps we could talk about it face-to-face?”

“Or is it like the butterfly effect? Might something small change things? Are there always consequences? If I flap my wings hard enough could I still maybe change my daughter’s world so that history doesn’t keep repeating itself? I don’t want her to be abandoned like I was, I want her to be loved. That’s why I had to do what I did. I’m dying, Carter. I’ve got cancer.”

“I know.”

What?

“Nobody knows, so how could you?”

“I saw the drugs in your bag. They’re the same ones my mum takes. What did you do to Eden, Birdy?”

“Eden, Eden, Eden. Why are you so obsessed with that woman?

Eden stole my daughter, my husband, my home; she stole my whole life from me. So I decided to steal hers before mine was over. Ten years ago I hired her to take care of my daughter, but instead she started fucking my husband whenever I wasn't around. I was so busy, and so damn grateful for her help, I didn't see what was going on right under my nose in my own home. My own bed. It was only when I visited my daughter at The Manor – ten years later – that the truth started to come out. I visited Gabby every day for a week – begged Mary not to tell her father in case he tried to stop me. I'd missed ten years of her life, I didn't want to miss a moment more. Every day she would whisper a new word. A new clue."

"Gabriella told you what Eden did?"

"Watching Gabriella come back was like witnessing a miracle. The doctors said seeing me again triggered something inside her mind. Despite the time that had passed for the rest of us, Gabriella was still trapped in a world of her own inside her head from ten years earlier. For me, my little girl was gone and a young woman had replaced her. For her, time had not passed in the same way, so she recognized me immediately. As though she had seen me the day before and I'd never left.

"My mother abandoned me when I needed her most. I still can't believe I did the same thing to my little girl. History has a horrible habit of repeating itself in families, but sometimes the past only becomes clear in the present, when the dust of our decisions has had time to settle. My history was rewritten, and my future was stolen, because of *Eden*. Gabriella started whispering each time I visited The Manor, and with Mary's help, I finally learned the truth. All of it.

"My daughter loved to play hide-and-seek as a child, just like I did. She was hiding in my wardrobe that day when she saw Eden and her father in bed together. She knew what they were doing was wrong and she was smart enough to keep quiet, but after Harrison left she was foolish enough to get caught. She told her babysitter that she was going to tell her mummy what she saw. Eden panicked, grabbed hold of her and pushed her over the banister at the top of the stairs. Gabriella landed on the stone floor.

"Eden thought my eight-year-old little girl was dead. She left her there for hours. Then, when it was dark, she dragged her broken body outside and left her lying in the road. Put her bike there too, to make it look like a hit-and-run. I think that was her plan. Then she called Harrison to say Gabby was missing. Harrison called the police – me, his wife the detective – and of course I drove straight home. In the dark. In the rain. Eden was waiting by the window for me to arrive. Just as I was turning into the road where we lived, she dialled my mobile. Which of course I answered, desperate for news about my missing child. Eden timed it perfectly, to distract me, and it worked. I took my eyes off the road to answer her call, the car hit the bike and I thought I'd hit my daughter. I thought I had caused my little girl's injuries, but it was the babysitter all along.

"For ten years Eden let me think what happened was my fault.

"She stole my life from me so I stole hers."

"So you *did* kill her?"

"No. By the time I got to the top of the cliff she was gone."

"But then who—"

"I still don't know. I think maybe someone else beat me to it. Got there first and pushed her over. When I read your transcript with Old Stu, I panicked. I thought he had seen *me* walking up the coast path that morning, that he might even be able to identify me. But it was obvious when I interviewed him that he didn't recognize me, and then he denied seeing a second woman at all. I really don't know what happened. We planned it all so carefully, it was supposed to be me but we all wanted her dead—"

"We?"

"Me, Harrison and Mary. We were all in on it. We all love Gabriella and hate Eden for what she did. The plan was to make Eden think she had lost her mind, and take away everything that she cared about, just like she did to me. It was only supposed to last for a couple of days, because any longer and we feared she'd find *someone somewhere* to back up her story and confirm she was the real Eden Fox. Her family had disowned her years ago, and she didn't have anyone else. She married Harrison when she was barely twenty, she had nothing in common with her old friends, and she was too young – and too stupid – to have anything in common with his. But we still worried someone might corroborate her story.

"We removed all traces of Eden from Spyglass. But we couldn't find the spare key for her Range Rover, so Harrison left a phone in the glove compartment, just in case she found the car key and managed to get away. The phone was only left there as a precaution, in case Eden strayed too far, to track her movements and lure her to the suicide spot when the time was right. Harrison sent her the text message, but he was never going to meet her there. It was always meant to be me. But when I got there she was already gone."

"So she jumped?"

"We don't know. Harrison and Mary both knew the plan, but they both said it wasn't them. Maybe Eden did the right thing for the first time in her life. Who cares. She's dead."

"Is she?"

I think maybe I hit him too hard.

"Of course she is. Have you forgotten the body on the beach?" I say.

"A body with a face that nobody could identify? You don't *know* that she jumped. You said you didn't push her. And the coroner's report was inconclusive until they can do further tests . . . so how do you know that Eden Fox is definitely dead?"

For a second I worry he might be right, but then I remember.

"The hairbrush I took for you to give the forensics team belonged to Mary, not Eden. We did that on purpose so that the DNA wouldn't be a match. The whole point was to kill Eden without anyone even noticing that she was missing. Mary was going to move in here and be a live-in carer for Gabriella. Nobody was even supposed to notice that the real Eden was gone. But then a dog walker saw more than he should, and you started asking too many questions, and she washed up closer to home than we hoped. So our plan had to change."

"But you still can't know for sure that the body on the beach was Eden."

"Of course it was her," I say, even though I'm starting to feel less sure.

"It could have been someone else. It's a popular suicide spot—"

"I know. My mother killed herself there, remember?"

"Did you or Harrison ever confront Eden about what she did to Gabriella?" he asks.

"I was going to, but when I reached the top of the cliff she wasn't there, so I never got the chance."

"But then how can you be sure that's what happened? After ten years, could Gabriella be . . . misremembering?"

It's a good question, but the answer is still "No."

"Lying then? How do you know what she said happened really happened?"

"Well, for starters, Harrison didn't deny sleeping with the babysitter that afternoon. And as for Eden pushing her over the banister and staging the accident, why would Gabriella lie? She has the mental age of eight. I don't think a child of that age could be capable of coming up with such an elaborate story. Why would she?"

67

GABRIELLA

I have always liked to play hide-and-seek. It's my favourite game.

At first, I quite liked the policeman who came to visit me at The Manor. I thought he was handsome and that he could be my boyfriend. But then he started asking too many questions I did not like. He knew things Daddy didn't want him to know. And if Daddy doesn't like someone then neither do I. So when the policeman chased Mary out of the room, I started screaming so that Ingrid the nurse would give me the sleepy pills. Staff at The Manor always give me sleepy pills when I scream. And if they don't give me what I want, I bite.

Sometimes hurting people is the only way to make them listen.

Ingrid gave me the pills, I closed my eyes, and she left my room. The sleepy pills don't work straight away – Ingrid is an idiot – and I wanted to know what happened to Mary. So I walked out of my room, down the staircase and out the front door. They only lock the doors at The Manor at night. As though you can only play hide-and-seek during the day. Which is very silly. I can play hide-and-seek anytime all day and all night long.

Mary often talked about her little red car. I know all the colours. I use them when I paint. Red can be called crimson, or scarlet, or ruby, but they are all still red. People have called me all sorts of names too, but I am still me. There was only one red car in the car park, so I hid beside it to wait for Mary. When she opened the car from a distance, while still running away from the policeman, I thought it might be fun to hide in the back. Behind the front seats. Beneath a blanket. I'm very good at hiding. So good that Mary didn't find me.

Then the sleepy pills started to work and I closed my eyes.

People seem to think that because I can't speak it means I can't hear, but there is nothing wrong with my ears. Nothing wrong with me at all now apart from my voice being a little bit broken. But people see what they want to see, hear what they want to hear and think what they want to think. Mary taught me that.

Daddy promised we would live together again one day in a beautiful house by the sea. He showed me a photo of a white house with wonky walls that was built into a cliff. He called it Spyglass and said it would be our home, so I started painting it over and over again. I got so good I didn't need the photo anymore. I knew the house by heart. When I woke up in Mary's car, it was dark and she was gone, and I was scared at first. I didn't know where I was. But then I looked out of the window and saw Spyglass!

I wanted to run inside, but then I saw my first mummy standing on the doorstep with the policeman, so thought it might be better to hide a while longer, in case they were there to take me back to The Manor. My first mummy was always at work at the police station. My second mummy taught me to paint – which was nice – but then she said I couldn't live with her and Daddy anymore and sent me away. She wanted him all to herself. She's gone now, which is good. I thought my first mummy might be coming back to live with us, but Daddy told me she is dying. I wasn't sure how to feel about that. Daddy said it was okay to cry, so I cried to make him happy and he said I was a good girl. I think Mary wants to be my third mummy, but I'd rather it was just Daddy and me.

When my first mummy came to visit me at The Manor it was as

though I woke up after a deep sleep and a bad dream. Strange noises came out of my mouth when I tried to speak. Daddy said I hadn't spoken for a very long time, so I tried to tell him what I wanted by painting the house where he said we would live. But he still didn't understand. Then Mary taught me to whisper my words. Me whispering seemed to make her and Daddy very happy, so I kept doing it. Mary would read me scary stories and I would tell her scary stories too. It was fun at first, but I don't want another mummy. Things will be much better when it is just Daddy and me.

I think I scared him in the car just now. I didn't mean to. I woke up again when I heard his voice. I came out from my hiding place behind the driver's seat, and told him that I love him to the moon and back. He used to say that to Eden all the time. But instead of saying he loved me too – like you are supposed to say when someone tells you they love you – he hit the brakes and the car skidded across the road. Daddy shouted and said some very bad words. I thought he was cross with me, which made me very sad so I started to cry. But then Daddy said we were going to be together from now on, always and forever. He said that it was good that I had hidden in the car because we were going on an adventure! He said it will be like a game of hide-and-seek, but that we are going to hide somewhere nobody will ever find us.

And I was so happy.

Until he said that Mary was coming too.

Eden is gone. Mummy is dying, hopefully soon. So Mary is the only problem left. And Mary was in the car too, sitting next to him. I wanted us to live at Spyglass together, like he promised. And I wanted it to be just us. So I cried again.

Then I got out of the car and I ran.

68

BIRDY

"The only way out is the tunnel, Carter."

"Not until you tell me the truth."

"I already did. Mary believed what Gabriella said too. She was as shocked as I was that Eden had left my daughter for dead in the street ten years earlier then let me – and the rest of the world – think that I was to blame. Together, we told Harrison. Then, once he'd had time to take it in and calm the fuck down, the three of us came up with a plan.

"We all wanted revenge for one thing or another, and there seemed to be a way for us to all get what we wanted. Mary wanted Spyglass, or at least what it would have been worth had my grandmother kept her word and left it to her. Harrison wanted to be rid of his wife but without having to divorce her – all of his money was tied up in his business, and he couldn't afford a scandal or a legal separation. There was no prenup when they got married, so Eden was entitled to half of everything Harrison owned – including his beloved company – and once he knew what she'd done, he didn't want her getting a penny of it. I didn't know that Harrison was the CEO of Thanatos until this week – he started the company long after we separated – but I know him. And I think it's fair to say his work has always been his one true love. I just wanted revenge. And I wanted to know that my daughter would be cared for when I am gone, which Mary promised to do in exchange for a large sum of money and annual salary for life.

"The three of us only met together in person once – at The Manor – and then we all played our parts. Harrison booked a viewing to see Spyglass and convinced Eden they should move there, already knowing that I would happily sell them the house. Mary played her role until the time was right, pretending to be Eden around the village. And I was supposed to meet Eden at the top of the cliff in Hope Falls. Say all the things I wanted to say to that bitch, then push her over. And I would have too. I've got nothing left to lose and I was looking forward to it. But either someone else beat me to it or she jumped."

"So you were just pretending to investigate her disappearance all this time?"

"No, I really wanted to know what happened to her. I never got to confront her or see the look in her eyes when she realized we all knew what she'd done. I pretended to be your new boss because I needed to know what really happened to Eden *and* I was supposed to steer you in the wrong direction and keep you from finding out more than you should. I failed big-time on that front."

"Why are you telling me all this?" Carter asks from the other side of the door.

I smile. "You've been asking too many questions. I reckon giving you the answers is the only way to make you stop."

"Then what? Aren't you worried I'll arrest you all when I get out of here?"

"No. I'll be dead."

"Even if that is true, I could still arrest Harrison and Mary."

"They'll be long gone and you'll never find them. They left over an hour ago. They're probably at the airport already."

"Then maybe I'll arrest Gabriella—"

"Carter, you're not going to arrest anyone. You are going to follow the tunnel to the sea, go back to your life and forget that any of this ever happened."

"Why on earth would I do that?"

"Because you said you would do anything for your daughter, just like I'll do anything for mine."

"What does that mean?"

"The original plan was that Harrison would give Mary this house. But then something unexpected happened; they fell in love. Everyone in the village already believed she was his wife, so they changed the plan to live here together. Gabriella was going to join them, once the real Eden was out of the way, but then there were complications. Including you. So the plan changed again. Harrison decided to sell his company and, for reasons I don't fully understand, now wants to move abroad. So they are leaving the country. Tonight. They're going to take Gabriella with them and start a new life together."

"You've finally been reunited with your daughter, and you're going to let her move to another country without you?"

"I told you. I'll be dead soon."

"You missed the small matter of murder. What makes you think I won't tell the world what really happened?"

"Now that the sale of Thanatos has gone through, Harrison's purchase of The Smuggler's Inn from the brewery will be complete. He made them an offer they wouldn't refuse for a pub that is now empty for half the year. But it won't be in his name, it will be in yours. So long as you keep your mouth shut, your family home belongs to your family again. Forever. Maddy can continue to run the place, and your parents can move back from Spain. Spend a bit more time with you and your daughter. If you agree to our terms, Harrison will pay off the mortgage on your cottage too."

"You think you can buy my silence?" he asks, sounding less happy than I expected. Why are people so ungrateful? The pain is getting worse again, so bad I squeeze my eyes shut. I guess today really is the day, and it would seem I am going to spend my final moments talking to Sergeant bloody Carter. I suppose it's marginally better than dying alone. I try one last time to explain the situation in a way his befuddled brain can understand.

"You told me Hope Falls was your home and that you never wanted to leave. Having spent a couple of days here, I feel like this is the capital of Bumblefuck, and you're the town mayor, but to each their own. I'm offering you everything you ever wanted."

"But you want me to lie?"

"The truth isn't as valuable as people think. Time with the people you love most is worth so much more than money or truth or doing the right thing. Trust me, when you get to where I am, you'll have a much clearer view of the world. Your life gets a whole lot less complicated when it's almost over. We're offering you financial security for you and your family forever. You can all be together again. And in terms of any moral dilemma, now that you know why we did what we did, surely you agree that Eden got what she deserved. If someone did that to your little girl, what would you do?" It is silent on the other side of the door for a while and I enjoy the moment of peace.

It doesn't last.

"What makes you think you're going to die? People can survive cancer," Carter says.

"We're all dying from the day we are born, it's only ever a matter of time. Life sentences us all to death in the end. The short version of a long story is that I know today is my last day because there is a company that can predict a person's date of death. That's how my grandmother knew when she was going to die. That's how I know."

It is quiet again, then Carter says, "I might be the mayor of Bumblefuck, but that sounds like bullshit."

I smile. "I couldn't agree more."

I take out all the pills I've been collecting these past few months.

Some of them from my own medicine cabinet, some from anywhere I could find them, enough to do the job. I've had a lot of time to think since Thanatos told me how little time I had left. Harrison would neither confirm nor deny that the prediction was true. Either way, I don't want a fucking AI algorithm deciding when I die. I want to go out on my own terms. When I want to. Maybe that's how my mother felt too.

Sometimes we inherit heartbreak.

Sometimes we inherit hate.

"But what about Eden?" Carter asks.

"What about her? I've done what I came here to do."

"You can't know that for certain. I get that the plan was to make it look like Eden killed herself. And you all *wanted* to kill her but *none* of you did. Think about it. Eden didn't strike me as someone who would take her own life. You told me to stick to the facts. Not to jump to conclusions. I'm just pointing out that you don't know for sure that Eden is dead. I'm guessing she knew about these tunnels. Isn't it possible that she could have been hiding for the last couple of days?"

"Your theories are so interesting. Please tell me less."

He's wrong, it must have been her on that beach. It being someone else roughly the same height and weight would be too much of a coincidence and there's no such thing. I swallow the rest of the pills and I'm already starting to feel sleepy. Like someone is drawing a curtain over my mind.

"Goodbye, Carter. For what it's worth, I think you're going to make a great detective one day. You already are."

I close my heavy eyelids, letting the drugs send me to oblivion, and surrendering to the darkness that has been calling me for a long time. I quickly drift into a deep sleep and slip inside a surreal dream. A person dressed head to toe as a female skeleton appears in the doorway of the library. It's obviously some strange manifestation of my memory after walking through the Day of the Dead parade earlier, but it's a disturbing final image for my tired mind to conjure. Her face is hidden by a mask, so the only real thing I can see are her eyes, which look wide and wild. She's wearing a wig, and appears to be dressed as some kind of bride come back from the dead.

"I hate you," she whispers, so quietly I almost don't hear it.

69

CARTER

I can't hear anything on the other side of the door anymore.

Birdy doesn't reply, even though I say her name, over and over.

The tunnels are now my only option.

I was always the fastest runner at school, and then again at the police academy. It's one of the only things I know I'm good at. But I can't run through the tunnels. They are too small, so small that in some places I have to crawl. I still go as fast as I can, following the sound of the ocean until I see light. Not daylight – it's the middle of the night – but the glow from the bonfire on the beach where some people are still celebrating the Day of the Dead. All of them are dressed like death – faces painted like skeletons or hidden behind masks – and nobody even seems to notice when I walk out from behind the rocks.

People are setting off fireworks on the beach, which happens every year, but strictly speaking, isn't allowed. It's dangerous when they've all been drinking, but I don't have time to stop. I hurry across Blackwater Bay, my feet sinking in the sand, and as soon as I am on the coast path I run. I run all the way to the village, passing The Smuggler's Inn – which is still in darkness even though it would normally open late, god knows where my sister is – then sprint up the hill. I don't have time to stop or catch my breath. Birdy is in danger. I don't believe in all that death prediction malarkey, but I remember all the bottles of pills I saw in her bag, and I'm worried about what she might be planning to do.

I hurry up the lane towards Spyglass, turn the corner and run straight into my sister. She's dressed up for the festival but has removed her mask.

"Maddy? What are you doing here?"

"I'm taking a walk. Jesus, Carter. You've got blood on you, are you okay?"

"Yes. No. Wait, I don't understand. Why are you up here? It's the busiest night of the year, but the pub is in darkness and you're out for a walk?"

"There was a power cut. Most people had left for the parade anyway, so I came up here to get some fresh air and enjoy the view of the fireworks."

Seems like a strange bloody thing to do. But the view *is* spectacular from up here. You can see all of Hope Falls *and* the fireworks. There are some loud bangs and an explosion of light in the sky right on cue.

"You look like you need to go to hospital. Do you need me to drive you?" she offers, her face full of concern. My big sister has always looked out for me.

"I'm fine. Just a bump on the head. Please go home, Maddy. I can't explain what is going on, but I need you to go home."

My sister never does what I say, but tonight she seems to make an exception.

The front door of Spyglass is open when I get there, so I hurry inside and make my way to the library. I'm breathless, sweating, shaking, and when I walk into the room I can't seem to process what I see. Birdy is slumped on the floor. I rush over and feel for a pulse but can't find one. The front door slams in the distance behind me, almost as though someone just left the house when I arrived, but maybe the wind blew it shut. I use Birdy's phone to call for an ambulance, then start CPR and try to remember my training.

"Don't you fucking die on me," I say beneath my breath. Then I pinch her nose and give her mouth to mouth, before continuing with compressions. "You're the most stubborn person I've ever met. The DCI Bird I know would never die on the day some bullshit company predicted she was going to. She'd tell death to fuck right off, and die another day just to prove a fucking point."

I breathe into her mouth again.

It isn't working.

Nothing I'm doing is bringing her back.

"You asked me earlier if our paths are already mapped out for us no matter what we do? My answer is no. We determine our own destiny. You decide what happens to you. Even if this bullshit death prediction is true, you can change it. Love can change anything. You didn't have anything to live for before, but you do now. Your daughter."

What I'm saying isn't working either.

Birdy was right, time is more important than anything else.

And I think I'm too late.

70

BIRDY

One year later

Everybody lies and everybody dies. Those are two of the only things you can be certain of in an uncertain world. Someone said that to me once, I can't remember who, but what they said is true and I think about it often.

I didn't die when I thought I was going to.

And, unless I get hit by a bus, I don't think I'm dying any time soon.

I'm in remission.

The doctors can't explain it, and I don't understand it, but I'm so grateful to get a second chance. When Carter found me in the library he called for an ambulance and did CPR until they arrived. I believe he saved my life. The paramedics said I was clinically dead for seven minutes, but then they resuscitated me. So in some ways, Thanatos was right – I did die on the day they predicted – but then I came back. When I was in the hospital – after they pumped my stomach – the doctors did a few tests. In the months that followed, my tumours started getting smaller. Maybe there is something to be said for sea air after all.

Life has changed a lot in the last year. Sunday and I have moved into Spyglass and made the place our home. Giving the house back to me was the least Harrison could do given the circumstances. He didn't tell me he was the CEO of Thanatos – I found out by accident – and then he still let me believe I was definitely going to die that day. Even after everything we had gone through together, his work was still more important than the mother of his child. Since he sold the company for a staggering amount of money, and now that we are on better terms, he confessed to me that the AI algorithm doesn't always get a person's date of death correct. But I almost died because of his lies.

Death is as uncertain as life.

Everything. Can. Change.

Everything.

Accepting that things change and learning to navigate wrong turns is the secret to a happy life. No prediction is ever one hundred per cent certain, that's why it's called *a prediction*. Accurately predicting a person's death is like predicting the weather; rarely accurate. Almost impossible to get right. But lies tend to be more profitable and easier to sell than the truth.

I've made a few changes to my life and I'm trying to take better care of myself. I'm choosing to live every day as though it were my first, and learning to appreciate the little things again. The things we think don't matter but do. Seeing the wonder all around us that I've been blind to has changed my perspective. I've started running with Sunday and I love how it makes me feel. We like to go out at dawn; it seems like a positive way to start the day. As we leave Spyglass this morning, and jog down the hill towards the village, I see clouds of my own breath. It makes me inexplicably happy, because it reminds me that I'm alive.

Stepping into Hope Falls still feels like stepping back in time, and I am part of the history here now too, even if nobody knows it. I wind my way through the network of narrow lanes and cobbled streets tightly packed with tiny terraced houses, pass The Smuggler's Inn – where Carter's mum and dad are the landlords again – and carry on running towards the seafront. I pass the church and glance at my favourite headstone in the graveyard. The one belonging to my grandmother. I don't know why she didn't try harder to find me after Mum died. Maybe, like me, she made the mistake of thinking it was kinder to stay away, thought that someone else would do a better job. History has an unfortunate habit of repeating itself in most families. What I do know is that thanks to the woman who died twice, I got a second chance at life.

I keep running, past the Driftwood Café and the art gallery, and towards the coast path, with Sunday trotting at my side. The sun is just starting to rise when we reach the harbour, and I am greeted by panoramic views of the sunrise over the ocean. Lines of bobbing fishing boats decorate the waterfront, and a flight of swallows swoops and soars above them. There are so many it's as though the sky itself is made of birds, blue shapes flying between them. By the time I turn onto the coast path, the sun is high in the sky over a turquoise sea. It really is beautiful here and I feel so lucky to call this place my home.

I run with the wind in my face and the sound of the sea in my ears and propel myself up the hill to the waterfall before heading further inland and onto the moor. I know some people run to get away from it all, but I run because it makes me feel alive and free, and I love that I always end up back where I started. Home. I'm even happier than normal to be home today. As soon as I get inside I plan to have a nice bath, put on my favourite loungewear – my joggers with the rainbow stripe and an old eighties sweatshirt – then I'm going to read a good book. With my own lovely little library at Spyglass there are always plenty to choose from.

When I reach the front gate I stop to catch my breath, stare up at the old house with a bird-shaped knocker reinstated on the front door, and am once again filled with a mix of gratitude and astonishment that I am somehow still here. Everyone got their happy ending in the end. Carter got promoted, he and his wife are mortgage free, and his parents are back at The Smuggler's Inn. Harrison sold his company and moved to Switzerland with Mary. Gabriella is being properly cared for by people who love her, and I came home to Hope Falls.

I like who I am now. We're all built from invisible scars, building blocks of heartbreak, shame, regret, disappointment making us taller, stronger, harder to knock down. And I'm grateful to have a perfect ending for the story of my imperfect life.

I hurry up the garden path to Spyglass and go to put my key in the front door.

It doesn't seem to fit in the lock, so I try again.

It still doesn't work and I don't understand.

I experience a strange sense of déjà vu even though this has never happened to me before. But it *did* happen to Eden. I know that because it was my idea.

I stare at the key, then at the door.

Then I have a word with myself and try one last time.

The relief I feel when the door opens is so overwhelming that at first I don't realize that the key didn't make it happen. Someone else opened the door from the inside and now she is standing there, staring at me.

"Can I help you?" she asks.

I don't speak. Instead I just stand there and stare back.

She's wearing *my* joggers with the rainbow stripe, and *my* eighties sweatshirt.

"I didn't say you could wear my clothes! Who do you think you are?"

She smiles and whispers, "I'm Gabriella and this is my house now."

My daughter lives with her father in Switzerland and visits me once a month. My little girl is nineteen, and I've been trying to make up for lost time. Sunday adores her just as much as I do and the feeling is mutual. Gabriella's voice is still quiet, but that's the only thing about her that is. We have matching senses of humour and tattoos –

she got a swallow like mine – and I think she's forgiven me for being gone so long. Life is an invisible cage for birds who don't learn to see the bars it builds around them. When the door is left open you have to fly. I think she locks the doors all the time because that's what they did at The Manor.

"Please stop locking the front door from the inside when I go out. There is nothing to be afraid of here," I say, giving her a hug.

"Sorry, Mum," she whispers.

Every time she calls me that it feels like my heart mends.

She's my angel. My reason for living. My everything.

Some people are a sky full of stars, others are a blanket of cloud. The sky can change with the slightest breeze, but people rarely do. They are what they are. My daughter is perfect and she's the best thing that ever happened to me.

"You won't leave me again, will you?" she asks.

"No. Never. Promise."

Cross my broken heart and hope to die.

Nobody can take her away from me now, and I know Harrison will always take care of us both financially. He loved me once and he loves Gabriella more than anything and anyone.

He never really loved Eden.

She was just my husband's wife.

MY HUSBAND'S WIFE

My husband's wife is an unforgiving woman. It seems strange to talk about myself in third person like that, but it makes it easier for me to come to terms with what happened.

It's been a whole year since I ran up that hill to the waterfall.

A whole year, and still nobody knows the truth.

What my husband did to me broke my heart and it changed me. Turned me into someone even more invisible than I was before. And more dangerous.

Marriage is a promise.

I think that promises are made to be kept, not broken, and I wish more people would try to remember that. Maybe if people didn't go around breaking their promises there would be fewer broken people in the world. I was still so young when I married my husband, and I dedicated my life to taking care of his daughter. I sacrificed any ambitions of my own, so that he could focus on his career, while I looked after *her*. He wanted us to live in Hope Falls and I thought we would be happy here. I made our new house feel like a real home, but he didn't appreciate it, not really. He didn't love me at all, he just used me to look after his precious little girl, and then he thought he could replace me.

I was going to jump that day at the waterfall. I was so tired, and confused, and upset about everything that was happening I couldn't think straight. I ran past Old Stu walking his dog, and I ran up that hill, and I was going to do it.

But then I saw her standing there.

With her long blonde hair. The "artist". Eden fucking Fox.

The slut who had seduced my husband.

I've heard what people in Hope Falls say about me.

Everyone thinks I'm just a plain Jane.

They think I'm a pushover; so did Eden, so I pushed her right over the edge of the cliff. I'm not stupid. I know Carter only married me because I was pregnant, but does that give other women the right to try to steal him from me?

I don't think so.

I'll never forget the utter humiliation and devastation I felt when I made Carter lunch one day and took it – along with our baby daughter – to surprise him at the police station. It was me who was surprised in the end, when I peered through the window and saw the back of that blonde slut's head. She was sitting on my husband's desk with her back to me and her tongue down his throat. Well, I took care of that bitch when I bumped into her at the waterfall. She had the nerve to deny kissing him – came up with some crazy bullshit story that it was another woman pretending to be her. I was so angry with her thinking I'm a fool I pushed her off the cliff.

Then there's the other one, Olivia Bird. I haven't dealt with her yet. She resigned as Carter's boss almost as soon as she started. He says he doesn't even speak to her anymore – he thinks I don't know why – and we're a happy family now. Very happy. But I know that Carter is lying about *something*. He often can't sleep, as though he has a secret burden on his mind. And I haven't forgotten the night Carter came home at 4:00 AM stinking of sex and another woman's perfume. She had the audacity to show up on my doorstep the next day, looking for him, introducing herself as his new boss, wearing the same stink. I played nice. I cooked them dinner. Then she lied to my face, in my home, and said they were joining the parade when really they snuck off to Spyglass together. I wore my Day of the Dead costume and I went there and I found her, but she looked dead already.

Otherwise I would have killed her too.

I'm still watching her.

I still might.

Because I'm not just a plain Jane.

I am a mother. I am a wife.

And I will not let some other woman steal my husband or hurt my family.

People always think it's the husband, but sometimes it's the wife.

ACKNOWLEDGEMENTS

Thank you to Jonny Geller for being the best agent in town. Thank you to Kari Stuart for being the best agent in America and my very own Mary Poppins. Thank you to Viola Hayden, Kate Cooper, Emma Jamison, Sam Loader, Atlanta Hatch, Natalie Beckett, Sophie Storey and everyone at Curtis Brown.

Thank you to the dream screen team that is Sylvie Rabineau and Sanjana Seelam. I am so grateful that I met you, and I'm so excited to see these characters come to life.

Thank you to Christine Kopprasch, my wonderful US editor, and one of my most favourite humans. And thank you to the whole amazing team at Pine & Cedar and Flatiron Books. With special thanks to Megan Lynch, Malati Chavali, Katherine Turro, Kate Keating, Marlena Bittner, Claire McLaughlin, Kate Lucas, Elishia Merricks, Maria Snelling, Isabela Narvaez, Emily Walters, Justine Gardner, Jeremy Pink, Jason Reigal, Laywan Kwan and Donna Noetzel. And huge thanks to Will Staehle for another stunning cover.

Thank you to Francesca Pathak, my brilliant UK editor, for so many things. You made a promise in my kitchen and you kept it. Huge thanks also to the marvellous team at Pan Macmillan – with special thanks to Lucy Hale, Laura Sherlock, Chloe Davies, Poppy

North, Claire Bush, Zoe Coxon, Rosa Watmough, Stuart Dwyer, Leanne Williams, Emily Sumner, Kate Bullows, Cormac Kinsella, Julia Finnegan, Gillian Mackay, Andrew Belshaw and Kieryn Tyler. And thank you to all my foreign publishers, who take such good care of my novels.

Thank you to the librarians, booksellers, journalists and book reviewers who have been so kind about my books. Forever thank you to my readers. I love seeing your beautiful pictures from all around the world, and your support means so much to me. Writers are nothing without readers, and I have the best.

Thank you to Harlan Coben for the phone call in my kitchen that made this a better book. Thank you to Tommy Harper for the phone call in Scotland that made me rewrite the ending. And huge thanks to Freida McFadden for reading an early version and for being so kind.

Thank you to Daniel, my first reader and favourite everything. This one is for you, to celebrate our twentieth anniversary. And to say sorry. People who don't know me often think I am unhappily married because I keep writing about unhappy marriages, but in real life I married my best friend. Finally, thank you to Boots, the best writing assistant, and dog, in the world.

ABOUT THE AUTHOR

Alice Feeney is the *New York Times* and *Sunday Times* multimillion-copy bestselling author of *Beautiful Ugly*, *Good Bad Girl*, *Daisy Darker*, *Rock Paper Scissors*, *His & Hers*, *I Know Who You Are* and *Sometimes I Lie*. Her novels have been translated into thirty-nine languages and have been optioned for major screen adaptations, including the forthcoming Netflix series *His & Hers*. *My Husband's Wife* was optioned by a major Hollywood studio almost a year before publication. Alice was a BBC journalist for fifteen years and now lives in the Devon countryside with her family. *My Husband's Wife* is her eighth novel.

www.alicefeeney.com

BEAUTIFUL UGLY

ALICE FEENEY

'I was consumed by this book, it's her best ever'
– Lisa Jewell

Author Grady Green is having the worst best day of his life.

Grady calls his wife as she's driving home to share some exciting news. He hears Abby slam on the brakes, get out of the car, then nothing. When he eventually finds her car by a cliff edge, the headlights are on, the driver door is open, her phone is still there . . . but his wife has disappeared.

A year later, Grady is still overcome with grief and desperate to know what happened to Abby. He can't sleep, and he can't write, so he travels to a tiny Scottish island to try to get his life back on track. Then he sees the impossible: a woman who looks exactly like his missing wife.

Wives think their husbands will change, but they don't.

Husbands think their wives won't change, but they do.

DAISY DARKER

ALICE FEENEY

'Clever, sinister, claustrophobic, beguiling and utterly compelling' – Peter James

Isolated on their private island in Cornwall, the Darker family have come together for the first time in over a decade. When the tide comes in, they'll be cut off from the rest of the world for eight hours. When the tide goes back out, nothing will ever be the same again. Nothing – because someone in the family is a killer . . .

As the autumn leaves fall, Daisy Darker arrives at her grandmother's house for her eightieth birthday celebrations. Seaglass, the Darkers' ancestral home, is a crumbling Cornish house perched upon its own tiny private island.

Every member of the family has their secrets. Nana, alone for so long. Daisy's absent father, Frank. Her cold-hearted mother, Nancy. Her siblings, Rose and Lily, and her niece, Trixie, full of questions and without a father of her own. Daisy has never had an easy relationship with her family, but some secrets are much darker than others. This will be a gathering that some of them won't remember.

GOOD BAD GIRL

ALICE FEENEY

'I was on the edge of my seat the whole time'
– Taylor Jenkins Reid

Sometimes bad things happen to good people, so good people have to do bad things . . .

Twenty years after a baby is stolen from her pushchair, a woman is murdered in a care home. The two crimes are somehow linked, and a good bad girl may be the key to discovering the truth.

Edith may have been tricked into a nursing home but, at eighty years young, she's planning her escape. Patience works at the home, cleaning up mess and bonding with Edith, a kindred spirit. But Patience is lying to Edith about almost everything.

Edith's own daughter, Clio, won't speak to her. And someone new is about to knock on Clio's door . . . and their intentions aren't good.

With every reason to distrust each other, the women must solve a mystery with three suspects, two murders and one victim. If they do, they might just find out what happened to the baby who disappeared, the mother who lost her and the connections that bind them.